~~~~~~~~~~~~~~~~~~~~~

AFRICA
GREEN

~~~~~~~~~~~~~~~~~~~~~

The further adventures of
Isabella Green

Kate Foley

Book 2 in the Green Family Saga

Previously published by PJ Skinner
(Kate Foley is a pen name)

ISBN 978-1-913224-34-9

Cover design by Jared Shear

Discover other titles by PJ Skinner

<u>The Green Family Saga</u>

Rebel Green (Book 1)

Fighting Green (Book 3) coming soon

<u>The Sam Harris Adventure Series</u>

Fool's Gold (Book 1)

Hitler's Finger (Book 2)

The Star of Simbako (Book 3)

The Pink Elephants (Book 4)

The Bonita Protocol (Book 5)

Digging Deeper (Book 6)

Concrete Jungle (Book 7)

Go to the PJ Skinner website for more info:
https://www.pjskinner.com

Chapter 1

The metal flap in the door squeaked in protest as the postman shoved the envelopes through the opening, slightly ripping one in his haste to finish his round and get out of the lashing rain. They landed on the doormat upside down; two brown envelopes spotted with raindrops, and a postcard of Sorrento. Seconds later, a young woman in a tight suit with big shoulder pads clattered down the stairs in high-heeled shoes. She swung herself into the hall around the smooth wooden banister and her mop of dirty-blonde curls fell across her face as she reached down to grab the post from the mat.

Frowning, she disregarded the postcard and one of the brown envelopes, but the postmark on the ripped one caused her heart to thunder in her chest. *Oh God, it's here.* Isabella Green sank down onto the bottom stair and held the envelope between her fingers, staring at the English postmark and trying to bend the contents to her will. She slipped her finger under the flap to prise it open and pulled out the letter, forcing herself to read the contents.

The first paragraph crushed her dreams in an

instant. 'Dear Miss Green, thank you for your recent application to work with the BBC. Unfortunately…' Hope extinguished, she crumpled the letter up into a tight ball and blew out a sigh.

'Is there anything interesting in the post?' said Graham Flynn, seated at the Formica table in their scruffy kitchen.

'No, just the usual, and a postcard from your mother.'

She threw the disappointing letter into the understairs cupboard and composed her features, taking the other envelope and the postcard into the kitchen. Dropping them on the table, she picked up a piece of overdone toast and walked over to the sink to scrape the burnt bits off.

'Don't do that. The crumbs stick to the sides,' said Graham, looking up from his Weetabix. 'Make me a cup of tea, will you?'

'Make it yourself. I'm not your servant.'

'Jaysus. What's got into you this morning? Did you get out of the wrong side of the bed?'

Isabella turned to watch him eat his cereal, always the same amount of milk and two teaspoons of sugar. She had suggested trying a slice of banana on it, but the idea had horrified him. *Why wouldn't he try something different?* The disappointment lurked in her chest, like a hole growing in her diaphragm, slowly getting bigger until it made her breath catch in her throat. *Is this all there is?*

She filled the kettle and switched it on. Then she sat at the table and buttered her toast, which she sprinkled with sugar, and ate two bites at a time. Graham finished his cereal and sat looking at her, his elbows on the table and fingers interlaced. He had a perfect side parting in his sandy hair, and that look on his face. Perplexed, hurt.

'Why are you eating sugar on your toast? Have you got your period?' he said, shaking his head. 'I don't understand you at all sometimes.'

'Me either,' said Isabella. 'I feel lost.'

'That's because we don't have any children. We should get married and have a baby. It will stop you being so self-absorbed, having someone else to occupy your thoughts.'

'I don't want to get married yet. I'm not ready.'

'Well, I am. And you're not getting any younger. It's time you grew up.'

'I don't want to get married, and end up like my mother, up to her neck in laundry. It's 1995, not 1965. What about my career?'

He raised an eyebrow, and she had to prevent herself from picking up a fork to stab him.

'Seven years writing stories for a pet tales magazine hardly counts as a career in journalism. That boat has sailed. Come on, darling, you have to be realistic.'

Rebellion bubbled in her chest, but she couldn't face yet another argument about the same thing. Maybe he had it right. Her high-flying ambitions had been knocked out of the sky years ago, and she hung on by a thread most days.

'I promise to consider it,' she said, finishing her toast.

He smiled and patted her hand.

'There you go,' he said. 'You'll be Mrs Flynn. A proper Irish housewife.'

There was no point reminding him she had been born in England and had no intention of changing her nationality. It never occurred to him that being English for her could be just as important as being Irish was for him. She sighed.

'See you later,' she said, putting on her raincoat and grabbing the biggest umbrella from the hall stand.

'Oi, I needed that,' he said.

'My suit will get wet.'

'I don't know why you bother getting dressed up for that dead-end job every day.'

'Dress for the job you want, not the job you have,' said Isabella, quoting her father at him.

But what job could she aspire to at this stage? Once she had convinced herself that she'd be a foreign correspondent or a newsreader on the television, if she just kept working and applying for jobs. Now she had been turned down for the umpteenth time, her hopes ebbed away. *Might Graham be right? Was she living a pipe dream?* She stepped out into the rain.

The bus pulled up to her stop in Rathmines as she ran a few breathless yards to catch it.

'Morning love,' said the driver, flashing a grin at her.

She smiled back and pushed through the throng of damp people into the area beside the doors. Her heart raced in her chest. That was a narrow escape. *How much longer can I fob Graham off? Do I even want to marry him?* She had once thought so. Men came and went until she met Graham at a party in Dublin. Despite his staid career as a chartered accountant, he seemed different and quirky. Ignoring social mores, she moved in shortly after meeting him.

It seemed to be the ideal relationship, but Isabella could not commit. Graham tolerated her immature tantrums and teased her into a less reactive frame of mind. He appeared to be the perfect foil for her. They lived the life of a married couple in a small terraced house in Rathmines and seemed to have it all. But Isabella craved excitement and adventure and applied for exotic jobs without telling him. *I should be happy, but I'm miserable. Where did I go wrong?*

Still musing on her future, Isabella arrived at work to find her colleague Sheila snivelling into a tissue. This was not unusual. Sheila could weep for Ireland, but solidarity forced Isabella to make her way over to Sheila's desk and put a comforting hand on her shoulder.

'What's up, pet? Shall I make you a nice cup of tea?'

'He's dead,' said Sheila.

'Dead? Who?'

Isabella put on what she hoped was a pained expression. Empathy was not her strong point, and this looked like a long one.

'Fintan, of course. Who do you think?'

Isabella tried not to look pleased.

'You're not serious? He's not even that old. How did he die?'

'They say he had a stroke,' said Sheila.

Isabella tutted.

'That's terrible. But why are you crying? You hated the boss.'

'I'm not a monster. The man is dead.'

'So, the filthy old man got his comeuppance? We should be celebrating.'

Sheila sniffed.

'Fintan wasn't that bad.'

'He was like a child with an open box of chocolates. He couldn't resist a poke and a probe at the tempting contents, including you and me.'

'Well, you never complained.'

'Not to him.'

But who could afford to lose their precious starter job in journalism? A rare opportunity for women comes at a price, and Fintan O'Neill knew it. Even a crappy pet stories magazine might be a stepping stone to greater things.

'I'm worried about our jobs,' said Sheila. 'Where will we go if they close this place?'

Shit. Of course. Will we all get fired?

'I hadn't thought of that,' said Isabella, frowning. 'Cheer up, it'll be all right. I expect they'll get a new editor.'

To Isabella's dismay, Graham took Fintan's death as a reason to stop using a condom, and she didn't have a good reason to refuse him. Isabella could not get a prescription for the pill as her doctor told her it was not available for unmarried women in Ireland, something she hadn't been able to check. *How ironic. If I don't want to get pregnant, I'll have to get married. Typical Irish logic.* As she lay in bed under his enthusiastic pounding, despair seeped out of her pores. *I don't even want children, but how do I tell him that? Am I just being selfish? Isn't having children what women do?*

She kept going to work and waited for the axe to fall on the magazine, but, to her relief, Fintan's replacement, Max Wolfe, burst into the office a week after his death, a tall man enveloped in a suffocating cloud of Brut. His coiffured hair bounced on his bullet-like head and a large aggressive moustache bristled from his upper lip. His jaw muscles showed white against his skull, visible clues to the inner conflict caused by being offered the stewardship of such a lowly publication. Max had big ambitions, and they didn't include publishing stories about lost pets.

'No more kittens,' he said in his first editorial meeting. 'No more pandering to the readers. We need to shake this place up and get some new subscribers. If you can't cope with that, the door's over there.'

The relief Isabella felt at the demise of Fintan O'Neill soon evaporated as Max's abrasive nature decimated the staff of the magazine. Several of the long-serving members found Max Wolfe's persona and ideas to be an anathema after Fintan O'Neill's loyalty to the magazine's original purpose.

'I can't betray my readers,' said one, as she packed her knitting into her cardboard box along with her soft toys and stuffed hearts.

Isabella inherited several cactus plants from another woman who claimed they would wound her cats if she took them home. She lined them up on the back rail of her desk to stop Max leaning over it and glowering at her.

'He's so in your face,' she complained to her sister, Liz. 'I can imagine his spit landing on me.'

But he didn't get near enough. For the first week, he ignored her, working his way through the other staff members, culling as he went. Each time he passed her desk, her chest tightened, but her turn never came.

'He can't fire everyone,' said Graham. 'Anyway, you can get a job in the supermarket if he does. It will tide us over until you get pregnant. After that, you can stay at home.'

Chapter 2

It had all started out with such promise. Isabella's high hopes for life had a strong foundation. As a child, she was the centre of attention, with her Shirley Temple curls and her tantrums. No-one in their right mind crossed Isabella Green. One of her death stares, as her mother, Bea Green, called them, silenced most dissent.

Isabella Green had never been a patient person. She rushed through her youth, missing out on its slow pleasures, because she needed to turn the page and see what came next, without absorbing the reasons it would be that way. Her mother had tried to change her, but it had been a wasted effort. Isabella resembled a butterfly in a bunch of flowers, flitting from one new interest to the next without ever exploring the depths.

A fascination with animals which grew stronger after the Greens had acquired their lurcher, Blue, was the only thing that held her interest over the years. As Isabella grew older, she chose veterinary sciences as her intended career, ignoring her parents' gentle suggestions that being a doctor might give her more scope. Opposition always made her stubborn streak emerge. The qualifications for a university place were tough but not unobtainable, and Isabella, despite the dumb blonde image she cultivated, possessed an able brain.

For once she stuck to her guns, but the novels of James Herriot put paid to her plans, or at least, the television series 'It shouldn't happen to a vet' based on them, about a vet in the Yorkshire Dales. The series caught the imagination of old and young in Ireland and soon the veterinary college raised their entry requirements to genius level in order to weed out the best from the flood of candidates.

Isabella did not have the dedication to get a string of A-grades. A solid 'B' student, and practical in nature, when she wanted to be, six A-grades were beyond her. Not that she gave up. She repeated the exams three years in a row, but there was always someone more academic than her who had a vet in the family or loads of money for the new statue in the forecourt of the Veterinary College. *How could James Herriot ruin my plans like that? Horrid little man.*

Finally, she gave up applying, and studied for a Natural Science degree at Trinity College instead. She specialised in zoology because her other options, the emerging fields of genetics and environmental sciences, were in their infancy, and had not yet developed into new job horizons. Despite its promise, the zoology degree left her more frustrated than ever.

'I can work in a zoo, shovelling poo, or I can go into teaching,' said Isabella to her parents. 'Neither appeals to tell you the truth.'

'Why don't you do a course in journalism?' said her father, Tom Green. 'Perhaps you can make money with that vivid imagination of yours and pay to go on safaris instead.'

At first, she had sulked, her go-to strategy up to that time in her life, but when no-one took any notice, she admitted defeat. After all, her father had offered to pay, and there being no grants in Ireland, this was no small thing. She had enrolled in the NIHE communications course in Glasnevin and shared digs for three years with a couple of girls from Kilkenny, who got married straight out of college, never to be seen again.

Despite graduating with top marks, Isabella could not get her foot in the door at any of the national newspapers. A friend of Tom Green's worked as an editor at the Kilkenny People, and he offered her a position which seemed to her to be a secretarial post. She turned it down with bad grace and soldiered on, applying to all the newspapers and publishing companies in Dublin and London with no success.

The opportunity at Tall Tales had materialised when one of her classmates from Glasnevin fell pregnant, and shooed Isabella into Fintan O'Neill's office as a suggested replacement, before he could protest. His eyes almost popped out of his head as he took in her blonde curls and golden eyes, and he didn't hear her answers to his questions. He offered her the job there and then. While his criteria for employing her rankled, there was never any chance of Isabella turning down the position. A rung on the ladder.

At first, Isabella had been reluctant to write for what seemed to be a glorified pet comic, but she had to eat. When anyone asked her what she did for a living, she told them she was a freelance journalist. Not a lie, because she might have been full time, but only on a consultancy basis, meaning the magazine could fire her on a whim. She made sure Fintan had no complaints about the standard of her work, while staying out of his reach as much as possible.

Despite her conviction about her abilities, and her drive and talent, Isabella found herself stuck at Tall Tales for years. Months went by as she tackled stories about kittens up trees, sheep giving birth in snow storms, and faithful dogs staying beside their masters' graves. She never lost hope of escaping to a national newspaper or even a spot on a television news programme, but the opportunities slipped by with the years, and seven years went by in the blink of an eye. She felt trapped, but how could she leave without admitting defeat?

When Max Wolfe had not yet called her into his office for a pep talk after a week in the job, a ritual to which he had submitted all the other members of staff, and which led to a further reduction in their numbers, Isabella's anxiety increased. Max had reduced the original team of ten to four, including her. *Had he finished firing yet?*

She stared at her screen and sighed as she proof-read yet another heart-warming story about a lost kitten. Despite Max's ambitions, kittens and puppies were still their principal source of material for the magazine. This one had got itself stuck up a drainpipe which had to be disassembled to rescue it. On her desk sat a photograph of the plumber holding the dappled kitten to his face and smiling, his teeth rotten with nicotine, and blackheads visible in his sweaty stubble. She shuddered as she remembered his toxic breath.

He wouldn't be looking so pleased with himself if he had known what would happen next. The kitten had objected to being squeezed and lashed out. The poor man had almost lost an eye, but of course, in the Tall Tales magazine of cute kittens and puppies, nature was not red in tooth and claw but pink and fluffy, and they would make no mention of the mishap.

In Isabella's world, the near miss would have been the story they used. She imagined the plumber being rushed off to hospital and operated on by a team of surgeons, one of whom was impossibly handsome. She could see the scene in all its detail.

'Can we save his eye, doctor?' said one nurse, breathless at his proximity.

'I think so,' he replied, the twinkle in his eye flashing, as he—

'Earth to Miss Green, are you still with us?'

The sarcastic tone of her new boss's whiny voice cut through her daydream, bringing her back to the drab room with its cheap desks and fluorescent lighting.

'Can you come into my office, please?' said Max, leaning out of his office door on the Monday after his arrival.

Isabella plumped up her curls and straightened her skirt. Her pulse quickened as she crossed the floor to his door. She took a deep breath and entered the lion's den.

'Miss Green, we meet at last,' said Max, pulling at his moustache. 'Sit down.'

Isabella sat on the edge of the chair. She twisted the Claddagh ring on her finger, not daring to look up. Max raised an eyebrow at her nervous twitching.

'I need you to go to Sierra Leone,' he said. 'There's a sanctuary outside the capital where they rehabilitate rescued baby chimps, and I want an exclusive article.'

Isabella's eyes opened wide, and she waited for him to laugh, but he didn't. Despite the exotic location, the assignment appeared to qualify as abandoned kitten territory. Was he pulling her leg? She gulped and said the first thing that came into her head.

'Baby chimps? Isn't that pandering to the

readers?'

He guffawed.

'Hoist with my own petard. No pandering included. This is a sanctuary for traumatized chimpanzees orphaned by the civil war,' said Max. 'The rebels ate their mothers.'

As if. A Maxism no doubt. Who ate chimpanzees? He prodded between his yellow teeth with a wooden toothpick and removed a remnant of his lunch time steak, which he scrutinised before popping it back into his mouth. His ashtray breath made Isabella gag, but she hid her reaction by reaching into her pocket for a polo mint.

'Can I have one of those?' said Max, holding out his hand. 'Where was I? Oh, yes, the chimp sanctuary. Well, I'd like you to investigate, and get juicy stories about the sanctuary and photographs. You can use a camera, I take it?'

Isabella frowned. Sierra Leone?

'Isn't the civil war still going on there?' she said.

'It's all over bar the shouting,' said Max. 'Anyway, there are loads of burly troops and mercenaries out there. Men in uniform. I'd have thought they'd be right up your street.'

She tried not to scowl.

'What's wrong?' he said. 'Are you chicken? I thought women's lib had banished all that.'

'No, not at all. It's just—'

'Just what? Speak up.'

'Just nothing.'

'Good. Maggie will sort out your tickets and hotel. You'll fly from London so you can pick up your tickets there, and buy a mosquito net and so on. I doubt you'll find them in Dublin. Do you have somewhere to stay in London or shall Maggie book you a room there?'

'My sister, Liz, lives there.'

'Excellent. Well, piss off home, get packed, and find your passport. I'll have Maggie drop the itinerary and plane ticket to London off at your home later this afternoon.'

He held the door open and Isabella walked back to her desk. Am I dreaming? She opened her desk drawer and fumbled for her keys before removing her coat from the back of her chair. Sheila's eyes opened wide.

'He fired you?' she said.

Isabella shook her head.

'Not quite. He's sending me to Africa.'

Sheila's mouth fell open.

'There's no fecking way I'm going there,' she said.

Chapter 3

Isabella shut the front door behind her, panting with triumph. *Oh, heavens. I'm going to Africa to be a proper journalist.* She kicked the mail aside and sprinted up the stairs into the bathroom. As she grabbed the bathroom chair, her reflection in the mirror made her stop and stare. The colour in her cheeks emphasised her unblemished skin, and her golden-brown eyes were twinkling with excitement and anticipation. *How long has it been since my eyes shone like that? I look ten years younger.*

She opened the door of the airing cupboard on the hall landing and pulled out the box step. She clambered onto it, teetering as she yanked her suitcase from the top shelf. The faded towels piled on the next shelf down vied for her attention. 'Take me, take me', they seemed to say. Isabella had read Hitchhiker's Guide to the Galaxy, and she chose her favourite, a pale green affair fraying on one of its long edges.

She opened her suitcase and lined it with the towel, but that was as far as she got. *What on earth do I need for Sierra Leone, besides a mosquito net?* She sat on her bed, flummoxed. Holidays in Marbella with Graham hadn't prepared her for this, but her brother Michael would know what she needed. *I'll call him and ask. Graham will have a canary when he sees the phone bill, but I'll be in Africa by then.*

She dug her address book out of her handbag and found Michael's number. It took several goes to get through and the line crackled and hissed over her brother's voice.

'Isabella? What a surprise! Talk about out of the blue.'

'I need help,' she said.

'Now that's not a surprise. Aren't you going to ask how we are?'

'Don't be mean. This is important. How are you?'

'We're fine,' said Michael. 'What do you need?'

'I'm going to Sierra Leone, and I don't know what to take with me.'

'Sierra Leone? That's a turn up for the books. How come?'

'My new boss has big ideas.'

'Maybe your by-line isn't so ludicrous after all.'

Isabella did not like to be mocked. When she started work at Tall Tales, she had insisted on using Africa Green as the name on her articles, the only rebellious act she indulged in, and one tolerated by Fintan O'Neill, who found it exotic. Michael had found her attempt at rebranding preposterous, and teased her mercilessly.

'I'm the one who lives in Kenya. Why are you called Africa?'

'It's aspirational.'

'Delusional more like.'

Now she felt vindicated.

'It was only a matter of time. Are you going to help me or not?'

'Have you got a mosquito net? Or repellent?

16

You'll need some khaki trousers and t-shirts. And a large brimmed floppy hat.'

'Not my usual wear, but I can buy them in London when I pass through.'

'Are your vaccinations up to date?'

'I didn't get any. I hate needles.'

'You'll need to be brave.'

'There may not be enough time.'

'Make time and get straight over to the travel clinic. It's vital.'

Michael was the family oracle on matters pertaining to Africa, having married Blessing, his childhood sweetheart from South Africa, and settled down in Kenya. Isabella trusted his knowledge, even if she didn't like the result. After she rang off, she took a bus to the travel clinic in the centre of Dublin and asked about the requirements for Sierra Leone.

'Hello, there. What can I do for you today,' said the smiley nurse at the reception.

'I'm going to Sierra Leone and I need my vaccinations.'

'Will you be getting boosters? Or is it your first time?'

'It's my first time,' said Isabella, biting her lip.

The nurse looked at her with pity.

'We'll have to give you the lot. Luckily, we've got them all in stock.'

Isabella tried to look pleased, and the nurse smiled.

'You'll feel grotty for a couple of days, as well as having the sore arms,' said the nurse. 'But, compared to the diseases they protect you from, it will be a breeze.'

The nurse took Isabella into a cubicle and left her

17

there while she took out a selection of vaccines. Isabella had to lie down when her legs wobbled at the sight of the syringes.

'I'm giving you a tetanus shot for good measure,' said the nurse. 'We can't be too careful.'

A new envelope sat on the welcome mat in the hall when Isabella got home from the clinic. The injections had been an ordeal, but now they seemed worth it. She tore it open to find a note from Max's secretary, Maggie, informing her that the first seat available to Sierra Leone left from London on Iceland Air a week from Friday. The envelope also contained a return ticket to London, leaving the following Wednesday. *What a let-down. I'll need to go back into the office for a week, and my emergency packing seems premature, too. O God, I forgot about Graham. What on earth will he say when I tell him? Surely he'll be happy for me?* But doubt crept into her mind, and she found her excitement fading.

It might have been a reaction to the vaccinations, but by the time Graham got home, Isabella had worked herself up into a panic. The day had gone by in a blur and she now felt foolish for getting so excited. A numbing nervousness had crept up her spine as she waited for the sound of his key in the lock. She sat at the kitchen table pretending to read the Irish Times, which she had picked up at the travel clinic and taken away by mistake.

'It's not like you to bother with a newspaper,' said Graham. 'Is supper ready yet?'

'I thought we might get a takeaway.'

Graham's brow furrowed as he took in this suggestion.

'But it's Monday. We eat takeaway on Fridays.'

'There's something to celebrate.'

Graham blinked. A wide grin appeared on his face.

'You're pregnant at last. That's fantastic.'

He moved behind her and put his arms around her shoulders. 'Now you can quit that shitty job of yours and we can get married.'

Isabella shook herself free.

'No, I'm not. How can you call my job shit? I pay the bills too.'

Graham deflated.

'I'm sorry. I was disappointed.' He sat opposite her. 'What's your news then?'

'I've got my big break,' said Isabella, watching his face fall. She willed herself to continue. 'I'm going to Sierra Leone, to research an article about a chimp sanctuary.'

A metaphorical clunk rang out as Graham's jaw hit the table. He stared at her with his mouth still open, disbelief writ large on his features. Then he laughed.

'You had me going there. I thought you were serious for a second.'

'I am. Max asked me to go next week.'

'And you said yes? Are you crazy? That country's a basket case.'

'There's a peace treaty, and the rebels handed in their weapons. It's not dangerous any more.'

'Who told you that? Max? Don't be ridiculous. I won't let my child be subjected to danger.'

'But I'm not pregnant.'

'How do you know? Be rational. It's too late to start a career.'

Isabella put her hands over her stomach. *Could I be pregnant? He's been trying hard enough.* Graham noticed her gesture.

'Don't go. It's too dangerous. What would I do if something happened to you? We're happy, aren't we? Let's get married and live a normal life.'

He reached out and grabbed her hands, looking deep into her eyes. A wave of shame engulfed Isabella. People had spoiled her all her life, and Graham had never let her down. *Is it time I grew up?*

'Max won't be happy,' she said. 'But I'll turn down the job.'

And she meant it. But somehow, she didn't speak to Max, and she didn't unpack her bag, hiding it under the bed instead. Graham did everything he could to make her feel loved and important, but was she about to miss out on the biggest adventure of her life? There seemed to be no answer to her dilemma. Despite her doubts, she had decided to tell Max the truth, before the deadline for her flights, but then her sister Liz called, her voice vibrating with excitement.

'Michael rang and told me your fantastic news. I can't believe it. You must be ecstatic. Why didn't you ring me yet? Are you coming through London?'

Isabella swallowed hard.

'I'm not going,' she said.

'What? Why not? Has Max changed his mind?' said Liz.

'No, it's Graham, well, us, I mean… He's not keen on the idea of me gallivanting off to Africa. He wants to get married and have children.'

'But you must take the assignment,' said Liz. 'You'll always regret it if you don't. Graham isn't going anywhere. You can come home afterwards and have babies.'

'But I already agreed—'

'Don't be ridiculous. Change your mind and go. It's a once in a lifetime chance to do what you've always wanted. How can you turn it down?'

And Liz was right, as usual. But telling Graham seemed impossible. He made a massive effort over the weekend to show her how much she meant to him, and even tried banana on his Weetabix to show he, too, could change. His desperation alienated her, making her more determined to go, but she couldn't find the right time to break the news to him. He didn't seem to notice the growing distance between them as Isabella drew away. She'd always liked his nonchalance with her, and now he had morphed into just another clingy boyfriend.

In the end, Isabella took the coward's way out. She booked a taxi to the airport and left the house while Graham was at work. She wrote him a note and leant it against a mug on the kitchen table. It read 'This is my last chance. If I don't go now, I'll never know what I am capable of. Sorry. Izzy'.

Chapter 4

Isabella pulled her thin coat tighter around her body as the rush of frigid air entered the sliding carriage doors.

'Mind the gap,' said the automated voice.

Mind the Arctic air, more like it. I hope Liz will lend me a coat for London shopping. She smiled at a woman sitting opposite her to receive a blank stare back. The unwritten rules of London life. In Dublin you couldn't help making friends on the bus.

The underground train arrived at Green Park and she took the Victoria line to Victoria. Liz lived in a mansion flat on Vincent Square, a short walk from the tube station.

'If I'm not in, ring the doorbell for flat one. The caretaker has a spare key. I'll tell her you might collect it,' Liz had told her.

Liz worked for a top-tier broker in the city, and often came home from work late. She never complained, only shrugged, and got on with it. Her hard won independence and pioneering spirit made Isabella feel inadequate. The City could be intimidating for professional women, but Liz's matter-of-fact manner, and her deaf ear to misogyny, soon established her a foothold. She had a natural instinct for broking, and her take-home pay grew with her reputation for making the right call.

Isabella lifted a weary arm to the bell and waited. The door clicked open, and she pushed it ajar, dragging her bag into the entrance hall. To her relief, an old-fashioned lift with accordion doors sat in the centre. After wrestling with them, Isabella pressed the button for the third floor. The lift rose, creaking and groaning in protest. Through the bars, a pair of polished brogues appeared and then the tailored wool trouser suit of her sister. Liz's smiling face slid into view.

'You're here, thank God,' said Isabella.

'It's a holiday in America. They shut the markets, thank Mammon. Fancy a glass of wine?'

The sisters sat side by side on the sofa, their stockinged feet up on the ottoman, which sat on a Persian rug with tattered fringes.

'Can't you afford a new rug?' said Isabella. 'I thought they were paying you a small fortune.'

'An enormous fortune, actually. And that rug is an antique. It's silk.'

'It's holey.'

'Don't be so parochial. Tell me about your assignment in Sierra Leone. Will you be interviewing the rebels?'

'I hope not. I'm doing an article on the baby chimps at the Tacugama Sanctuary.'

Liz snorted.

'Baby chimps? Maybe, change your name to Chimpanzee Green instead?' she said, giggling.

'Don't be mean,' said Isabella. 'Anyway, it's important. The rebels are slaughtering chimpanzees and selling their babies as pets. I want to expose the trade in protected animals. Max says he can use any interesting articles I write, or pass them on to other magazines in the group.'

'Now that sounds more like it. Someone important might spot your talent.'

'I'm hoping to do an exposé if I find any corruption.'

'That sounds great, but, remember, not everyone is ready for Africa Green, fearless female journalist. If the government is involved, they won't want you interfering.'

'I'll be careful, I promise.'

'And don't outshine Max, if you want to keep your job.'

Isabella sipped her chardonnay. Trust Liz to be right again. Her sister could infuriate her.

'How's Sean?' she said.

Liz bit her lip.

'Oh, you know. He never changes.'

'And that's a bad thing?'

'You should know. How did Graham take the news?'

Isabella blushed.

'I chickened out,' she said. 'I didn't tell him.'

Liz's eyes opened wide.

'Won't he be wondering where you are?' she said, taking a mouthful of wine.

'I left him a note.'

Liz choked as her wine went down the wrong way. She coughed and spluttered, bright red in the face. Isabella thumped her on the back, laughing. Finally, Liz recovered and turned to face her.

'We're not much good at romance, are we?' she said.

'It's odd when you consider how in love Mummy and Daddy still are,' said Isabella. 'Maybe we're looking for the perfect relationship.'

'So, how come I'm still with Sean?'

When Isabella awoke the next morning, Liz had gone to work, leaving a set of keys on the kitchen table. After a quick glance into Liz's sad fridge, she bought a bacon sandwich at the corner café. Thus fortified, she made her way to Piccadilly and entered Hatchards. Being unsure which section held books on chimpanzee behaviour, she approached the desk and asked a thin young woman with greasy hair where they might be.

'You could try the politics section,' she said, smiling at her own wit. 'But perhaps the section on the natural world might be better.'

Isabella soon found what she was looking for; The Chimpanzees of Gombe: patterns of behaviour by Jane Goodall. A friend from university had recommended it to her, but he had not mentioned its size. *Six hundred pages? When will I ever read all that?* Notwithstanding, Isabella opened the book and examined the pictures, fascinated by the facial expressions of the apes and their different physiognomies. Time passed as she read page after page, arms aching with effort. Then somebody tapped her on the shoulder. The assistant stood there with a leaflet in her hand.

'Are you going to read it all in store?' she asked.

Isabella jumped.

'Oh, no, I mean, of course not. Is that the time? Gosh, my appointment begins in half an hour.'

'Do you want me to ring it up for you?'

'Yes, please.'

'By the way, I've put a leaflet inside the flap for you. Jane Goodall is giving a talk in July at the Linnean Society. Since you are so fascinated by her book, you might enjoy it.'

'Oh, that would have been wonderful. Unfortunately, I live in Dublin.'

'Dublin? You don't sound Irish.'

'I do when I'm with my friends.'

'Ah, a chameleon, a useful trait. That will be twenty pounds.'

'Twenty pounds? I'm not sure I…'

'There's a cash machine outside.'

'No, it's okay, I have my credit card.'

By the time Isabella got back to the flat after carrying the book around all day, her arm felt a foot longer. *Poor planning, I should have bought the book last.* After packing the repellent and mosquito net and other essentials, the book would not fit in her suitcase. *I don't want to lug it around in my rucksack.* Plan B then. She opened the book on the kitchen table and took notes on the most important observations about chimpanzee life, which she collated into sections;

- individuals show preferences in their diet for more meat or fruit
- begging for food is a common behaviour in which an individual asks another for food, especially of a rarer or more highly prized sort such as meat or sweet fruit
- the ability to avoid looking at interesting things to avoid bringing a rival's attention to them
- aggression varies between individuals, even when of the same age, size, and sex
- large groups can split in two, leading to lethal violence between the two groups until all the males of one group are eliminated

- alliances formed between related or even unrelated individuals to intimidate lone rivals
- some individuals (both male and female) are more interested in one-on-one "consortships" away from the group when the female is fertile, and other individuals stay in the group and have multiple partners
- some females prefer to find a male from another group of chimpanzees when in oestrus, but other females mate with a male from the same group
- the strong attachment between mother and child lasts into adulthood
- when a mother dies (e.g., from disease) with offspring who were not yet old enough to make their way as adults, others in the group will care for them; sometimes these were their grown siblings, but sometimes not.

Isabella was still bent over the book when Liz got home late carrying a feast of Chinese food with her. The smell wafted up Isabella's nose, reminding her she had not eaten since her bacon butty at breakfast.

'You have no idea how good that smells,' she said.

'Oh, I do. I'm starving. Sorry I'm late. Is this research?' Liz said, gesticulating at the table.

'Yes, I bought a book to take with me, but it's too big. I thought I could take notes and leave it with you, if that's all right?'

Liz picked up the book and read the back cover. She frowned.

'Sure, but…'

Isabella sighed.

'I thought you'd disagree.'

Liz pursed her lips.

'You're going to Sierra Leone,' she said. 'I'm willing to bet a copy of that book would be like gold dust in the sanctuary.'

'I hadn't thought of that.'

'The owner is just some random guy who took in a baby chimp and never looked back, right? I bet this book would be an amazing resource for him.'

'I guess so.'

'There you go. And you can put it on expenses too.'

Isabella frowned.

'But it's so heavy.'

'I'll lend you my wheeled suitcase. Stop fussing and serve us some of the food. I'll get the wine.'

About half way through dinner, the telephone rang. Liz picked it up and answered through a mouthful of food.

'Hello? Yes, she's here.'

Isabella's eyes widened, and she shook her head. Liz passed her the phone and pointed to the kitchen. Sighing, Isabella took it inside and shut the door. She raised the receiver to her ear.

'Hello,' she said.

'Hello? Is that all you have to say for yourself?' said Graham, choking on his words. 'How could you do this to me?'

'I'm sorry. I had to give it a go.'

'Why?'

'If I knew, I'd tell you. I just didn't want to spend the rest of my life, up to my neck in nappies wondering what if. Surely you can understand that?'

A long silence. Had the line gone down? Graham cleared his throat.

'How long will it take, to find out?'

'I'm not sure. A few weeks, a month. Can't you wait for me that long? I thought you loved me.'

'I do. It's just, well, it's not normal. I should've known…'

His voice tailed off.

'You should've known what?'

'Nothing. Will you call me from there?'

'I'll try. The phone service may be ropey.'

'Okay. I'll wait, but don't take the piss. I'm a man and I have my needs.'

Like a takeaway on a Friday and no banana on his cereal.

'It's just this once, darling. I need to get it out of my system. I'll be back soon. Honest.'

'Okay so, look after yourself and take your antimalarials.'

'I will. Love you.'

'Love you too.'

Isabella replaced the phone on the receiver and sat down. She picked up her fork and poked the remains of the Chinese food on her plate. Liz drummed her fingers on the table.

'Well?' she said.

Chapter 5

The hovercraft rumbled its way across the estuary from Freetown airport, bucking over the waves and causing Isabella to feel nauseous. She swallowed and tried to see out of the small, dirty windows towards the horizon, her stomach churning. *Why did no one warn me I would be in a boat? Not that I expected the scrum for the luggage either.* She tugged her rucksack to her tummy, pressing the weight of the book in it against her. *How much longer?*

After what seemed like an eternity, the vessel glided onto the shore at Man of War Bay and the passengers disembarked. Isabella dragged her suitcase down the gangway, green about the gills, muttering to herself as she ignored the waiting taxi drivers. Maggie had booked her a hotel located a short walk from the hovercraft port, so Isabella set out along the road, dragging Liz's suitcase over the broken pavements.

The damp heat crept into her clothes and her cheeks glowed red with exertion. Isabella had spent her life complaining about the climate in Ireland, rain, rain and more rain, and she had been unprepared for the heavy heat of the Sierra Leonean capital. Torremolinos had been hot, but not like this. She stopped in the shade of a large tree, panting with exertion. *Should I go back for a taxi?* A thin boy, with dust in his short afro, appeared at her side, making her jump.

'Can I help you, Miss?' he said.

Isabella examined him. He didn't appear dangerous, and there was no way he could run off with the heavy suitcase. It must weigh more than him.

'I don't have any leones yet.'

The boy grabbed the handle from her.

'Oh, that's okay,' he said. 'I take dollars, sterling, francs. Where are you going?'

Isabella fumbled in her handbag for the itinerary.

'It says here, the Animal Kingdom Resort,' she said, frowning. 'Funny name for a hotel.'

'It's close by. Follow me.'

He started off down the road, his feet slapping in his battered flip-flops, tied onto his feet with electric flex. His stained t-shirt was transparent with wear and his shorts were held up with string. Open sores on his legs and his arms spoke of neglect and a poor diet. Isabella wondered how anyone could treat a child that way. His breathing, laboured under the burden of pulling her suitcase, crackled in his lungs.

They stopped at the entrance to the hotel and he waited for her, his hand outstretched.

'What's your name?' she said.

He looked at her with suspicion, his thin face snot-smeared and tired. She raised her eyebrows.

'You'll laugh at me,' he said.

'I promise not to.'

'It's Ten,' he said. 'My mother ran out of names.'

The hurt in his voice cut Isabella to the core.

'Oh.'

'That's why I'm on the streets. She couldn't feed me.'

'Where is she now?'

'Dead.'

He snivelled, head down, staring at the ground.

'Give me my money,' he croaked.

Isabella crouched down beside her suitcase and reached out to lift his chin. He flinched at her touch. *Christ, he thought I would hit him. Poor little fecker.* She sat down on the hotel steps and patted the step beside her. He perched on the edge of the step as if ready to flee.

'Would you like to show me around town tomorrow?'

She saw him hesitate.

'What's your day rate?' she said. 'Do I get a discount for being blonde?'

His brow wrinkled as he fought to imagine a figure.

'How about I give you five pounds now and we can negotiate the rest tomorrow? Buy a fresh pair of shoes, I can't be seen with a scruffy assistant.'

His eyes opened wide as she held out the note, and he grabbed it and stuffed it in his pocket before she changed her mind. He saluted her.

'I'll be here at dawn,' he said.

Isabella laughed.

'How about nine o'clock?'

'And what shall I call you?' he said.

'Africa, my name is Africa Green.'

'Okay, Miss Africa, I will see you tomorrow.'

He didn't seem to notice her weird name. *I guess it's not so strange compared to his.* After she watched him flap down the street, Isabella entered the hotel and approached the reception desk, a cheap homemade affair with peeling laminate. A man with a name badge that read Pete Hawkins looked up from the old magazine he had been reading. He had army tattoos on his arms and a handsome, shaved head. His grey eyes had dark blue rings around the pupils and sadness in their depths.

'Yes?' he said, with badly concealed aggression.

'I think you have a reservation for me? I'm Africa Green.'

He sighed and pulled a scruffy log book towards him, pretending to run his finger down the bookings. The labouring ceiling fan did not alleviate the heat in the lobby and a bead of sweat ran down Isabella's face. She wiped it off with her sleeve. *Like this dump is going to be full.*

'I've found a booking for Green, but it says Isabella here.'

Isabella blushed.

'Well, yes, that's the name in my passport, but Africa Green is my byline and I'm here on an assignment.'

Pete raised an eyebrow.

'And who do you write for?' he said.

The blush deepened until she resembled a red traffic light at night.

'Tall Tales.'

'A pet magazine?' he said, smirking. 'You won't find many puppies and kittens out here, love.'

'Actually, I'm writing an article about Tacugama, and the rebels.'

'Really?' he said, raising an eyebrow.

He pulled out a form and pushed it across the desk.

'Fill this out with your real name. Are you paying in pounds or dollars?'

'I've got sterling travellers cheques.'

'You can pay with those and I'll give you the change in leones.'

'That would be great. By the way, I've asked a young lad to show me around town tomorrow, what's the going rate?'

Pete rolled his eyes and shook his head.

'I wouldn't recommend it. How old is he?'

'I don't know. He looked about nine or ten.'

'Twelve or thirteen, then. Pay him about five quid in leones and that's more than fair. Are you sure he's not a thief? Most of them are.'

Isabella bit her lip. *I've already paid him that much. Will he come back or just keep the money?*

'No, but he needs the money. I'll take my chances,' she said, more vehemently than she meant to.

Pete laughed, and the smell of alcohol wafted across the desk.

'Don't get snotty. I'm a hearts and minds man myself.'

'Were you in the British army?'

'Yes, the Royal Anglians, but I left...'

He seemed about to say something else, but he clammed up, avoiding her glance, and shuffling some papers. She put her rucksack back on.

'Where's my room?' she said.

'It's on the first floor up the stairs. Number twenty-two.'

He didn't offer to help her with her suitcase, and she didn't want to ask.

'Great, thanks.'

She hauled her bag up the stairs, careful not to look back and catch his eye. He might be handsome, but he seemed bitter and twisted and had been drinking. By the time she got to her room, her clothes were damp with exertion. *Did Ava Gardner sweat like a horse? What was the saying? Horses sweat, men perspire and ladies merely glow?* Perhaps ladies didn't have to carry their own suitcases. The heaviest thing Isabella had seen Ava Gardner lift was a martini.

When she had unpacked a few essentials and put on a dry shirt, Isabella sat on her bed with the pillows banked behind her back and made notes about her first impressions. She had intended to skip supper but, as the light faded, her stomach growled in protest and mosquitos appeared from nowhere, intending to make a meal of her instead.

She slid off the bed and pulled her long linen trousers and baggy t-shirt from her suitcase, spraying them with her repellent. Travel had creased them, but she didn't bother looking for an iron. The Animal Kingdom had air conditioning, and from the sound of it, a large generator, but there the luxuries ceased. She brushed her hair, tying a bandana around her forehead and under the curls to lift them from her neck, put on some red lipstick and admired her blonde bombshell reflection in the mirror. Her tawny eyes held excitement, and she grinned at herself.

In the lobby, Pete did his handover to the night shift, a local lad.

'Hi Madam. My name is Demba. How can we help you this evening?'

'I'm Africa Green.'

Pete snorted, but Isabella ignored him.

'Is there somewhere local I can get something to eat?'

'Pete's going to Alex's. You should go with him,' said Demba, receiving a black stare from his companion, who sighed.

'I'll show you where it is,' said Pete.

'That sounds great,' said Isabella, ignoring the inferred snub. 'I just need a quick bite to eat.'

Pete cocked his head to one side.

'Are you Irish?'

'No, but my parents brought me up there, so I have a slight brogue.'

'It was the long 't's that outed you. Let's go then.'

Chapter 6

Alex's bar sat on Man of War Bay near the hoverport. The sound of people laughing and glasses clinking echoed up the street towards them. As they walked towards the entrance, Pete caught his toe on a paving stone in his haste to distance himself from Isabella, pitching forward out of balance. Isabella grabbed his arm and stopped him from hitting the ground. He jerked it from her grasp.

'I don't need any help,' he said, wincing as he steadied himself.

'Who says you do?' said Isabella. 'I've got quick reactions. Did you hurt yourself?'

'No. I'm fine.'

He pushed his way past Isabella, ducking as he entered an archway covered in climbing plants, which released a cloud of perfume as he blundered through. Isabella drank in the smell and did a couple of deep breaths to calm her annoyance. She followed Pete past the bar and onto the covered veranda which stretched left and right, full of plastic tables and chairs. The tables had paper tablecloths held in place by cheap metal napkin holders and vases with plastic flowers in them.

Unused to being snubbed, Isabella joined Pete at a table beside the folding screen at the edge of the veranda. Stray patches of sand had invaded the tiled floor and crunched underfoot as she sat down. He gave her a hostile look.

'I didn't ask you to sit with me,' he said.

'Were you expecting me to sit on my own?' said Isabella.

Pete shrugged.

'I'm not a babysitter,' he said.

'It's nice here,' said Isabella. 'I didn't expect it.'

'Were you expecting natives with bongo drums or what?'

Isabella did not answer. Instead, she gazed around at the mixture of people sitting at the tables, trying to see what they were eating, and guessing at their conversations. She pulled out her notebook and scribbled in it. As she had expected, Pete didn't like to be ignored.

'It's my favourite bar,' said Pete. 'I can get home in a couple of minutes, and they show the Premier League on cable too.'

A frazzled waitress arrived, wiping the sweat off her brow with her apron. She took their order and hurried off into the kitchen before returning with their drinks. Now that she had ordered food, Isabella's stomach grumbled with hunger. She watched Pete down a couple of beers in quick succession while she made notes in her journal and sipped a Sprite. Despite her determination to dislike him, she found herself mesmerised by his forearms. Their muscular form and prominent veins brought her a tug of lust.

Then he burped, interrupting her reverie, and wiped his mouth with the back of his hand, challenging her to mind. She turned her head to face him, her golden eyes fixed on his grey ones, trying to see past the confusing show of studied indifference and terror of being ignored. He looked away, folding and unfolding a paper napkin, his calloused hands battered and scarred.

'So how did you end up at the Animal Kingdom?' she said.

'It belongs to my brother-in-law. He's Lebanese and comes here to trade diamonds. When I left the service, I found it hard to settle in England and he offered me a job out here.'

'Oh, I see,' said Isabella, but she didn't.

Who would choose to run a hotel in such a dangerous country? Maybe he drank too much, and they didn't want him around. She tossed her mop of curls and tightened the bandana, lifting them off her neck. Despite the ceiling fans cutting thick swathes through the turgid air, she felt as if she were sitting in a hot bath. A drop of sweat ran down the side of her face. She looked around the restaurant, trying to distract herself.

A burly man, with Pacific Island features and build, held court at one of the plastic tables across the restaurant from her. The waiter had placed three iced tankards of Castle lager in front of him. Condensation ran down the outside and stained the paper table cloth. The other men at the table hung on his every word, looking around at each other in affirmation when he made some quiet point, and leaning forward, straining to hear him above the din of the crowded room. Isabella's companion noticed her gaze.

'The court of King Faletau,' said Pete, sneering.

'Who's he?' said Isabella, scrabbling for her pen.

'Manu Faletau. Ex-SAS. He's a mercenary who washed up here with the other flotsam from the armies of the Globe. He works for anyone who'll pay enough.'

The hairs on Isabella's arms stood stiffly to attention as a shiver ran up her spine. *An authentic story, one I can get my teeth into, after all the tales of stranded ponies and abandoned kittens.* Not that she didn't like animals. Her heart bled for most of them.

Isabella pushed her chair back, intending to head for the table where Faletau was sitting.

'The toilets are that way,' said Pete, grabbing her arm and gesticulating. 'Where are you going?'

'To do my job,' said Isabella.

'Slow down there,' he said, 'I thought you were here to write about Tacugama.'

'I am. I just want to meet him. Can you introduce me?'

'Forget it.'

'I don't need your help,' she said. 'I'm going, anyway.'

He shrugged and stood up.

'Okay, but show some respect, he's used to it.'

She adjusted the waistband of her khaki trousers and pulled down her t-shirt. Flashing her set of perfect white teeth, she strode over to the Tongan's table with as much verve as she could summon. Manu Faletau looked up as she approached and raised his eyebrows. His appraising glance surveyed her with laser-like intensity. As she later told Liz, he had x-rayed her in a second. A shudder of anticipation ran through her body. This could be a scoop. She stuck out her hand.

'I'm Africa Green,' she said.

He looked at her hand and raised an eyebrow.

'Are you now?' he said, appraising her. 'Hi Pete, how's tricks?'

Pete's bravado evaporated. He shuffled and

looked at the floor.

'Not bad, sir.'

'So, Miss Green, what can we do for you?' said Faletau, leaning back in his plastic seat and making it creak in protest.

'I'm a journalist with, um, here on assignment.'

'She's writing about baby chimps,' said Pete. 'And her name's Isabella.'

She spun around to glare at him and the men laughed.

'Don't mock her, chaps, we need the press on our side,' said Faletau.

Another roar of laughter. Isabella's cheeks burned with shame. Pete joined in, enjoying her discomfort.

'A very important assignment. Are you going to Tacugama?' said Faletau.

'Yes, the day after tomorrow.'

Manu's eyes fixed on hers and she struggled to return his gaze.

'Be careful out there. Some rebel soldiers are still refusing to give up their weapons. We're going on a helicopter recce on Friday to scout out the camp of the most dangerous group.'

'Can I come?' said Isabella, surprising herself and everyone else at the table.

Manu raised an eyebrow.

'It might be dangerous,' he said.

'Oh, I don't care,' said Isabella. 'Won't I be safe with you?'

What am I doing? That Sprite must be spiked.

A rumble from Manu's chest erupted from his mouth in a guffaw of laughter.

'You are a cheeky baggage, aren't you? Sure, tag along. We'll be leaving at four thirty, so we can approach out of the setting sun and surprise them.'

'Where is the heliport?'

'I presume you're staying at the Animal Kingdom? We'll pick you up on our way there. Do you want to come, Pete?'

'No thanks, I've done my last recce,' said Pete.

'Have a beer with us, Africa.'

Isabella shook her head. She needed to process before jumping in head first.

'No, thank you. I'm tired after my flight. I'm going to bolt my food and go back to my room,' she said. 'Stay here with your friends, Pete. It was nice to meet you, Mr Faletau.'

'Call me Manu. We'll see you tomorrow.'

Isabella went back to the table where a plate of fried fish with rice sat waiting for her with a napkin lying on it to keep the flies off. She gobbled her food, desperate to get back to her room and digest the day. Now and then loud bursts of laughter from Faletau's table made her look up from her food. She finished her meal and signalled at the waitress for the bill.

'The gentleman over there already paid for your bill,' said the waitress. 'But you can leave me a tip if you like.'

Isabella turned to see Manu waving at her. She waved back and smiled at him, and he nodded in acknowledgment. As she left through the bar, she noticed Pete coming out of the toilet. He was gazing at her with a longing which sent chills up her spine, the hunger in his eyes undisguised. A dangerous man. She resolved to stay well clear.

Chapter 7

Pete walked back to the hotel earlier than usual, unwilling for Manu and his cohort to witness his habitual descent into the drunkenness which cloaked him from the nightmares that came looking for him like enemy star fighters probing his weakness with their lasers. He stumbled through his routine, brushing his teeth, and throwing his clothes onto a chair, before sliding naked under his army issue mosquito net, impregnated with permethrin and bad memories.

He tried to think positive thoughts as he sank into sleep, but the sight of Isabella pouting at his unnecessary put-downs invaded his head. Another person alienated, and for what? Like he didn't need more friends? And there was something special about her, a vulnerability under the fake hard shell. He wanted to crack her like a warm Smartie and find the liquid chocolate centre within. But even his thoughts of Isabella couldn't hold off the demons who came for him later, unprotected by drinking, naked in his bed.

The nightmare always started the same way. He moaned in his sleep as he retraced his stops along the dusty trail through the foothills of Iraq. Ahead of him, the platoon leader scoured the culvert bordering the road for tell-tale signs of recent activity unrelated to goats. The tire tracks of the Scud missile carriers stuck out like a sore thumb in the desert and could be followed to the prize. Pete's unit was tasked with taking them out of commission and then slipping back over the border.

They had been out walking for hours in the baking sun, chasing down targets spotted from the air, only to find they had been moved again. Exasperation grew with the heat, and water supplies were already running low. No audible grumbles of dissent came from members of the unit, but the slumped shoulders and dragged feet spoke volumes of their moral. Pete's eyes were red with exhaustion in his sunburnt face. The bone-dry air had chapped his lips, and he resisted the temptation to lick them and get a mouthful of silt.

Out of habit, he counted the days until the end of his tour of duty. Only thirteen days remained. Lucky for some? He hoped so. The Iraqi Scud Missile units had become more active, emboldened by their success. His unit was now stranded in no-man's-land, working off the end of their tour in a hostile and dangerous country. Their patrols had become less frequent as the situation rendered them more futile. What was the point of risking their lives for a patch of dusty hinterland that they would soon abandon? Their now infrequent raids were merely a signal to the Iraqis that the British had their number, and not to take liberties until they had gone.

He trudged along the trail, deep in thought. A cramp grabbed his guts, and he stopped and bent over double. A drop of sweat rolled down his nose and plopped onto the sand. He swung his rucksack off his back and on to the ground in front of him. He fished in the front pocket to retrieve an anti-spasmodic, groaning in pain as another cramp seized his colon. Most of the patrol members were several yards ahead of him. Before he could ask the unit to halt for a second, a metallic click penetrated the still air as someone's foot depressed the trigger on the antipersonnel mine. The last thing he saw was his friend Fred spin around in shock before the landscape exploded.

The world filled with bright light and pain. Horrible screaming penetrated his eardrums, despite the ringing in his ears. He lay still for a moment, fighting for consciousness. All around him, bodies writhed on the ground. He patted himself down, checking for his four limbs and between his legs. He let out a relieved breath. All present and correct. His rucksack had taken the main force of the blast and lay shredded beside him. *Have I escaped unscathed?* He tried to get up, but a terrible pain made him look down at his side, which had been pierced by a piece of shrapncl. His radio lay on the ground in front of him and he reached for it, grunting with effort.

After radioing their position, he checked on the other members of the patrol, shouting their names. Only two men answered, but no one stood up. The mine had maimed most of them below the knee except for the soldier who had trod on it, blowing him to pieces. Pete reached Fred by pulling himself along in the dirt, but Fred had died in the explosion and his eyes were still open in surprise. Pete lay beside Fred's body and focused on staying alive. He pulled some dressings out of his rucksack and taped them over the wound, grimacing with pain.

He couldn't tell how long they lay there, as he passed out shortly afterwards. The whomping sound of the helicopter landing nearby alerted him to their rescue and the next thing he knew, he found himself in the medivac tent. The pain seeped back into his body as the morphine stopped working. He lay there fighting the nausea, listening to the cries of agony from the other voices in the tent until he could bear it no longer and screamed, too.

***

Down the hallway, Isabella woke with a start as a loud yell of pain reverberated through the hotel. She sat up in bed, looking around in alarm, her heart thundering in her chest. *What the hell was that?* No other sounds broke the silence, and she was about to lie down again when a low moan echoed down the hall. It sounded like Pete. *Could he be in trouble? Maybe he had got drunk and fallen down the stairs? It's not like I owe him anything, but what if he has injured himself?*

Sighing, Isabella put on her shoes and crept out of her room, along the passageway. The floorboards creaked under her feet and a group of punch-drunk moths mobbed a bare light bulb in the hall. She shuddered as one crunched under her foot. She stopped to listen for a moment. The moans had stopped, but she could hear someone crying behind a door. She reached out her hand to open it, but Demba appeared beside her and caught her hand.

'Don't,' he said. 'Mister Pete would be ashamed if you saw him like this.'

'Pete? Oh, I heard the screaming. Is he alright?'

'Nightmares,' said Demba. 'Something that happened in his army days. He won't talk about it.'

'Is that why he drinks so much?'

'I guess so. Go back to bed, Miss. I know how to deal with this.'

He opened the door and Isabella glimpsed Pete's muscular form bunched into a foetal position under a mosquito net. She turned away, unwilling to invade his privacy despite her curiosity. Demba slipped into the room and put his hand on Pete's back, rubbing it in a circular motion, muttering placatory sentences. Pete moaned and struggled with his sheets, but his movements became less jerky as he relaxed. Demba turned around and, seeing her standing there, gestured that she should leave.

Isabella started back down the passageway, still hearing Demba's soothing tones floating out of Pete's room. She felt ashamed for her earlier disgust at his behaviour. *What on earth could have caused this sort of continuing trauma? As a soldier, he must have witnessed some horrible scenes. Maybe they haunted him still?*

The horrors of war were not new to her. She had almost lost her brother Michael to a terrorist bullet in her youth, something which had made her grow up fast in that respect. She would never forget the cold hospital rooms with their plastic chairs, and the white faces of her parents as they waited for Michael to come out of surgery. Their friend Liam had died in the same attack, which knocked the stuffing out of the entire family. Liam's funeral still ranked as the saddest day of her life, and one of the few where she didn't want to be the centre of attention. She still blamed herself for his death, but she had told no one about her lingering guilt. She locked it up in the deepest recesses of her mind and pretended life went on despite his death.

Isabella lay in bed listening for Pete to call for help again, but only the juddering racket of ancient taxi engines, and the high-pitched squeaks of bats feasting on mosquitos outside her window, broke the silence. She shut her eyes and turned on her side, but it took a long time before she could fall asleep again.

Chapter 8

The next morning, resisting the temptation to inquire about Pete, Isabella asked a bleary Demba to change some money into leones for her. Then she stepped outside the hotel, expecting to find that Ten had swindled her, and abandoned to her own devices. To her relief, he waited for her on the steps outside the hotel. Instead of a new outfit, he sported a black eye and his knees wept from deep grazes. He avoided her eyes as she took in his dishevelled appearance.

'What happened to you?' she said.

'Nothing,' said Ten. 'Are you ready to go?'

'Not yet. I need breakfast. Where can we eat?'

'What about here?' said Ten, indicating the hotel with a thrust of his jaw.

'The cook is hung over,' said Isabella, which was not true, but the thought of seeing Pete again made her nervous.

They ate at Alex's. Ten ate all of his breakfast and half of Isabella's and then sat back with a euphoric expression on his face, his belly distended. He stared out to sea, mesmerised by the small boats zipping back and forth.

'What happened to your eye?' said Isabella, hoping to take advantage of his mood.

Ten frowned and his expression closed again,

shutting her out.

'Do you want a tour or not?' he said, slipping off his chair, his flip-flops slapping on the floor.

Isabella shrugged. They had all day to find out about each other, and there was no way she could make her way around without him. She summoned reserves of patience and paid the bill. They went out into the street and Ten stuck his arm out at a passing taxi, which pulled in to the kerb beside them. The driver leered at Isabella, but Ten snapped out some instructions and he turned his attention back to the road.

Once they had passed over the bridge towards the centre of town, the traffic snarled up and crept along the narrow streets full of potholes and houses with faded wooden fronts interspersed with old colonial buildings crumbling where they stood. In the centre, several government buildings in a 1970s block style filled the holes between them. The pavements heaved with street traders and people hurrying to work or to the markets.

The taxi stopped at a chaotic roundabout, provoking loud horn blasts and abusive language from the cars stuck behind it. Isabella and Ten descended from the taxi beside an enormous tree with massive buttress roots and large thorns on its trunk. Ten went over to it and leant his forehead on the trunk for an instant before turning to Isabella.

'This is the Cotton Tree,' he said. 'The first settlers in Sierra Leone prayed under this tree when they got here from Nova Scotia.'

'Nova Scotia? Are you sure?'

Ten frowned.

'Do you think I'm stupid?'

'No, of course not, I'm just surprised, that's all. I

know nothing about Sierra Leone.'

'Anyway, it's been the symbol of freedom in Freetown ever since.'

Isabella looked up into the immense leafy canopy and tried to imagine the first settlers sitting under its ample shade.

'I like those weird fleeces on the seed pods,' she said. 'What sort of tree is it?'

'It's a ceiba but some people call it a cotton tree because of the fibres.'

'Do they make anything with them?'

'We use it to stuff pillows and mattresses.'

Isabella picked up a fallen seed pod and felt the fibres between her fingers. Then she put it in her rucksack. Ten rolled his eyes but did not comment. He led Isabella to the Tourist Office, but it looked like it had been closed for a while. Isabella pressed her face against the glass. Inside, the desks looked as if they had been abandoned in a hurry, the brochures fading in the window and cobwebs in the corners. A poster on the wall of the office offered tours to Bunce Island. It had a photo of a ruined building overgrown by vegetation on it.

'What's Bunce Island?' said Isabella.

'They used it as a place to keep slaves ready for transport across the Atlantic. We can go there on a day trip. It's a nice island,' said Ten.

'Nice? But what about the slaves? Don't you hate the traders?' said Isabella.

'Who sold them the slaves?' said Ten. 'Other black men.'

'But they abolished slavery in the 19th century.'

'And who rules Sierra Leone now? The descendants of freed slaves. They returned here from

America wearing western clothes and lording it over us locals. The powerful man still rules here. Look what happened to me last night.'

'What did happen to you?' said Isabella, seizing her chance.

Ten spun around to face her, his face contorted.

'Are you stupid?' he shouted. 'It's not important.'

'It is to me.'

Ten sighed.

'I bought myself some new shoes with the money you gave me, and I wore them home. Some bigger boys beat me up and stole them, and they took the rest of the cash.'

'That's terrible.'

'It's my fault. I should have hidden the shoes before I got home.'

'Where do you live?' said Isabella.

'It's none of your business,' he said.

His small chest heaved with emotion as he struggled to contain himself. Isabella waited for him to calm down.

'How did you know about the return of the slaves? Did they teach you that at school?'

'School? I've never been. My mother couldn't afford to pay for the uniforms.'

'But you can read and write?'

'Enough.'

But he avoided her eyes and his face closed again. Releasing the pent-up rage had subdued him and he sat on a wall, swinging his feet and recovering his equilibrium. His pain seeped out of his pores and invaded the air. Isabella hadn't felt so useless and distressed in years. The combined pain of Pete and Ten penetrated her selfish mindset and made her feel responsible for them in a way she couldn't explain. *But how can I help?*

She tapped him on the knee, avoiding the grazes.

'Ten? Huh, that must be short for Tensing,' she said.

The boy turned to her in disbelief.

'Is that a real name?' he said.

'Are you kidding? Tenzing Norgay is famous as hell. He was the first man to climb Mount Everest.'

Seeing his incomprehension, she elaborated.

'The highest mountain in the world.'

Ten sniffed.

'Really? The first?'

'Yup, cross my heart and hope to die.'

The radiant smile on the boy's face brought her close to tears. His chest swelled.

'I'm named after a famous explorer?' he said.

'I guess you are,' said Isabella.

They spent several hours exploring the bustling streets of Freetown. Isabella used up an entire roll of film, taking photographs of street vendors and crumbling colonial balconies overflowing with flowers. They ate sandwiches at a café near a shop which offered telephone and fax services for overseas numbers. When Ten got into the taxi with her for the journey home, Isabella fought her natural inclination to ask him more questions, and let him luxuriate in the novelty of private transport.

The traffic was even worse on the way back to the hotel. Isabella took out her notebook and began making notes for an article on Freetown, which she hoped would appeal to Max. Ten pretended to look out of the window, but he couldn't contain his curiosity.

'Are you writing about me?' he said.

'Do you want to read it and find out?' said Isabella, offering him the notebook, and then seeing the panic on his face, she took it back. 'I could do, but you'd have to give me permission.'

'But who would be interested in me?' said Ten.

'Lots of people from other countries where there is less poverty who wonder how a boy fends for himself in a dangerous city. But you don't want to tell me, so...'

Ten avoided her glance, pulling at a thread on his battered shorts.

'Would you really write an article about me?' he said.

'I might. If you told me things.'

Ten frowned. Isabella waited, breath held.

'Can I think about it?' he said.

They pulled into the hotel just as the sun disappeared behind the hills above Man of War Bay. Ten jumped out and held the door for Isabella, which made her smile.

'Do you want to come to the chimp sanctuary with me tomorrow?' she said.

Ten looked at the ground and scuffed his flip-flops on the pavement.

'No, I'm busy. Can I have my money now?'

Isabella did not mention the fact she had already paid him. She took the equivalent of five pounds out of her bag and handed it to him. He put the money in his pocket and then took most of it out again.

'Can you keep this for me,' he said. 'Because...'

'Sure, I'll put it behind the desk in an envelope and tell Pete and Demba that it's yours. Are you sure you don't want to come to Tacugama and see the chimps?'

'They're just bushmeat. I can see them in the market.' said Ten, and he marched off, leaving her speechless.

Chapter 9

The waxy leaves of the trees bordering the road to the sanctuary shimmered in the sun as the ancient car weaved its way through the large potholes and fell into smaller ones. Isabella winced as her kidney took the brunt of the impact when the car lurched into one of the larger holes. The driver caught her eye in the mirror and shrugged.

'Sorry, madam, my wife done chop all my money. None left for shocks.'

'Has she also chopped the front seat? The back seat is pretty uncomfortable.'

She tried to smile to mitigate the effect of her complaint.

'I'm sorry, madam. I had to sell it.'

'It's not so bad,' she said, lying. 'Are we almost there yet?'

The sanctuary gate hung off one hinge and took all of Isabella's strength to open. The taxi driver had remained in his cab, parked in a small clearing down the road.

'I'm afraid of those monkeys,' he said. 'You don't know what they're thinking.'

'I'll be careful,' said Isabella. 'I might be a couple of hours. Is that okay?'

'You're paying,' said the driver, sniffing.

A waft of fetid air, smelling of sour milk and excrement, hit Isabella as she approached the line of ramshackle cages on the right-hand side of the road. Hoots and squeals indicated some of them at least were occupied. Isabella peered into the first, half afraid of what she might see, but the door on the back wall hung open and dead vegetation rotted on the floor. The adjoining cage was also empty.

She had more luck with the next block, which consisted of a pair of cages, side by side, separated by a brick wall with a metal door in it. The occupants of the cages could pass from one to the other through the door. Stout pieces of rebar made up the grid at front of the cages through which she could see a line of baby chimps sitting along a raised concrete bench, hugging each other for comfort. Her appearance in front of the cage caused consternation. Several of the chimps bared their teeth at her. *Are they smiling? They don't look happy.*

A flood of raw emotion coursed through her as she examined them, one by one, through the filth-caked bars of the cage; one with a weeping sore, one with rheumy eyes, another missing a finger. The injustice of it made her blood boil with frustration and pain. She had been so busy planning the trip and doing her research she hadn't considered the effect the project might have on her. *How can I stay aloof from such suffering?* She turned away to take a couple of deep breaths, but the smell invaded her sinuses.

Just then, a sallow skinned man emerged from one of the two Nissan Huts at the end of the road. He shaded his eyes and walked towards her, a grin widening on his face. She composed herself, straightening her shirt, and fixing on a smile.

'You're Isabella?' he said.

She nodded, and he shook his head. 'I had imagined someone who looked like Mary Poppins.'

He pronounced it like Merry and Isabella had a vision of Julie Andrews and her permanent smile. Merry, definitely.

'Yes, that's me,' she said. 'Sorry I'm late.'

'Late?' he said. 'I don't think there's such a thing in Sierra Leone. My name is Hasan Fakeem.'

'It's nice to meet you, Hasan. I'm so fascinated by your work here; I can't wait to hear about it. What shall we do first?'

'Why don't we take a tour and I'll explain how the project is set up?'

'Great. Let's start here,' said Isabella, taking out her notebook and pen, and balancing them on a stanchion holding the iron railing in front of the cage.

'Sure, well, you're standing in front of a cage containing the latest batch of orphans. They're kept away from the others for a month's quarantine in case they are carrying any contagious diseases.'

'What sort of diseases?'

'Mostly of human origin; colds, flu, that sort of thing. They pick them up in the villages where the rebels sell them.'

'How long have these chimps been in this cage?' said Isabella, scribbling in her notebook.

'Most of them have been here over a month now, but there are several issues which have caused this. The first is a lack of space for new arrivals.'

'What about the other cages?' said Isabella, gesticulating at the buildings back along the path.

'They need repairing. Chimps are super strong and very intelligent. They will escape if the cage is not tamper-proof. We don't have the time or the funds to do it.'

'So, each time you get new orphans, the entire group has to do quarantine again?'

'Got it in one. We used to get two or three orphans a month, but since they drove the rebels out of the cities, they have lived by killing bushmeat and selling the babies.'

That word again. Isabella dropped her pen.

'What did you call it?'

'Bushmeat. All animals are the same to them. Chimpanzees are no different to gazelles as far as they are concerned.'

Isabella turned to look into the crowded concrete cage with its bare bench. She swallowed to prevent herself from crying.

'What happens after quarantine?' she croaked.

'Come with me.'

Hasan walked over to a bank of raised earth and mounted some rickety steps to a viewing platform. Isabella followed him up, steeling herself for whatever was next. At the top, a waist high barricade made of green roofing material lined the edge of a three or four metre drop into a moat of grass around a small hillock covered in scrub and trees. Ropes and tires hung from a climbing frame with several levels. Loud hooting rose in volume as Hasan and Isabella came into view from below.

'This is our dominant group of male and female chimpanzees of all ages. We rescued the vast majority of them as babies, but some juveniles were being used as photographer's props on the beach before the civil war.'

'You're just in time for feeding,' said Hasan. 'It

59

will give you a good idea of the hierarchy in our group.'

Isabella put a hand on the barrier to test its stability. It wobbled, but appeared sturdy enough. She leaned over to get a better look at the chimpanzees. They were smaller than she remembered from her childhood visit to London Zoo. The moat filled with hooting apes as a young man brought a plastic dustbin up onto the viewing platform. In the centre of the group, a large male sat with his hand out, oblivious to the surrounding chaos. He had not only size but presence.

'Do you see the chimp with his hand extended? That's Lucius, the alpha male. He gets first choice at the food. There is a strict pecking order in the group, as you will see. Okay, Joe.'

The young man nodded and threw dozens of sweetcorn cobs into the moat. Lucius picked up two large bundles and took them to the bottom of one tree, where he ate unmolested. The rest of the troop screeched and fought, with some of the more timid members of the troop hanging back from the fray. The larger males rushed away with some cobs in their hands and others stuffed into their mouths. Some chimps scaled the climbing frame and sat on the platforms eating their prize.

Soon, half eaten corn cobs littered the ground and the lower ranking members of the group scavenged among them, cringing and ready to flee. The juvenile chimps got nothing and were reduced to begging from their mothers. Isabella noticed a tiny chimp with a white triangular tuft of fur sticking up from her backside. She had sidled up to Lucius and was stealing food from his pile. To her surprise, he did not stop it, but when a larger juvenile with no tuft tried the same thing, Lucius batted him away, causing him to squeal in pain.

'Why does Lucius let the one with the white tuft steal his food?'

'All babies have a white tuft on their backside for a couple of years. The adults are tolerant of bad behaviour until it disappears. After that, they get relegated to the lowest rank in the hierarchy and learn fast to wait their turn.'

Lucius spotted Isabella and locked eyes with her. She felt her guts churn at the challenge she saw there.

'Look away,' hissed Hasan.

But Isabella held Lucius's gaze. Defiant, she stood taller. Before she could react, a rock hurtled through the air and hit her on the shoulder. She gasped in pain and surprise, stumbling backwards. Hasan stopped her falling, his face a picture of concern.

'It's my fault,' he said. 'I forgot to warn you about his nasty habit.'

Isabella tried to control her quivering lip, but a tear escaped from her eye, betraying her distress.

'Let's go down,' she said.

A small Indian woman, feeding a baby chimp, smiled when they approached her. She noticed Isabella rub her shoulder and grimaced.

'Lucius?' said the woman. 'You poor thing. Hold Fidget while I get the arnica.'

She handed the small chimp to Isabella and headed for the bungalow.

'That was my wife, Gupta,' said Hasan. 'She's forgotten her manners. Do you want me to take him?'

Isabella shook her head as she felt Fidget's little fingers grasp her t-shirt. She prided herself on her understanding of animals. She could almost hear them talk to her. *Why else would I have tried so hard to be a vet?* Despite the setback with Lucius, she had the chance to prove it.

'No, it's okay, I can do this,' she said, setting the chimp on her hip and holding the bottle at an angle so he could drink the milk.

Fidget didn't care who held him, guzzling down the milk as if afraid that another chimp might come and steal it from him. He gazed up at Isabella and tried to grab her blonde curls with his grubby fingers.

'He likes you,' said Hasan.

'Would you take a photograph of us please?' said Isabella, now feeling in control again. 'My camera's in the front pocket of my rucksack.'

Hasan pulled out the compact camera and stepped backwards.

'Just point and click,' said Isabella.

'Say cheese,' said Hasan.

'Cheese,' said Isabella, but at that moment, she felt a trickle of liquid which turned into a stream running down her shirt and over her trousers.

Gupta came bustling back with the arnica. She noticed the yellow stain creeping down Isabella's clothes and her hand flew to her mouth.

'Fidget,' she said, trying not to giggle. 'You naughty boy. You shouldn't pee on the guests.'

Isabella held the baby chimp at arm's length while he emptied his bladder and then Gupta took him back. Resentment and embarrassment bubbled in Isabella's chest.

'I'm so sorry,' said Hasan, who couldn't look her in the eye. 'We can give you a t-shirt from the gift shop if you would like.'

Isabella just wanted to leave before something else happened. The mishaps had punctured her dignity, and she felt unable to continue the interview with pee-soaked trousers. *I'm a fraud. What the hell am I doing here?*

'No, that's all right,' she said. 'I need to go anyhow.'

'But we haven't told you about our work or—'

'I've got to go now,' said Isabella, grabbing her rucksack. 'I'm sorry.'

She almost ran back to the taxi, so desperate was she to leave. Gulping in ragged breaths, she forced open the gate and leaned on it for a few seconds, gathering her composure. The taxi driver snored, curled up in his back seat, and did not appreciate being shaken awake.

'I was having an erotic dream,' he said. 'You ruined the good bit.'

He looked her up and down, his brow wrinkling.

'And what's that smell? You're not sitting on my seat smelling like that.' He reached inside and pulled out a filthy old newspaper. 'Here. Sit on this.'

Chastened, Isabella did not speak on the journey home, which was made interminable by a puncture 'caused by her bad karma'. Her head spun with shame about her behaviour and she almost asked him to return to the sanctuary so she could apologise to the Fakeems. By the time she got back to the hotel, she needed a sympathetic ear for her troubles.

Pete lifted his head as she came in, taking in her bedraggled appearance and defeated air.

'What happened to you then, Africa? Did things get a little too real for you out there?'

Isabella flashed him a look of hatred.

'The sanctuary was a nightmare. I had a rock thrown at me which hit me in the shoulder, a baby chimp peed on me, and I had to wait on the roadside for over an hour while my driver fixed a puncture.'

Pete grinned.

'Is that all?' he said. 'I knew you were all hat and no cattle. You think you're some sort of animal whisperer with your fake empathy and your bogus name.'

Isabella's mouth fell open, but Pete hadn't finished.

'Did you think it would be like the movies? All khaki two-piece suits, and a g and t in the afternoon? I can't believe your boss sent such a naïve idiot to a war zone. Did you sleep with him to get the gig or—'

Isabella slapped him in the face with all her force. It was difficult to tell who was more shocked by her reaction. She recovered first.

'And who do you think you are, criticising me, you drunk has-been? I've seen better soldiers in my brother's toy box.'

They stood toe to toe at the desk, and then Pete roared with laughter, rubbing his cheek in wonder.

'You pack some punch, Africa. Do you fancy a beer at Alex's? I bet you're starving after all your adventures.'

'I'll need a shower first,' said Isabella.

'Good plan. I'm not eating dinner with some woman smelling of chimp pee. What about my reputation?'

Isabella tried not to smile as she mounted the stairs, but the spat with Pete had brought colour back to her cheeks and a sparkle to her eyes. *What a cheek! I'll show him. And I'm having a gin and tonic.*

Chapter 10

Isabella lay in bed the next morning nursing a hangover and a guilty conscience. Nothing had happened with Pete over dinner, although it could have. Their fractious friendship did not quite conceal a serious sexual chemistry that threatened to bubble over. At one stage Pete had brushed her arm with his hand to knock off a mosquito and she had almost fainted with desire. She had never experienced genuine passion before. Her relationship with Graham had led them into a comfortable partnership, but it never passed through the valley of unadulterated lust.

Get a grip, Isabella! I need to call Graham and Max and get anchored back home. What is the point of ruining everything for something resembling a holiday romance on steroids?

Ten, who had taken to hanging around the hotel helping Pete out with odd jobs, took her to the telephone exchange near the Cotton Tree, where a contact of his instructed her in the use of the faxes and ordering international calls. She sent her handwritten pages of notes to Max with some trepidation, and put in a call to Graham first, to give Max time to consider her proposal. She used his work number, hoping to avoid a scene by abusing her knowledge of his controlled office persona.

As she waited for the call to come through, she hopped from foot to foot, trying to distract herself.

'Who are you going to talk to?' said Ten.

'My boyfriend in Dublin,' said Isabella.

'Your boyfriend? I thought Pete was your boyfriend?'

Isabella blushed to the roots of her hair. Outed by a ten-year-old.

'Don't be silly, Pete's not my boyfriend.'

Ten raised his eyebrows.

'He thinks he is,' said Ten.

'No, you're wrong, I—'

The clerk at the desk yelled out, 'booth 6 for Isabella', and relief flooded her as she escaped the interrogation. Ten tried to come in with her, but she shut the door in his face.

'You're not invited,' she said. 'Wait outside.'

This did not go down well. Ten reverted to his closed face persona and stomped outside. Isabella lifted the receiver as if it were a grenade with a loose pin.

'Hello?'

'Isabella?'

'Yes, it's me. Sorry for calling you at work, I'm pretty busy out here.'

'That's okay. They patched you through to the boardroom so we can talk in private.'

'Oh? Great.' Isabella swallowed. 'How have you been?'

'Just the usual work and stuff. Missing you, of course.'

A silence. Isabella realised she should reciprocate.

'Oh, me too. Loads,' she said.

'What are you doing out there?'

'I've got to go back to the sanctuary at least once to complete the story. And there's a secondary thread I may pursue...'

She trailed off.

'Another story? But when are you coming back?'

'Well, that's the thing. I'm going to stay out here a little longer than planned because of the wealth of stories waiting to be told. Max is very excited.'

He'd better be, or my plan is in shreds.

'Longer? How much longer?'

Graham's peeved tone reverberated down the line from Dublin.

'Hard to tell. A couple of weeks, I expect.'

Not what I have in mind at all, but hopefully it will be easier to take in small chunks.

'Weeks? I can't believe it. I want you to come home right now. You never should have gone. I—'

Isabella replaced the receiver on the cradle, hoping he thought the line had gone dead. Why did he insist on treating her like a truant? She didn't want to argue about a decision she had already made. If he didn't like it, he'd have to lump it. Perhaps if I send him a letter with drawings and love hearts?

Her second call came through almost immediately to the same booth. She took a deep breath and picked up the receiver.

'Max?'

'Well, hello there, my intrepid reporter. How's it going on the dark continent?'

'Wonderful,' she said. 'Well, difficult, but amazing.'

'I didn't ask about your love life,' said Max, laughing.

'Oh, Mr Wolfe, it's such a great opportunity. You wouldn't believe how many fantastic stories there are out here. Have you read my proposal?'

'Proposal? It read more like an ultimatum. Do I have any choice?'

Isabella laughed.

'Not really. Today I'm going on a recce in a helicopter with a bunch of mercenaries. I should get an interesting story out of it.'

'I won't ask you how you swung that.'

'It's amazing what blonde hair and red lipstick will do to an ex-military man,' said Isabella.

'I know,' said Max, and Isabella realised she had missed the obvious clues to his background.

'So, can I stay longer?' she said.

'You're there now. It would be more expensive to fly you there twice. Just send me the articles in good time, and keep your expenses to a minimum. We have more money now that I have reduced the number of staff, but the budget is still limited. I'm thinking of doing an African column in the magazine with these. Like a sort of diary. It might go down well.'

'With my by-line?' said Isabella.

'Of course.'

'I won't let you down.'

'You're right there,' said Max. 'If you want to keep your job.'

After she had paid for the calls and the sending of the fax, Isabella left the telephone exchange to find Ten sulking on the steps, throwing lumps of pavement at a flock of pigeons.

'Don't do that,' she said.

'Why did you shut me out of the booth?' said Ten.

Isabella sighed.

'Because I wanted some privacy. Anyway, you do that to me all the time. You never tell me anything about your life. How come you think you should know all about mine? By the way, have you thought about doing that article I asked for?'

Ten drew his eyebrows together and glared at her. She laughed. Touché.

On the way back to the hotel, Isabella replayed her call with Graham over and over in her head. Short and not so sweet. She hadn't expected his reaction. *He was so tolerant of her eccentric ways. Why didn't he understand how much she needed this? Had she been going out with a stranger the whole time?*

'I'll do it,' said Ten.

'Do what?' said Isabella.

'The article, of course.'

'Well, that is brilliant news. We can't do it today though, because I'm going on a trip.'

'Where to?'

'I don't know. We're going in a helicopter.'

Ten's eyes came out on stalks.

'A helicopter? Can I come? Please?'

'It's not my decision. To tell you the truth, I doubt it, but you can ask.'

Manu Faletau's jeep screeched to a halt outside the hotel seconds after Ten and Isabella entered the hotel lobby, his horn blaring with impatience. Isabella slapped her forehead.

'Tell Manu I'll be down in a couple of minutes. I have to get something from my room,' she said to Ten.

'Who's Manu?' said Ten.

'The big grumpy Tongan.'

She ran through reception and up the stairs. She changed into long trousers, sprayed herself from head to foot with repellent and selected an unused film for her camera. Then she thundered back down the stairs. Pete and Manu were deep in conversation at the reception desk, and her noisy arrival made them frown.

'Christ, I thought it was a herd of buffalo,' said Pete.

'Let's go,' said Manu.

Isabella stuck out her tongue at Pete as she got into the back of the open jeep, immediately regretting it. Are we in the playground now?

Ten tried to follow her, but Manu pulled him back down to the pavement.

'And who is this?' said Manu, poking Ten in the chest.

'Ten Adams,' said Isabella. 'He's my assistant.'

'Well, he can't come with us,' said Manu. 'It's a secret mission. I don't want any spies on my helicopter. Go play with eight and nine, kid.'

He roared with laughter at his own joke. The other guys joined in. Ten shrank with misery. Isabella shrugged at Ten from the jeep and tried to convey her sympathy, but his lips set in fury at the cruel joke.

'Sorry, Ten. Next time,' she said.

Sulky now, he backed away from the jeep, bumping into Pete, who had been observing the scene. Pete put his hand on Ten's shoulder and, to Isabella's surprise, Ten didn't throw it off. He stood stiffly, unused to the gesture of support. Manu jumped in beside the helicopter pilot and shoved the jeep into gear. They set off, wheels screeching.

Isabella held on to the side with all her strength as she sat on the hard bench opposite the burly guys in their Kevlar vests.

'I'm Whitey,' said the smaller of the two, and

hooked his thumb at his companion. 'And that's Chopper. The passenger is Trevor. He's the pilot.'

Trevor turned around and gave her a thumbs up.

'He's saving his strength for the helicopter,' said Whitey. 'Here. You may need this.'

He threw her a spare Kevlar vest. She put her arms through the sleeve holes, almost falling out of the jeep as Manu threw it around a corner. She pulled up the zip, but the bulky padding rose under her chin, making her feel suffocated, and she unzipped it again. I must be out of my mind. There's still time to back out of this.

But she didn't. She marched up the steps into the hold of the ancient helicopter in a subconscious imitation of the others and sat with her back to a small round window. Trevor lifted the craft off the ground. It shuddered and rattled over the take-off pad before they were off, swooping over the shanty towns and out of the capital.

'Why wouldn't you let Ten come with us?' said Isabella. 'He wouldn't have been a bother.'

'He has a surname common in the forces opposed to the government. Some kids spy for the rebels. I couldn't risk it,' said Manu.

Isabella opened her mouth to protest but thought better of it. Ten had been secretive about where he lived and with whom. There was no way of knowing if he collaborated with the rebels to earn money for food.

The sun sunk lower in the sky as the helicopter followed the course of a river through the farmlands and over a forest. Anticipation and dread seized her as Chopper set up a machine gun on a swivel attached to the side of the helicopter and fed a clip of bullets into it. She wanted to take notes, but her fists had balled up in fright. *Why hadn't Pete warned her about the nature of the recce? He probably thought it was funny to let her find out what Manu had in mind.* The helicopter switched to silent mode, the gyro making a whomping sound as they flew low, out of the sun, over a scruffy compound containing tattered huts and men sitting outside them drinking.

Manu grabbed the door handle and slid it open. Chopper, who had seated himself behind the machine gun, swung into the doorway and fired in large arcs at the compound. Spent cartridges flew in the air, making Isabella jump when one landed hot on her hand. She slid along the bench, out of harm's way. Whitey and Manu ignored her, focused on their prey now, shouting directions and cursing when a rebel escaped the hail of bullets. Isabella dug her nails into her palm to stop herself from crying. *This is what foreign correspondents do? They must be mad.*

When the shooting stopped, Chopper swung back out of the doorway and disassembled the weapon. Manu noticed her on the bench and beckoned her forward to the door. She forced herself to stand and tottered over to the door way.

'Hold tight to this.' Said Manu, pointing at a handle on one side of the door. 'We're going to do one more pass over the compound to recce the damage.'

Isabella grabbed the handle, torn between watching the destruction and looking away. Manu held onto a handle on the other side of the door. They both gazed down as they approached the compound again; Manu in triumph, Isabella in horror. Bodies littered the ground. Pigs, people, and chickens indiscriminately slaughtered by Chopper.

'Do you see their guns?' said Manu. 'You may not

be comfortable with our methods, but these rebels kill local people every day, and chop off their hands so they can't vote.'

He wiped his brow with a filthy hanky and was about to elaborate when a shot rang out from the ground. The bullet hit Manu in the arm, releasing his grip on the handle. His eyes opened wide in shock and he tipped towards the open door. Isabella lunged outwards and gripped his belt, jerking him backwards just enough to make him fall inside the helicopter instead of outside. Manu landed on the floor on his backside.

'The bastards shot me,' he said, holding his arm.

Whitey pulled him up by the shoulder straps and put him on the bench. He examined Manu's arm.

'It's only a flesh wound, boss. You'll live.'

Manu pointed his finger at Isabella.

'You're bad luck,' he said. 'I've never been shot before. Next time I'm leaving you at home.'

'That's harsh,' said Chopper.

'She saved your life, boss,' said Whitey. 'If she hadn't grabbed your belt, you'd be lying on the ground with the chickens.'

Manu snorted.

'Maybe,' he said. 'But Vishnu had my back.'

Isabella put her hands on her hips.

'Vishnu? Isn't he a Hindi god? I thought Tongans were Christians.'

Manu frowned.

'My mother is a Hindu. Anyway, it wasn't my karma to die today.'

'I should have let you fall,' said Isabella.

Manu's eyebrows flew up, and then he guffawed.

'Okay, okay. You got me there,' he said. 'I owe

you one.'

Chapter 11

When she could avoid it no longer, Isabella swallowed her pride and made a trip back up the hill to Tacugama. Despite protesting that they did not want to waste their day off, Pete and Ten came with her. They sat in the back of the taxi, elbowing each other, and giggling like two small boys on a day out, which they sort of were, thought Isabella. Ten had flourished under Pete's wing. They had established an odd partnership, which consisted mostly of finding ways to annoy her, but she tried not to mind.

Isabella had noticed a subtle change in Pete. He appeared to drink less when Ten was around. Ten's shrieks of joy when Pete wrestled him made her heart fill.

'He's twelve, you know,' said Pete. 'Almost thirteen. Soon he'll be hitting puberty. It's a tough time for boys without a father.'

Isabella raised an eyebrow.

'Are you volunteering?'

She regretted her question before it left her mouth and it struck home. Pete avoided her inquiring glance, his face darkening.

'I'm just being a human,' he said. 'The lad needs support.'

She didn't apologise to Pete because she felt

rather jealous of the amount of attention Ten received compared to her. She suspected Ten had told Pete about Graham because he behaved differently to her after she came back from her epic trip in the helicopter. At first, she thought he might be cross about her saving Manu and becoming the favourite of the mercenary crew, but his veiled references to her need to return home to Dublin made her think he knew. What an absurd love triangle. Me, Pete and Ten. *Maybe I should talk to Pete about it, but what would I say?*

When they arrived at the sanctuary, Ten loitered at the gate, unwilling to enter, but Pete gave him a friendly shove.

'I don't know what we're doing here,' said Ten. 'They're just food.'

'You need to watch out,' said Isabella. 'The food knows how to fight back.'

Hasan's face lit up when he saw Isabella.

'You've come back,' he said. 'Gupta will be so pleased. She blamed herself when you left.'

'I'm so sorry about leaving like that. It wasn't my best moment,' said Isabella.

'And who are these two fine gentlemen?'

'I'm Pete Hawkins, and this is Tensing Adams.'

Hasan shook their hands.

'You're welcome to Tacugama,' he said. 'Wait here beside the babies, while I tell Gupta you have arrived.'

Hasan disappeared into the Nissan hut at the end of the path and reappeared a moment later. Beside him, Gupta waved from the door. Isabella stood back as Hasan explained the plight of the young chimps in the quarantine cages to Pete and Ten. Pete's brow furrowed as the catalogue of woes hit home. Ten pretended not to be interested but Isabella saw him offering a finger to one chimp who hung on to it with grim determination.

Then they headed up to the bank overlooking the adult chimp enclosure. Their appearance on the viewing platform induced hopeful hoots for food from the adults in the enclosure. Ten leaned on the fence and peered down at the apes, a sneer on his lips.

'I wouldn't do that if I were y—'

A rock whistled through the air, narrowly missing Ten's head.

'What the hell?' said Ten. 'That brute threw a rock at me.'

'Maybe he doesn't like being called food,' said Isabella.

She looked around to see that Lucius had spotted her and appeared fixated. He hooted at her and stuck out his hand. Without thinking, she hooted back, and then felt embarrassed at her amateurish attempt, looking down at the platform. Pete raised his eyebrows at Hasan, who shrugged and grinned.

'What was Lucius saying?' said Isabella.

'I do not know,' said Hasan. 'But that's unusual behaviour. Lucius doesn't like anyone. As you know, he usually throws things at visitors.'

'Maybe it's my blonde hair?'

'Hmm, I guess it might look like a baby's tuft. I don't know. You did the right thing by looking away. He'll take that as a mark of respect.'

Isabella could feel the ape staring at her, willing her to look up again, but she didn't.

'How will you introduce the orphans from the cages to the group?' said Pete.

Hasan shrugged and shook his head.

'I don't know. There are already too many chimps in the enclosure. Any more and the group might split into two and start killing each other.'

'What are you going to do?' said Isabella.

'I'm not sure,' said Hasan, sighing. 'We have a plan, but it would cost money we just don't possess. Follow me.'

Hasan descended the staircase and headed behind the empty cages, where a patch of scrubby forest crawled up the hillside. He gestured at it without enthusiasm.

'We own this land, up to the summit. It would be an ideal place to start a new group of chimpanzees using the young orphans, and some of the lower ranking females from the main enclosure. The older individuals would teach the orphans how to be a chimp and it would rescue them from the constant bullying and bickering in their group. It would also have the knock-on effect of reducing tensions in Lucius's group.'

'What do you need to make it suitable?' said Pete.

'Rehabilitate the old cages as buildings for sleeping quarters and isolation cages, and surrounding the area with electric fencing to keep them inside the enclosure. We'd have to upgrade the generator as well. Inshallah.'

'How much would it cost?' said Isabella.

'Too much. We are losing the battle for funding. Soon I'll have to refuse any chimps they offer us.'

'But won't they die?'

Hasan shrugged.

'I can't save them all. Would you like some lunch? My wife Gupta has made a potato leaf stew.'

Potato leaves? Aren't they toxic?

'That sounds delicious, thank you,' said Pete.

'Yes, please,' said Ten, rubbing his stomach.

Hasan led the way into the cottage at the far end of the complex. A delicious aroma crept into Isabella's nostrils and made her stomach rumble.

'You must be Pete, and Tensing,' said Gupta, who was ladling stew into a heavy pottery bowl. 'Would you like to wash your hands, Isabella? The bathroom is through the curtain.'

Isabella pushed her way into a spartan toilet with a shower head in one corner and a chipped basin in the other. In between them sat a flat ceramic toilet with a hole in the middle. Isabella tried not to gag at the smell as she hovered over it. *I hope I don't fall in.*

She emerged, wiping her hands on her trousers, to find Hasan and Gupta seated at a table with Ten and Pete. On it were the bowl of stew and another of rice. A jug of freshly made mango juice sat in the middle, fat drops of water glistening on its outside.

'Help yourself,' said Hasan.

'It smells fantastic,' said Isabella. 'Are there really potato leaves in it?'

Gupta laughed at her expression.

'Sweet potato, of course. We don't want to poison you.'

Isabella helped herself to a bowl and was about to dig in when she slapped her forehead.

'Oh dear, I forgot about the driver,' she said. 'He'll be starving. Can I take him some food?'

Ten stood up and grabbed a plastic bowl.

'I'll do it,' he said.

Isabella raised the food to her lip and sipped the gravy. The taste made her feel quite faint with hunger.

'Oh my gosh, this is fabulous.' She coughed. 'It's

pretty hot.'

'That's the peppers. It has a secret ingredient too; ogiri.'

'What's that?'

'Fermented sesame paste.'

'Wow! This is such a different taste. We eat less spicy food in Ireland anyway, although I do like Chinese food. How long have you been here?'

'Ten years. I don't know how long we can keep it up, though,' she said. 'Donations ebb and flow with the civil war, and we need someone else to help us with the chimps, but we're snowed under with bills. We can't afford to pay anyone right now.'

She shrugged and sighed. They ate in silence.

'What about volunteers?' said Isabella.

'For what,' said Hasan.

'To help in the sanctuary.'

'Volunteers? Fat chance. People can't afford to work for free, they need to feed their families.'

'I could do it,' she said, before she could stop herself.

Pete's jaw almost hit the table. He stared at her in disbelief.

'You?' said Hasan. 'For how long?'

The doubt in his voice clashed with the hope in his eyes as they searched hers. Am I just trying to impress Pete?

'I'm not sure, but I have holidays coming up and I need a change. I've been stuck in an office for the past seven years.'

'Do you have any training?' said Gupta.

'I'm a zoologist,' said Isabella.

Hasan's mouth hung open and Gupta patted his hand to make him shut it.

'Allahu Akbar. A zoologist? But we can't pay you,' she said.

'Can you give me bed and board? It's too far to come from Freetown every day.'

'There are plenty of rooms in the Nissan Hut next door. We could rig up a bed if you buy a mattress in town. But I should warn you; conditions are primitive. The bathroom—'

'I'll cope. I've been camping. It can't be that different.'

A lightbulb went on in her head.

'Could I bring someone with me?' she said.

Gupta laughed.

'You mean Ten? He'll have to help if he wants to get fed.'

'He'll help,' said Isabella. 'I just need to persuade him.'

'What about school?' said Hasan.

'He's a street kid,' said Isabella. 'I don't know if he can read and write.'

'Probably not,' said Hasan. 'Are you sure he's trustworthy?'

'No, I can't say I know yet, but have you anything to steal?'

Seeing their faces, she blushed traffic light red. *What a thing to say, you idiot Green!*

'I'm so sorry,' she stuttered. 'I didn't mean…'

'Don't worry. You are right. We have impoverished ourselves to save the chimps. Bring him along and we'll see if he is a good worker.'

'I can teach him in return for his help,' said Gupta. 'But what will you do for money? We can't pay you anything.'

'I'll write stories for my magazine. We can do the

article about Tacugama first, and I'm sure there are more animals here that would interest our readership,' said Isabella.

'What about Tiwai Island?' said Hasan. 'It has eleven species of monkey, including some rare ones, and a small troop of chimps.'

Gupta's eyes widened.

'The pygmy hippos,' she said.

'I'd forgotten those,' said Hasan.

'Pygmy hippos?' said Isabella. 'I don't believe it. How impossibly cute. My boss will be thrilled.'

'It's difficult to get there,' said Pete. 'You'll need help.'

'Are you offering?' said Isabella, but he didn't answer.

'I think we have a deal,' said Hasan, stretching out his hand.

Chapter 12

Ten stared at Isabella as if she had three heads.

'You want me to go to the chimp sanctuary with you? Are you crazy?'

Taken aback, she hedged.

'It would be safer for you than the streets of Freetown, and you could learn to read and write. Gupta is a—'

'I'm not your project. I'm a man. Men don't sweep floors and feed babies. That's women's work. You're just farming the chimps like cattle. The rebels will come and kill them all for food.'

'I didn't mean it like that. It's a job. I only want to help you get ahead in life. You lost your mother when you were too young.'

'It's none of your business. I'll join the rebels soon and they'll treat me like a man.'

'The rebels? But—'

'But what? They'll give me a gun, and a woman, if I want one.'

Pete had emerged from the kitchen drawn by the sound of the argument. He wiped his hands on a dishcloth and a smell of garlic penetrated the lobby. He couldn't help smiling at Ten's ambition, but Isabella's face told him another story.

'Steady on, Ten. There's no need to be rude,' he

said.

'It's my fault,' said Isabella. 'I should have asked Ten before I told Hasan.'

'Yes, you should. You pomwis with your bleeding hearts always interfere in things you don't understand. There is a war on. You should go home before someone kills you,' said Ten.

Ten drew himself up to his full height and scowled at her. Despite dwarfing him, she wilted under his scorn. She didn't wait for his next outburst, and ran upstairs to finish packing her bag. Pete watched her go and then turned to Ten.

'Did you have to do that? She cares about you,' said Pete. 'How many friends have you got besides us? Can you afford to alienate her?'

Ten looked at the floor.

'I thought you were on my side,' he said. 'You're a soldier. You should understand.'

Pete shrugged.

'I do. That's why I got out of the army.'

He left Ten in the lobby and ran up the stairs after Isabella, without considering what he wanted to say. Her bedroom door hung open, and she stood in the window, folding, and refolding a t-shirt. She turned as he entered, bright tears staining her cheeks. She brushed them off, sniffing.

'What do you want?' she said. 'Have you come to gloat?'

Pete hesitated and folded his dishcloth, mimicking her.

'I wanted to tell you not to worry about Ten. I'll keep an eye on him for you. Maybe he'll change his mind.'

He bit his lip. Isabella sighed.

'Maybe.' She looked down at the t-shirt. 'Am I just a stupid pomwi?' she said. 'With my colonial ideas and old-fashioned solutions to intractable problems.'

'If you are, that makes two of us. Listen, Manu owes you a massive favour, one he can't easily repay, and he knows it. I thought he might squeeze some money out of his backers for the new enclosure at Tacugama. The government has made the chimpanzee the national animal of Sierra Leone, so it would go down well with them if Manu and the boys helped upgrade the sanctuary.'

Isabella blew her nose in a piece of old tissue.

'Really?' she said.

'I can't promise anything. Why don't you come to Alex's for dinner on Friday and we'll work on him together?'

For a split second, Isabella considered running into his arms, but the moment passed.

'It's a deal,' she said.

The taxi journey to the sanctuary did not get any easier the second time, but Isabella noticed the grinding gears and worn shock absorbers of her chariot. Her determination to impress Manu, Pete, Ten and even Graham buoyed her throughout. She made the taxi stop on the way there, so she could buy a thick foam mattress, some cheap polyester sheets, and a couple of new pillows. At least she would be comfortable at night, even if the heat became oppressive.

Isabella asked the taxi driver to sound his horn from the car park and soon Joe appeared at the gate. Seeing her struggling with the mattress and bed linen, he helped her to carry it to the second Nissan Hut, where he placed it on the rough wooden frame in her bedroom. Splinters still littered the floor where someone had sawed the wood and banged in the nails. Isabella put her rucksack on the bed and went next door to ask Gupta for a brush.

She knocked on the door and, when there was no answer, she let herself in, planning to borrow the brush and replace it later. To her surprise, Gupta appeared from the bedroom dressed in a breath-taking red sari, her face pink with embarrassment.

'Oh, it's you. Thank goodness,' she said, and sank onto a chair. 'I thought it was Hasan.'

'You look wonderful,' said Isabella. 'Like a princess. Is it silk?'

'It's my wedding dress. Please don't tell Hasan you saw it. He thinks I sold it years ago. It's the only beautiful thing I have left. We've sold everything else to keep the sanctuary going. I put it on sometimes to feel glamorous.'

'I promise not to tell anyone. It must be hard for you here in the sanctuary.'

'I spend my whole life covered in chimp spit and excrement but I wouldn't change it for the world.'

'How did you get here?'

'When Hasan and I first married, our families expelled us for marrying outside our religions. We went on a cheap honeymoon to the beach where we came across a young chimp, Lucius, posing for photographs with the tourists. His owner did not know how to feed a chimp or how to take care of one. Hasan bonded with Lucius over the few days of our holiday and we couldn't leave him there to die. So, we bought him and took him home. He soon grew too big to keep in a house, but we persuaded the Ministry of Agriculture and Forestry to provide the land and to fund the setting up of the sanctuary. And the rest is history.'

She wiped a hair out of her eyes.

'Have your family forgiven you for marrying Hasan?'

'My mother sends me money sometimes, but my father refuses to see me. He says he no longer has a daughter. He might thaw if I had a grandson, but...'

She waved her hands around. Isabella sensed her pain, but could not find any words to explore Gupta's obvious reference, and changed the subject.

'I didn't know marrying a Muslim mattered so much to Hindus. I'm a protestant myself, but I went to a convent because it was the only choice. The nuns were nice to me there though, so I didn't mind.'

'Where do you live?'

'Ireland.'

'But isn't that where they are killing each other over religion?'

Isabella sighed.

'Only in the North. I don't understand why. I never have.'

Gupta shook her head.

'Religions,' she said. 'I'll never get what all the fuss is about. We're all worshiping the same God, after all. I'll change back into my work clothes now. What was it you wanted?'

'Oh, the broom. I'm going to sweep out my room.'

'Would you like to meet Lucius?'

'Up close?' A shiver ran up Isabella's spine. 'As long as it's safe.'

'Lucius is like many males of the species. Bravado on the outside and a soft centre inside.'

Isabella swept out her room with excitement and

trepidation bubbling up inside her. She avoided breaking a large new spider's web, reasoning that it would catch the mosquitos for her. Dust particles flew into the air, dancing in the sunlight. Most of the splinters fell out of her room through the gaps in the floorboards returning to the earth below. The small amount that remained, she pushed into a corner for later collection. She surveyed her work. *I haven't swept the room. I've just moved the dirt around.*

She emerged sneezing from the Nissan hut to find Gupta waiting for her outside. They headed down past the orphans' cages and turned right to enter a door below the viewing platform. It led into the passage along the sleeping quarters dug into the banking.

'Wait here,' said Gupta. 'I'll get Lucius to come in by himself.'

Isabella waited beside the cages, trying to stay calm as her pulse raced and an adrenaline surge made her feel nauseous. A grid of soldered rebars separated the sleeping quarters from the passageway. Behind the grid, a climbing frame with several platforms reached from ground to ceiling. Sleeping nests made of old blankets and straw spilled over onto the floor. Old tyres which served as swings hung on chains from sturdy beams. Small metal doors at the bottom of the walls gave access to the outside and to adjoining cages.

One of them slid open with a bang, making Isabella jump. Lucius ambled into the room and looked around, checking inside the tyres for hidden snacks. Isabella stood stock still, holding her breath. The door slid shut again, and moments later Gupta reappeared at her side.

'Ready?' she said.

Isabella nodded, unable to speak. Lucius seemed

much larger close up. His physical presence intimidated her and removed all romantic notions about Tarzan and his friend Cheeta from her head. She felt foolish for her naïve assumptions about Africa and the sanctuary. *Ten said some harsh things about me, but had what he'd said been so far from the truth?*

'He's much bigger than I'd imagined,' said Isabella.

'Lucius is enormous. He's about twenty percent bigger than the other males. We don't know why. It's probably just genetic.'

Gupta handed her some slices of mango.

'His absolute favourite,' she said. 'Don't give it to him all at once.'

The smell of the mango invaded Isabella's nostrils. She licked her finger, and the sweet, tart taste of the juice made her drool.

'Wow. It's delicious. I've never tried a mango before,' she said.

Gupta laughed.

'It's not for you. But if you like, I'll get you one later.'

'Oh, yes, please. I—'

Lucius lunged closer to the grid and smacked his lips together. Isabella stumbled backwards, dropping the mango on the floor, her heart in her mouth. Gupta picked it up and gave it back to her.

'Don't be nervous. Just offer him a piece. Go on. He won't hurt you.'

Trembling, she stepped forward and held out a piece of fruit. Lucius stretched his massive hand through the grid and took it between his black nails. He sniffed it in appreciation before popping it in his mouth and making sucking noises. Isabella grinned at his pleasure. His hairy hand requested another piece, and then another, until they were all eaten.

Isabella held out her hands so he could see they were empty. Lucius reached out towards her, hooting softly. She couldn't move. He touched her hair, pulling it without malice. Isabella, careful not to look him in the eye, stepped a little closer, mesmerised by the encounter. Then he withdrew his hand and retreated to a corner, where he poked a pile of faeces with his finger and sniffed it. Isabella let go of the breath she had been holding.

'Wow,' she said.

'He likes you,' said Gupta. 'You're privileged. Don't screw it up.'

Isabella searched for something profound to say, but the sensation of Lucius's massive hand touching her hair had befuddled her.

'Can I have a mango?' she said.

After supper, Isabella wandered out to gaze at the night sky. The myriad of stars made her feel insignificant, but it reinforced her determination to make a difference before she got reabsorbed into the universe. The combined challenge generated by the attitudes of both Pete and Graham goaded her to ignore the hardships and rise above them. She stared up at the moon and made a vow to stick it out, no matter what.

Chapter 13

Isabella's encounter with Lucius set the tone for her time in the sanctuary. His acceptance of her gave her the licence she needed to get involved, and she set about learning how to feed, rehabilitate and re-introduce the orphan chimps to group life. While she often felt rather useless compared to the nimble locals, used to the rough and tumble of looking after thirty opinionated adult chimps, she felt drawn to the orphans in quarantine. Their bewildered loneliness at finding themselves orphaned, and shut in a cage for reasons they didn't understand, touched her in a way she hadn't expected.

Loud hooting from the neighbours ensured no-one got a lie-in at Tacugama. Isabella stumbled out of bed every morning feeling like a truck had run her over. She gulped down a cup of tea and ate a couple of fried eggs and rice before making up the bottles for the orphaned chimps with Enfamil, a powdered formula intended for human babies. Hasan had a supplier who sold him large tins of formula which had gone out of date, at half price, and he kept large supplies of it in the shed with the fruit rations.

The ritual of measuring out the powder and shaking the bottles settled her into her morning routine and blew the last of the cobwebs away. Once the bottles were ready, she headed to the shed beside the quarantine cages, causing mass hysteria in the orphan ranks as they saw their breakfast approaching. In the wild, their mothers do not wean chimps until they are between three and four years old, so the orphans needed milk as a major part of their diet. The younger chimps liked to be held while they drank their milk, but the older chimps grabbed a bottle and fed themselves.

Joe often swept out the cages at this time, taking advantage of the distraction. If he tried to sweep the floors at other times, the orphans liked to redistribute the straw and faeces as quickly as he piled them up. Since chimps did not like water, Joe had no problem hosing down the cage once he had swept away the dirt. Some of the older chimps liked to play chicken with the water sprayed from the hose, but most of them scampered to other parts of the cage while he cleaned the floors.

Isabella took the baby chimps out of the cage for feeding in relays and put one on each hip in slings designed by Gupta. Baby chimps spend most of their first 6 months glued to their mother's front before moving to her back. The physical contact is important for their mental health, so the chimps at Tacugama were all fragile and confused, and clung to each other, battered soft toys and any human who came near. Some of them had the habit of wrapping their arms around themselves and rocking in a corner.

Isabella's heart broke to see them so lonely. She found it hard to stomach the callous indifference of those responsible to the misery they caused. The juvenile chimps provided some solace to the babies of the group, but they spent a lot of time indulging in wild horseplay around the cages, upsetting the babies who came off worse. Isabella and Gupta had at least two of the smallest orphans clinging to them for most of the day. The two women had bonded over their shared knowledge of the clandestine sari and often sat together, putting the world to rights.

'How are these babies going to survive in an adult group?' said Isabella, wiping spit off her arm.

'There are several older females in Lucius's group who assumed the role of adoptive mothers for the youngest orphans. When we build the second enclosure, we will introduce them to the babies and see who adopts who. The young females are pretty good with the babies. They practice on them, like girls do with dolls.'

'Chimps are so like humans,' said Isabella. 'But they're a mystery sometimes. I saw the young males ganging up on one of the older females the other day and beating her up.'

'I wish I knew why they did that,' said Gupta

'Maybe it's in the book—'

Isabella clamped her hand over her mouth.

'What now?' said Gupta.

'In the excitement of arriving and getting started, I completely forgot,' said Isabella. 'I brought you a present from England, a book on chimpanzee behaviour by Jane Goodall.'

'You did? Where is it now?' said Gupta.

'I haven't seen the book since I arrived. It must be at the bottom of my suitcase. I'll search this evening.'

'How about lunchtime?'

Isabella smiled.

'Okay, lunchtime.'

While Gupta prepared a salad and some fried

shrimp for their lunch, Isabella tipped her suitcase out on her bed. The book fell out from the bottom compartment where she had packed it in London and landed on the mattress. She picked the book up to examine, but it had not suffered from being left in the damp air. She returned to the kitchen and presented it to Hasan and Gupta, who were as excited as children on Christmas morning.

'Alhamdulilah. Jane Goodall is a great lady,' said Hasan, reading the biography. 'I thought we were the only ones who cared.'

They ate a quick lunch and then spent several hours reviewing the contents.

'There, you see,' said Gupta, pointing at a paragraph. 'I told you that behaviour was natural.'

'How fascinating. I thought I had imagined it,' said Hasan.

They beamed at each other. Isabella envied their mutual passion. *Why couldn't Graham make an effort to encourage her ambitions? He only has one dream for me, that of marrying and having children. He followed his chosen path into accountancy and had a career he loved. Why can't I?*

The days went by in a blur of bottle feeds and health checks. Isabella mucked out cages and comforted orphaned chimps. She made them try out new foods like leaves and fruit, often pretending to eat them herself and making smacking noises with her lips to show how tasty they were. The orphans were like human toddlers, being volatile and needy in equal measure. She soon identified the bullies and the victims, the strong and the weak, from among the group.

'The larger juveniles are going to need separating

from the other orphans soon. I don't know what we'll do,' said Gupta, picking up a squealing youngster who had been bowled over in a game and needed a cuddle. 'We can't afford to fence off the area for the second group, and then there are the buildings for sleeping and so on.'

She sighed, wiping her brow with the sleeve of her t-shirt. Isabella bit her lip.

'I don't want to offer false hope, but I think I can help with that,' she said. 'I need to go to Freetown tomorrow to fax my article to Max, and there's someone in town who owes me a favour.'

Gupta laughed.

'Already? You've only been here five minutes. Are we talking about Pete?'

Isabella blushed.

'No, he promised to help me too, but I, um, sort of saved someone's life, and he owes me big time.'

Gupta raised an eyebrow.

'You sort of saved someone's life? How does that work? I think we need a coffee.'

They sat outside the Nissan hut under a decrepit umbrella made of palm leaves and sipped the strong coffee stiff with sugar. A spider dropped in front of them on a silken thread, almost taking a bath in Isabella's cup.

'Whoops, there you go little fellow,' she said, grabbing the thread and sticking it to the umbrella pole in the centre of the table.

Gupta tapped her fingers on her thigh.

'So? Are you going to spill the beans?'

Isabella took another sip of the vile coffee, grimacing as she swallowed it. She put down the cup and pushed her hair off her face.

'I met some mercenaries in town on my first night out with Pete. I mean, you know, he showed me where to eat near the hotel.'

'Sure,' said Gupta.

'Yes, well, they were eating at a nearby table, and they knew Pete, who is a soldier, and we got talking.'

'So did you save them from food poisoning, or what?'

'Oh, no, I went on a recce with them in a helicopter.'

Gupta snorted.

'You did what?'

'It seemed like an exciting story for Max, and I didn't ask where they were going so…'

Isabella trailed off.

'I thought you were a little eccentric, but I had no idea you were insane,' said Gupta. 'What happened?'

'I have to admit, I nearly got cold feet, but I couldn't find an excuse at short notice, so I ended up sitting in the back of the helicopter while they shot up a village.'

'Kasam se, go on.'

'One man got shot in the arm and almost fell out of the door. I grabbed his belt and pulled him in. That's it. Nothing heroic, just instinctive.'

'Aren't you a dark horse?' said Gupta, shaking her head. 'You had me fooled.'

Isabella laughed.

'You can't imagine how terrified I was. I'm such a coward, I was too afraid to refuse.'

'He doesn't sound like the type of guy who'd have much empathy for our troubles. How are you going to get him to come?'

'I don't know, but he's a Hindu, like you. Have

you got any suggestions?'

Isabella finished writing her next article for Max that evening. She read it through and smiled to herself. *Pretty good, even though I say it myself. How sad I can't send him the photographs I've taken. Perhaps Max could publish them in a later edition of the magazine? I'll fax the article tomorrow and I had better ring Graham too. He must be worrying about me.*

Chapter 14

The next day, Isabella got ready to take a bus into Freetown, bringing with her the finished article for faxing. She had not slept a wink, tossing and turning all night, dreaming of doors slamming in her face as she tried to escape from an enormous house in the woods. She awoke, sweating with effort and stress, and took a cold shower to calm herself down. The sun had already evaporated the mist off the ground, and she put on her coolest linen shorts and top before going into the kitchen next door.

'And where are you going, all dolled up?' said Gupta, looking up from the bottles.

'I'm not dolled up. It's scorching outside, so I'm wearing the coolest outfit I have. Do you want anything in town?' she said to Gupta.

'No, thank you. Hasan and Joe are doing a run later today, so they have my list. Don't you want to get a lift with them?'

'I'd rather get this done as soon as possible. And it gives me all day if the phone lines are down in the morning.'

Gupta narrowed her eyes.

'So, it's not because you want to spend more time with Pete then?'

'With Pete? No, why would you say that?'

'Oh, no reason.'

A blush stole into Isabella's cheeks. As if. But she had to admit that he had wandered into her thoughts a few times over the past few days. She shook herself.

'He's a drunk. Why would I be interested in him?'

Gupta smirked and took a sip of her tea.

'No reason.'

As the bus inched through the outskirts of Freetown, Isabella wriggled with impatience, willing the traffic to part so she could get to the telephone exchange quicker. She felt sure that Graham would have calmed down and be ready for a better chat now he had got used to the idea of her staying longer. She had so much to tell him.

'Hello, darling.'

That was more like it.

'Hello, have you missed me?' said Isabella.

'Oh, it's you,' said Graham.

'Of course, it's me. Who else would you be calling darling?'

'I knew it was you. I'm just joking. What happened last time? I waited and waited but you never called back.'

'Oh, did you? I'm sorry. The telephones here can be out of order for days, and I have to travel from the sanctuary on a rickety old bus that takes hours.'

'You're staying at the sanctuary? Isn't that odd?'

'Well, I'm helping them—'

'You're what? Are they paying you?'

'No, not as such. I'm learning—'

'They're not paying you? What on earth is wrong with you? Why do you let people take advantage of you all the time?'

'That's not fair. I offered to help them. It's educational for me and I love the chimps, especially Lucius.'

'Who the hell is Lucius? I hope you're not making a fool of yourself.'

Isabella sighed.

'Lucius is the alpha male, the leader of the chimps.'

'A chimp? You're mooning over a chimp? I don't believe you.'

'Try to understand. I'm living my dream right now. I just need a little more time, that's all.'

'You're away with the fairies, more like.'

'Don't you miss me? I miss you, a lot.'

'Don't change the subject. I want you to come home now. This is turning into a farce.'

'I can't come yet, but I promise to let you know when I've booked my flight to London. Maybe you could meet me there? We could have a few days together and go to the theatre.'

'Why would I want to go to London, when there are theatres in Dublin? Come home soon, or don't bother coming at all.'

The line cut off, and Isabella held the receiver to her chest, trying to take in the conversation. Somebody knocked on the door of the booth, making her jump. A small, cross-looking man put his head inside.

'Are you finished? There's a queue, you know.'

Isabella stumbled to the desk and paid for her call and the fax to Max. She didn't feel up to a chat with him over the article, so she left without calling him. Close to tears, she sat in the local coffee shop, waving away the begging street children, stony faced. A lurking sense of misgiving had replaced her optimism about making up with Graham. *Did he mean what he said, or was it just emotional blackmail? And saying hello darling before she spoke was weird, too. How did he know it was her on the line, anyway?*

She got into a taxi, her heart heavy, and gave the driver the name of the hotel.

'Are you on holiday?' said the driver.

'Sort of,' said Isabella.

'Do you like Sierra Leone?'

Do I? Or am I just being stubborn?

'It's wonderful. Do you know any shortcuts? I'm in a hurry.'

By the time the taxi rolled up to the Animal Kingdom, Isabella had used all her reserves of politeness. The driver would not take a hint, no matter how monosyllabic her answers, and he had forced her to talk to him all the way there. She paid him and he gave her his business card.

'You might want to have dinner with me,' he said.

I might not.

'Thank you, but my boyfriend works in this hotel, and he is ex-British army so I don't think that would be a good idea.'

The driver sped off, leaving her holding the card.

'Hey, it's the wandering scribe,' said Pete, when she walked into the hotel. 'What are you doing in town?'

'I've just been to call Graham and send Max an article by fax.'

'And how did that go?'

'I faxed the article to Dublin without a hitch.'

'I meant your call to Graham. How's he taking your desertion to Sierra Leone?'

'I haven't deserted and I don't want to talk about

Graham, if it's all right with you.'

Pete brushed a dead fly off the desk with a dishcloth. He looked up and feigned disinterest.

'No bother. I was only being polite. I don't care what you said to him.'

'Good. I'm here to collect on the dinner you promised me,' she said, blushing with effort. 'With Manu, I mean.'

Pete grinned.

'Now that's the best idea I've heard all day,' he said, winking. 'I'll be off shift at seven if you can keep yourself occupied until then. Your room's free if you want the same one.'

'I'd like that, thank you.'

Isabella lay on her bed after a relaxing shower, luxuriating in the cool air from the air conditioning unit which rattled in its frame. The phone call with Graham had unsettled her. He sounded offhand and didn't say he missed her, even when prompted. He put down the phone before she had time to say goodbye. *Or perhaps the line got cut off? Didn't I play the same trick on him last time?*

Needing to escape from thought of Graham, she put on her swimming costume and wandered down to the beach to sit in the shade of the palm trees. Red crabs scuttled back and forth, scooping up sand in their claws and disappearing under the roots whenever she moved. She tried to read her book, but her mind wandered to the dinner with Manu and Pete. *I need to be persuasive to pull it off. Manu didn't seem keen to admit he owed me anything, but I'm sure he was showing off in front of his team.*

As the sun went down, she picked up her towel and shook the sand out of it, starting the crabs. She slipped on her flip-flops and ambled back to the hotel. There was no sign of Pete at the reception and she told herself she didn't care. Graham's rejection of her overtures had hurt her feelings, but that didn't mean Pete represented a new beginning.

Back in her room, she stood up to brush her hair, admiring the freckles across the bridge of her nose in the bathroom mirror. They looked like war paint. Her hair had become blonder in the sun, and her signature red lipstick stood out like blood on her face. *I feel like I've been here for months. How odd to feel so at home after such a short while.* Time to go into battle.

Chapter 15

Isabella bounced down the stairs into the lobby to find Pete waiting for her. He had showered and shaved, and the smell of aftershave permeated the air. The way he looked at her made her smile and blush. They stood in awkward silence, searching for a banal ice breaker.

'You scrub up well,' she said.

'One of us had to look good,' said Pete. 'Ouch.'

'Let's go, Prince Charming.'

Ten stepped out of the shadows as they left the hotel and stood in front of them, hands on his skinny hips, resentment seeping from his pores.

'Where are you going?' he said.

'Gosh! You gave me a fright. How are you?' said Isabella.

Ten ignored her.

'Are you taking her to Alex's?' he said to Pete. 'Can I come?'

'Another time, buddy. This is business,' said Pete.

Ten pouted.

'I don't know why you like her. She doesn't like you,' he said. 'She already has a boyfriend.'

'He knows that, Ten,' said Isabella. 'We're just friends.'

'He calls your name at night, you know,' said Ten.

'Get lost,' said Pete. 'You're not funny.'

Ten glared at them in fury and stomped off towards the back of the hotel.

'See you tomorrow,' said Isabella, but he didn't turn around.

They walked to Alex's on the narrow pavement in the balmy night air, their arms and hands brushing. Ten's revelation about Pete shouting her name in his dreams had a profound effect on Isabella. Despite the heat, she felt her hairs stand on end at the contact. Pete's physical presence made her feel ill with desire, and she fought the inclination to take his arm so she could smell him closer. *For God's sake, Isabella, you have a boyfriend. Stop fantasizing.* Pete seemed oblivious to her quandary and let her enter the archway first.

'Game on,' he said.

But which one?

Isabella spotted Manu and his crew lounging on their seats at the table nearest the beach. Chopper had them all enthralled with a well-worn tale about Angola, and Whitey interjected with gory details to embellish the story. When Pete and Isabella approached the table, a shadow passed over Manu's face.

'So, you brought Irish with you?' he said.

'I'm not Irish,' said Isabella. 'I just live there.'

'All right, keep your hair on. I'm just surprised at Pete hanging around with you, when he hates the Irish.'

Isabella's eyes opened wide. Pete shook his head.

'Don't listen to him,' he said to Isabella. 'He's just stirring.'

'I'm only telling the truth,' Manu said.

'And what's Ireland got to do with anything?' said

105

Pete. 'We're here for a beer and a good time. Or should we sit somewhere else?'

Whitey patted the seat beside him.

'Sit here, Africa. I'll protect you from the grumpy Tongan.'

'Sit between us,' said Chopper. 'That way, you'll be safe from both the grumpy buggers.'

Isabella grinned.

'Now, there's an offer I can't refuse.'

She sat on the plastic seat, which felt cool compared to the night. Pete pulled up a chair between Whitey and Manu and ordered a round of beers. A silence fell on the group as the moon came out from behind a cloud and shot a path of golden light across the sea towards them like an invitation to adventure. Isabella watched as Pete breathed in the warm night air with his eyes closed. She felt ashamed of her instant dismissal of him as a drunk. *How does he enjoy his days, when the nights hold such terror for him? When will I learn to be less judgemental?*

The waitress arrived with the drinks and Pete opened his eyes, catching her staring at him. He winked and handed her one of the cold beers from the tray held by the waitress. She lifted the chilled glass to her lips to cover her confusion. In her haste, the beer sloshed over her upper lip and the foam sat on her lip like a comedy moustache. Manu snorted with laughter.

'You're one of the boys now. That 'tache suits you.'

Isabella wiped the bubbles off her lip, but not her grin.

'I'm trying to look like your mother,' she said.

A moment of shocked silence was followed by an explosion of laughter around the table.

'Hail, the queen of banter,' said Chopper.

Trevor chinked his glass against hers.

'Kudos,' he said.

Manu looked like he had been shot again.

'She's dangerous,' he said, rubbing his beer belly. 'Women should be illegal.'

Isabella let everyone have a couple of beers and a feast of scampi and fried fish before broaching the subject of the sanctuary, calculating her request would go down better on a full stomach. She caught Pete's eye and mouthed 'now?' He nodded.

'What are you guys up to this weekend?' she said.

'I haven't made any plans,' said Whitey.

'Drinking,' said Chopper. 'And a visit to Paddy's Bar for a gawp at the trannies.'

'You're obsessed,' said Trevor.

'Desperate more like it,' said Manu. 'I'm going to clean my weapons and drink whisky.'

Isabella took a deep breath.

'I wondered… It's just…'

'Spit it out,' said Manu, glowering.

'I need some help,' she said, almost choking on her words.

Manu took a toothpick from the jar at the centre of the table and clamped it between his teeth, daring her to continue. Whitey elbowed her.

'What sort of help?' he said.

'At the sanctuary. We need to build a fence around the second enclosure for the orphan group.'

'What's wrong with the first enclosure?' said Manu.

'The orphans are too young for the politics in there. If we put them in with the adults, who are already a bit cramped for space, they will not survive,' said

Isabella. 'And some of the weaker chimps in there are already being bullied and need to move out before they get killed in a fight.'

Chopper's brow wrinkled as he took this in.

'I thought chimps were peaceful vegetarians.'

'Actually, they can be tribal and kill each other. Sometimes even eat each other,' said Pete.

'My illusions have been shattered,' said Trevor. 'Next thing you'll tell me is that Santa doesn't exist.'

He scratched his stubble, and they all waited for Manu to say something.

'No way,' said Manu, shaking his head. 'There's no bloody way I'm spending my free time making Wendy houses for baby chimps. I'm a soldier, not a nanny.'

Manu sounded so like Ten, Isabella almost laughed. She bit her lip.

'What about sewa?' she said. 'Isn't it a duty? I thought you were a Hindu.'

Manu's face darkened with rage.

'I never thought I'd have a Christian tell me about my religion,' he said. 'You've got some cheek.'

Isabella looked around the table for support. Chopper and Whitey wouldn't meet her eye and Pete looked as if he might faint, but she did not back down.

'I saved your life, or maybe karma did,' she said. 'You need to repay the debt.'

'As the officer class would say; hoist by my own petard. Where did you get this information from?' said Manu. 'I doubt they teach Hindu studies in Dublin.'

'The owner's wife, Gupta, is a Hindu. She told me what to say.'

'Hindus run the sanctuary? Why didn't you say so in the beginning? Of course, I'll help.'

'We need some materials too,' said Isabella, ignoring the fact Hasan was a Muslim, and wincing at her own bravery.

Manu shoved a napkin across the table.

'Make me a list,' he said.

'I've got one here,' she said, pulling a sheet of paper out of her pocket.

'Why doesn't that surprise me?' said Manu.

He read the list, mouthing the words like a schoolboy.

'That's some list,' he said, shoving it into his pocket. 'I'll have to call in some favours.'

'Can you do it?' said Isabella.

'I'll bring the Irish Rangers with me. Can you feed them?'

'How many men?'

'Thirty.'

'We can feed them,' said Isabella, with a conviction she did not feel. 'Gupta can make a curry.'

'It's a deal,' said Manu. 'And don't look so amazed boys, you're coming too.'

A chorus of faux moans greeted this announcement.

'This round is on me,' said Isabella.

'And the next,' said Manu.

The team spent the rest of the evening calculating and recalculating the materials needed for the fence and the nursery. As usual, their competitive natures overcame their reluctance to help with the project. Pete surprised Isabella by doing all the mathematics, his head bent over a series of napkins, which were soon covered in calculations. The beers kept coming until Manu stood up.

'We'll see you soon then,' he said. 'I'm not sure

when, but we'll be there. Tell Gupta I like my curry as hot as Hades.'

Pete and Isabella waved them off and sat in silence for a moment. Pete swallowed the last of his beer and looked into her eyes.

'Do you want to come for a walk on the beach?' he said.

'Now?' said Isabella, regretting it.

Pete looked at the floor and shuffled his feet.

'I just thought—'

'No, yes, of course. I didn't—'

'Let's go then.'

He pulled back Isabella's chair with some ceremony and stuck out his elbow so she could slip her hand through. She could feel his heart pounding through his t-shirt and knew her own matched it beat for beat. *Is he drunk? Do I care?*

Chapter 16

The sand shimmered in the moonlight as Pete and Isabella walked arm-in-arm along the curve of the strand. Isabella felt all her troubles lift and float away with the mosquitos which threatened but did not bite, deterred by her repellent. Bats swooped and clicked over their heads, and small crabs scuttled sideways to avoid being trodden on, running into the gentle waves lapping the shore.

Pete headed for the dryer sand at the top of the beach and plonked himself on a bank near the promenade. Isabella sat beside him, leaving a space between them, as the thought of sitting in close contact with him made panic rise up her throat. He gazed out to sea and a contented sigh escaped his lips.

'Is it true?' she said.

'Is what true?'

'That you shout my name in your dreams?'

'I don't know. I'm asleep.'

Isabella waited.

'I'm plagued with vivid dreams right now. That's why…'

'That's why what?'

'Why I drink so much. I'm trying to suppress the nightmares.'

'Hm. I'm not sure I'm flattered to feature in them. Would it help if you told me about it?'

A small figure pushed his way in between them and sat on the sand. The moment seemed lost. Isabella sighed.

'What the hell, Ten?' said Pete. 'Scram, short stuff. You're not invited.'

Ten's face fell and his bottom lip quivered. Isabella felt guilty for wanting him to leave so she could be alone with Pete. *What if he went back to the slums and disappeared forever?* There would be other times, and Ten needed them right now. She patted his knee.

'That's okay,' she said. 'You can stay on one condition.'

'What's that?' said Ten.

The light from the moon picked out the suspicion written all over his face.

'Everyone has to tell a sad story.'

'Seriously?' said Pete.

'About their life,' said Isabella.

'No way,' said Ten.

'Only if you start,' said Pete, looking Isabella in the eye. 'And if it's good enough, I'll play too.'

Isabella took a deep breath.

'Okay, I'll go first, but only if you both promise to tell your story too. Do you swear?'

'Yes,' said Pete, and Ten nodded.

Isabella stared out to sea, trying to find the words. *Where do I start? With the truth.*

'When I was a little girl, my brother and his friend got shot by the IRA.'

Pete gasped as if winded. Ten blew out through his lips.

'You're lying,' he said. 'Who is the IRA?'

'No. I wouldn't lie about something like this. The IRA is a terrorist group in Ireland. They're like the rebels in Sierra Leone, except they are fighting for a united Ireland.'

Pete snorted.

'Freedom fighters? That's not what I'd call them.'

'Rebels are heroes,' said Ten. 'Always.'

'Are you two going to let me tell my story or not?' said Isabella.

'Go on,' said Ten. 'I want to hear.'

Isabella grabbed her knees for support and looked out to sea, remembering.

'The IRA had recruited our friend Liam, but he didn't last long with them. He hated the violence and the killing of innocent people, and he had run away. He came to our house for shelter. Michael, my brother, went for a walk in the woods above our house in Ireland, and Liam followed him there.'

'If Liam belonged to the IRA, why did he come to an English family for shelter?' said Pete.

'Oh, he used to live next door to us. He liked my mother's cooking, and debating politics with my father. He disappeared one day and joined the IRA. Next thing we heard, they had moved him to the border with Northern Ireland to smuggle weapons across to Belfast. When Liam got cold feet and phoned for help, my father drove up there to rescue him.'

'Why did they get shot?' said Ten.

'Well, we're not sure. Michael took Blue, our dog, for a walk in the woods, and Liam ran after him. We think it's because he knew about the IRA training ground down one path, and he wanted to stop Michael from going there. One of them spotted the boys and thought Michael was a soldier.'

'Why?'

'Because he had joined the cadets at school, and had a military haircut. He was seventeen, but he looked twenty. Anyway, some men grabbed hold of them and shot them on a rifle range. Blue ran home and barked at me, but I thought she was just being annoying and I shooed her away. My father heard her barking outside and knew something had happened. He followed her to the forest and found Liam and Michael lying on the ground in a pool of blood. Liam had already died, but my father called an ambulance for Michael and they took him to the hospital. We had to wait for hours in the hospital until he came out of surgery. I thought I'd lost him and I felt guilty for not realising that Blue had tried to tell me something. I should have known. She never barked. Liam died because of me, and Michael nearly died too. I always complained about his bond with my other sister, instead of loving him, and in one second of bad luck, I almost lost him forever.'

She sniffed, and a tear ran down her cheek. A small hand took hold of hers and squeezed it. She squeezed back, unable to speak. Pete coughed.

'You don't know that,' said Pete. 'If the IRA meant to execute them, the only surprise is that Michael survived at all. You can't blame yourself.'

Pete put his arm around her shoulder, squeezing Ten, who squeaked in protest.

'Okay,' he said. 'My turn. I fought the IRA in the streets of Belfast. They used snipers on rooftops to pick us off when we were on patrol.'

'Wait,' said Ten. 'The same IRA?'

'The same.'

'But I thought Britain lived in peace. I thought…'

He trailed off.

'One day,' said Pete. 'I patrolled the Catholic enclave with my troop, and a sniper shot at us, killing a baby in a pram. The mother screamed and screamed. We tried to staunch the bleeding, but it was hopeless. The baby had died instantly. The mother became hysterical, and she blamed us instead of the sniper. There was nothing we could do. I've always felt guilty even though it isn't my fault.'

He stopped and looked out to sea, swallowing hard. Isabella reached over and touched his face, finding it wet. Pete turned to Ten.

'Your turn,' he said. 'No cheating.'

Ten stood up, but he sat down again, chewing his cheek in anguish.

'Okay,' he said. 'But don't look at me.'

Pete and Isabella turned to look at the sea, while between them, Ten battled with himself. Finally, he cleared his throat.

'My mother died of malaria when I was nine. I didn't know she had become ill because she had already sent me to live on the streets.'

He paused. Isabella held her breath, dying to ask why any mother would do that to a nine-year-old, but knowing it wouldn't help.

'When I heard she had gone hospital, I knew it had to be bad because she had always refused to go to there in the past. They wouldn't let me in to see her because I had no proof I was her son. I sneaked past the doctors into the ward and I found her lying on a mattress with a high fever. They found me beside her and tried to throw me out. I begged them to help her, but the hospital had no medicine. So, I went to the chemist near the hospital to steal some chloroquine...'

He trailed off as a large sob caught in his chest.

'It's alright,' said Isabella, taking his hand again. 'You don't have to tell us.'

Ten shook his head.

'The owner of the chemist's shop caught me and he called the police. They threw me in jail for the night.'

He wailed, tears streaming down his cheeks. Pete flashed Isabella a look which rent her heart in two. She cried, holding Ten's hand. After a while, he stopped and blew his nose on his t-shirt, gasping for breath.

'When I got back to the hospital, her bed was empty. They told me she had died. And the worst thing is, I killed her.'

A sharp bark escaped from Pete. He kneeled in front of Ten and grabbed him by the shoulders.

'Never say that. You were nine years old, for God's sake. You did your best. Poverty killed her. Not you.'

He pulled the boy close and held him tight, the two of them crying with big ragged sobs. Isabella sat watching them, stunned by the outflowing of emotion. She had hoped to bring them all together with secrets but she had instead opened a Pandora's box of emotions which flowed like a tsunami taking all barriers down with it.

When the tears subsided, Ten sat back down between them and they all sat in stunned silence with their thoughts. Pete put his arm around Ten and Isabella and pulled them closer. A sort of miracle. Nothing is solved, but everything is possible.

They sat looking at the bats swooping low over the sand, their wings glinting in the moonlight. Isabella thought about Liam and wondered if he could see her now. *If he had lived, would he have saved himself? Got a job, married?* The moon went behind a cloud, and Pete shook himself, standing and offering his hands to Ten and Isabella. Ten refused, but Isabella let him pull her up.

'I've got to work in the morning,' said Pete.

'And I've got to go back to the sanctuary and tell Gupta we're entertaining the troops. Will you come with Manu?'

'Wouldn't miss it,' said Pete.

They walked to the hotel and Ten headed for his room at the back. Before they could enter the lobby, he turned.

'Can I come with you to Tacugama?' he said.

Isabella hid her surprise.

'Sure, I'll be going mid-morning. Do you want to have breakfast with me at Alex's?'

'Okay.'

Ten disappeared into the night. Isabella pumped the air with her fist.

'It won't be plain sailing,' said Pete.

'Nothing ever is. I'm just not used to being wrong so often.'

'Perhaps you never noticed before? Ouch!'

'You're one to talk. I don't know why I put up with you.'

'But you do.'

He leaned over and kissed the top of her head.

'We're an odd, traumatised family. We all need to learn to be patient with each other,' he said.

'Family?'

'You know what I mean.'

And she did.

Chapter 17

Gupta's eyes opened wide when Isabella arrived at Tacugama with Ten in tow. She rushed forward and threw her arms around him, but he wriggled free, torn between embarrassment and enjoyment.

'Don't do that,' he said, his face like thunder.

Isabella rolled her eyes behind him, and Gupta contained a laugh. She held out her hand for him to shake.

'I'm sorry for hugging you,' said Gupta. 'It's how I greet people. I'll get your room ready.'

'I'm not staying long,' said Ten.

'But you need a bed, right?'

Ten nodded, shamefaced.

'I'm going to make a cup of tea,' said Isabella. 'Do you want one?'

'Is there something to eat?' said Ten.

'There's always something to eat for young men who are growing fast,' said Gupta.

The ghost of a smile crept across Ten's face. Isabella led him into the kitchen where she poured water over the tea leaves and left the tea to steep while she measured milk powder into the bottles for the orphans. Ten watched her in a mixture of wonder and disbelief.

'Who's going to drink that?' he said.

'You'll see,' said Gupta, coming in with an armful of laundry. 'Isabella, give the lad some biscuits. We are going to feed the youngest chimps with bottles. You can come into the orphans' building with us, but don't be surprised if they're frightened of you. It takes a while before they trust someone new.'

'Won't they attack me?' said Ten.

'Where did you get that idea?' said Gupta.

'No, they will just be nervous,' said Isabella. 'If you're afraid, you can wait outside.'

'Afraid? I'm not afraid of anything. Of course, I'll come in.'

Ten helped Gupta carry the bottles, and they walked towards the cages where loud hooting came from the sleeping quarters behind them. He shrunk back from the noise, hovering behind the women as they entered the passageway, an overpowering smell of small, fetid bodies hitting them. He put down the basket of milk bottles and mango slices, and held his nose, leaning back against the wall away from the cage. Gupta smiled at him.

'Will you please help us by manning the doors to the cages and sleeping quarters? There are two sliding doors in the alcove on the left. The one at the far end is our direct way in and out of the cage, and the one beside it on the right is used to let us in and out of their sleeping quarters. This door between the two sleeping quarters, leads to the holding area, which has one door on the left, one on the right and two at the end. The left-hand one is to let the chimps in and out of the sleeping quarters into the holding area, and the left-hand one on the front wall is to let them in or out of the cage. Most mornings, we let them through the holding area into the cage where they spend the day playing together. Then we take the chimps out in pairs to give them their bottles, with one of us guarding the doors. If you do the doors, we can take two each into the holding area and feed them faster.'

'What about these other doors on the right-hand side?' said Ten, fully engaged now.

'They're for the second cage which needs repairs, so we can't use them now,' said Isabella.

'Okay then. We'll go into the holding area now. Can you stay outside and monitor us through the bars, please? Once we are inside with this door closed, I need you to open the door to the sleeping area on the left by taking out the bolt and sliding the handle towards you. Once we are through the door, slide it shut again. We will go in and put a chimp on each hip. Once we have two chimps each, please open the door and let us into the holding area. Be sure to shut the door behind us or the other chimps will come into the holding area and try to steal the milk,' said Gupta.

'But what if one gets through before I shut the door?'

'Just do your best. If you put some pieces of mango through the bars while we pick up the babies, none of the bigger chimps will be interested in the doors.'

Ten nodded, but he did not move towards the cages.

'Are you sure you want to do this?' said Isabella. 'You could just watch instead as it's your first morning.'

'I'm not stupid. I can open a couple of doors,' said Ten.

'Nobody said you were,' said Gupta. 'Okay, grab the basket, Isabella, and let's get started.'

Ten adapted well to his new position of responsibility, opening and shutting the doors with no alarms or escapees. Contrary to Gupta's expectations, the orphans did not shy away from Ten, and Fidget, who had gained status in the group with his bravery, showed signs of wanting to be picked up by the newcomer.

'What do I do?' said Ten.

'Would you like to feed Fidget?' said Gupta.

Ten wavered. Fidget whined through the bars and tried to grab Ten's hair. With Ten's help, Gupta retrieved Fidget from the sleeping quarter and handed him to Ten in the passageway.

'Take a bottle and sit down. He won't run away. He's too small for that sort of behaviour.'

Fidget grabbed the bottle and sucked on it with contented grunts. His grubby hand reached up, and he enlaced his fingers in Ten's short curls. Ten's eyes opened wide.

'My little sister used to do that,' he said.

'Resistance is futile,' said Isabella under her breath to Gupta, who smothered a laugh, and then slapped her forehead.

'I nearly forgot,' she said. 'How did it go in Freetown?'

Gupta's eager expression made Isabella hesitate. Manu had promised, but she didn't know him well enough to trust him to turn up. He might have felt obliged with the eyes of his men on him at the restaurant. *What if he changes his mind? Or a flare up in the fighting prevents them from coming?*

'I told them about you, and I think they're going to help, but I'm not sure how soon it will be.'

Gupta's face fell.

'You can tell me the truth. Did they refuse? I'd prefer the truth. We need to deal with our over-crowding problem before it gets acute.'

'They didn't refuse. They offered to help, but until they come up with the goods, I'd prefer not to rely on them. I'm sorry, but I can't promise they'll come through,' said Isabella.

'You tried. It's not your fault. Everyone says they'll help, but when it comes down to it, they always have something better to do or to buy. At least you tried, and you're here helping, which is what counts. We'll think of something. We always do.'

Despite her attempt at optimism, Gupta's mood took a turn for the worse over the next few days. Hasan tried to cheer her up with amusing tales of the goings-on in Lucius's group, but she moped and sat in her room with her precious sari when he wasn't around. Isabella and Ten took on extra duties to give her some space and waited for her to get back to her old self.

Ten tried not to enjoy his new role at the sanctuary, but his barriers crumbled after only a few days. Isabella noticed that the adult chimps responded to Ten's aloof style by teasing him, and the babies flocked to him, grooming his tight curls and wrapping themselves around his arms and legs. He spent hours in the cage comforting the younger orphans and crooning to them.

'He's an odd lad,' said Gupta, watching him with Isabella. 'Where did you find him?'

'He carried my suitcase from the hoverport and the rest is history,' said Isabella. 'He ended up on the streets when he was only eight years old, and his mother died when he was nine, so he had to grow up too fast.'

'Poor mite. No wonder he responds to the orphans, he is one himself.'

'I hadn't thought of that. Of course, he fits right in.'

Lucius remained aloof, treating Ten like an interloper, while still cosying up to Isabella, who had taken to visiting him every evening when he came inside to the sleeping area. He pressed his body up against the rebar so Isabella could groom him and make gentle grunting noises. She risked offering him a hand, which he took between his stubby fingers and sniffed, turning it over to examine the palm. His breath warmed her palm as he held her hand inches from his massive jaws, poking it with his finger.

Hasan, who spent his days searching for supplies with which to supplement the adult chimps' diets, shook his head at their peculiar bond.

'Lucius doesn't like anyone. I wonder if it's your blonde hair? Perhaps he thinks you are a baby human?'

'I don't know, but there's something about him which draws me in. If he were human, I'd say he had charisma.'

'He could tear you limb from limb if he thought you were a threat to the group. Always remember, he is a wild animal with survival instincts that override any loyalty to humans. If the time came, he would choose.'

Isabella spent her evenings trying to collate her observations from the day's goings on. Often, exhaustion sent her to bed before she wrote anything down. Ten had sprouted like a young bamboo and he slept day and night when he didn't have chores. There was never any respite from the constant demands of the chimps. Besides feeding and monitoring of their health, the team had to think up constant entertainments to keep them focussed, so they did not fight.

'It says here that males stay with the same group all their lives, but some females move to fresh groups when they reach adulthood,' said Gupta, reading their new bible, Jane Goodall's book. 'We should take it into account when we decide who should form the basis of the family group for the new enclosure behind the cages.'

'I don't know how you think that's going to happen,' said Hasan. 'There's no way we can afford to set that up. And what about the sleeping quarters?'

'How long have the orphans been in quarantine?' said Isabella.

'Exactly a month, but I don't know what to do next,' said Hasan.

'Why don't we try to fix the damaged cages on the nursery block and separate the older orphans into one side and the babies in the other. We could put two older females in with each group.' said Gupta. 'And two males who suffer from bullying. That should start socialising the older orphans who are getting out of control and hurting the babies. They have to learn about group life, or they are going to have a nasty shock when we put them in with the adults.'

'And then what?' said Hasan.

'One step at a time,' said Gupta.

Chapter 18

When it came to surrogate mothers and fathers for the orphans, several obvious choices existed among Lucius's group. Sarah, who had lost her last baby and had become arthritic, already spent her days babysitting and keeping the peace amongst the squabbling teenagers. Her daughter, Greta, had followed in her mother's footsteps, and always had a baby on her back or latched to her front. After much discussion, Hasan decided to separate the orphans into their groups first, and then to add an adult to each group. Since a grid of rebar formed the boundary between the two adjacent cages, the groups could still see and communicate with each other.

Ten's knowledge of the orphans' friendships and social groups proved to be invaluable in deciding which chimps they should put in what groups.

'You can't put Brian in there without Daisy,' he said. 'Daisy will pine. She spends all day with him.'

'But she can see him through the bars,' said Hasan.

'She's too little to understand, and she just lost her mother.'

'Ten's right. We can put Brian in with the larger orphans after Daisy forms an attachment to Sarah,' said Gupta.

Ten beamed.

'Can you check the lists for me, please,' said Hasan, pushing the notebook over to Ten's side of the table. 'I want to get this right.'

Ten stood up, knocking his chair over in his haste.

'Just ask me if you don't know. I don't need to read your lists,' said Ten, and walked out.

'What got into him?' said Hasan. 'I thought he'd be pleased that I asked him to help.'

Isabella shook her head. What a mercurial boy. Either furious or ecstatic. You never knew which Ten would turn up. Gupta tutted and patted Hasan's hand.

'I think it's obvious,' she said. 'Ten can't read.'

'But he's almost thirteen,' said Hasan. 'How is that possible?'

'He's never been to school,' said Isabella. 'His mother couldn't afford his uniform, or the books.'

'But we have to help him,' said Hasan.

'I've known for a while, but it's a delicate matter,' said Gupta. 'He's so sensitive to criticism. Leave it to me. I'll pick a moment.'

Suddenly, Ten ran back into the Nissan hut. His eyes shone with excitement.

'They've come. You've got to come and see this,' he said. 'You won't believe it.'

Gupta looked at Isabella, who feigned ignorance, shrugging. Please let it be Manu.

'What is it?' said Gupta.

Hasan, who turned to Isabella. 'Do you know anything about this?'

Isabella winked at him.

'Oh my God, you did it. Why didn't you tell us?' he said.

'Tell us what?' said Gupta, looking around in confusion.

'You'll see,' said Isabella. 'Let's go.'

She pushed Gupta through the door and the three of them ran past the cages, triggering an eruption of disgruntled coughing from the orphans who had been expecting their fruit ration. A bunch of smiling soldiers stood at the sanctuary gates, carrying bags of cement on their shoulders. Manu, Chopper, Trevor, and Whitey were among them, Manu looking sheepish, carrying a lump hammer and a goat carcass. Gupta stood looking at them with her mouth open.

'Did you do this, Isabella? I can't believe it. We were done for,' said Gupta.

'I called in a favour, but on one condition.'

'What's that?' said Hasan, opening the gate wide and shaking hands with the soldiers.

'I promised Gupta would make a goat curry for supper.'

Gupta put her hands on her hips and raised her eyebrow.

'You did what?' she said.

'I said you'd cook supper for everyone.'

Gupta smiled.

'And what sort of hostess would I be if I didn't? I'll need help though.'

'That sounds like me,' said Isabella.

'I presume this goddess is Gupta,' said Manu, pushing Isabella out of the way. 'Pleased to make your acquaintance, madam.'

Gupta blushed and fluttered her eyelashes at him.

'That's enough introductions,' said Hasan, frowning. 'If you two deal with the orphans, and the supper, I'll show the boys what we need to do.'

Isabella tried not to look for Pete, her heart racing. Manu caught her searching and laughed.

'Lover boy's on his way, Irish. He's driving the second truck. We raided a village last week where the rebels had stockpiled building supplies. It looks as if they were going to build a palace for their leader, but we took the lot.'

Isabella ignored the reference to Pete and her origins. *Manu was Manu. Take it or leave it.* And he had turned up with the most amazing quantity of materials, and about thirty-five men, so she couldn't complain about his lack of commitment. Gupta stood to one side, mouth open as she watched the men carry rebar, telegraph poles, reinforced wire netting and an old generator up the road to the derelict block where Hasan directed operations.

'Come on then,' said Isabella, pulling Gupta's arm. 'We have a curry to make.'

'But where's Pete?' said Ten.

'He'll be here,' said Isabella. 'Why don't you help Hasan with the fence?'

Ten frowned.

'Manu doesn't like me,' he said.

'Manu doesn't like anyone,' said Isabella. 'Ignore him. Show him you don't care what he thinks.'

Ten shrugged and trudged off towards the group of men who were drawing up plans with sticks in the dirt. Soon he became animated, and one man slapped him on the back.

'My work here is done,' said Isabella.

'No, it isn't,' said Gupta. 'Come with me and cut up the goat.'

Soon Gupta had dug out a blackened caldron from the back of the visitor's Nissan hut, and they hung it from an improvised frame over the fire pit beside the huts.

'It's like a scene from Macbeth,' said Isabella.

'It will be, if supper isn't ready on time,' said Gupta.

The women set about dismembering the carcase and cutting the meat into cubes. Isabella peeled a bag of onions, weeping her eyes out until her face felt swollen and puffy. Pete chose that moment to put his head through the door.

'Is it my imagination, or do I make you cry every time I see you?' he said.

Isabella laughed and threw a bad onion at him.

'Go away and help Hasan. Can't you see we're busy in here?' she said, but she gave him a radiant smile.

'That man is dangerous,' said Gupta. 'If I weren't a married woman…'

'I hope you're not talking about Manu,' said Hasan, who popped his head around the door. 'I didn't like the way he looked at you, habibi. It may be grounds for divorce.'

'Don't be silly. You're the only man for me,' said Gupta, giving his bottom a playful pat.

Once they had added all the ingredients into the caldron and the fire had been lit, Gupta and Isabella fed the now indignant orphans and sat outside watching the men hammer the telegraph posts into the ground and set them with cement.

'Ten's right about Daisy and Brian,' said Gupta.

'He's right about most things,' said Isabella. 'Maybe that's why his behaviour irritates me. He could be so much more.'

'That's rich. Coming from someone who hasn't

taken advantage of her opportunities,' said Gupta.

Isabella spun to look at her, certain she would see a smile of complicity, but Gupta's face held no redemption. How could she say that? She doesn't even know me. But Gupta had hit the nail on the head. Ever since she had arrived in Sierra Leone, Isabella had felt the world open out in front of her, revealing all she had missed by taking the easy way out. Her pride had been hurt when she couldn't get into veterinary college, and that defeat had resulted in her lack of determination and her use of self-sabotage. Living in a comfortable rut had reduced the chances of humiliation and disappointment, but it had also killed any possibility of success or adventure. *Why did I stay so long in a dead-end job? What possessed me to move in with my insipid boyfriend?*

Gupta put her hand on Isabella's shoulder, waking her out of her reverie.

'I'm sorry,' she said. 'I shouldn't have said that, but the world is at your feet and I'm jealous of everything you could have, if you only went out and got it. Ten has limited opportunities, and he's terrified to take the ones on offer in case they evaporate, and yet you seem resentful of him. I don't get it.'

Isabella blushed.

'I hate to admit it, but you're not the only one who's jealous. Pete and Ten have a special bond, and I feel left out. Is that dumb? Just look at them.'

Out by the fence, Pete had grabbed Ten and rubbed Ten's tight curls with his fist while Ten roared with laughter. Joy radiated from them both and infected the rest of the crew.

'You should be happy for them. Two damaged people are finding new joy in the world. I saw the way

Pete looked at you in the kitchen. He's not in love with Ten.'

'In love?' said Isabella. 'I didn't mean that—'

'What did you mean then? You looked at him the same way. Come on, the cauldron needs stirring and we have to make the rice and salads.'

By the end of the day, the crew had erected the new fence around the enclosure and attached to the derelict cages, which had a new lean-to passageway with a zinc roof running along the front of it. They had oiled the old sliding doorways and repositioned them in their rails and swung old tires from the ceiling on chains. They hammered temporary sleeping platforms made of shipping pallets to a frame offering different levels for nesting.

'Wow,' said Gupta. 'I never thought I'd see this.'

'We fixed the second cage in the orphan block too,' said Ten, who had several fingers bandaged and a big smudge of dirt on his face.

'Amazing,' said Hasan. 'I don't know what to say.'

'He's a good worker,' said Manu. 'That curry smells fantastic.'

'I'm afraid we don't have enough plates, but Joe cut some flat waxy leaves for us to use if that's okay,' said Gupta.

Silence reigned as the group tucked into their food. The goat curry burned Isabella's mouth as she perched on a pile of pallets next to Pete, who wolfed his food down like he hadn't eaten in a week.

'Do you want to finish mine,' she said. 'It's too hot for me, and I haven't been hammering fence posts all day.'

'If you're offering, I won't turn you down,' said

Pete. 'Will you be coming back to town with me?'

'Not this time. We need to get the new group sorted out, and it's a lot of work. I don't want to leave Gupta and Hasan in the lurch.'

He raised his head from his meal and looked at her, an appraisal which made her feel odd.

'You're growing on me, Irish,' he said.

'Don't call me that.'

'Only kidding. Nicknames are a sign of affection. I've got to go now but I'll be back to help next weekend.'

'You will?'

'Of course. I won't let you take all the credit for saving the sanctuary.'

Isabella jumped up and hugged him. Before she knew how it happened, he had stood up and kissed her on the lips, the hot curry making them buzz under his touch. They lingered over the kiss for an instant and then she stepped back to look at him, almost tripping over Ten, who had come over to say goodbye.

'Oops, sorry Ten, I didn't see you there,' said Isabella.

Ten seemed rooted to the spot, and he opened his mouth, but nothing came out.

'I'm off to town now,' said Pete, sticking out his hand to shake Ten's. 'I'll see you both next weekend.'

Ten did not take Pete's hand. He turned on his heel and marched off towards the Nissan huts.

'He saw us,' said Isabella.

'What if he did?' said Pete. 'We're adults. I can kiss you if I want to.'

'Can you indeed?' said Isabella. 'You can kiss me if I want you to, and no other reason.'

'And do you?'

She blushed.

'Sometimes,' she said, and slipped her arms around his neck.

'Irish, leave that man alone. He needs to drive us back to town.'

Manu. What a pain that man was. The weekend couldn't come fast enough.

But Pete didn't come that weekend, or the weekend after. Isabella and Ten moped and quarrelled.

'You shouldn't have kissed him,' said Ten. 'It's your fault he didn't come back.'

'Maybe he didn't come back because you were rude to him. You're not the only one with feelings, you know.'

'Honestly, I don't know which of you is more immature,' said Gupta. 'Can't you just get along? Pete will be here soon.'

But he didn't come.

Chapter 19

Hasan and Joe started work installing the electric fences at the top and bottom of the barriers around the new enclosure, leaving Gupta, Isabella and Ten to start preparations for the introductions of members for a new group. Ten had reverted to his aloof ways with Isabella, but she had become accustomed to his moods, and her policy of ignoring him seemed to bear fruit. They sat at the table discussing their priorities for the move and for once, he engaged.

'Now that we have the new enclosure, there is no need to separate the orphans into two groups,' said Gupta. 'Since all the adults already know each other, the most important aspect of forming the new clan will be the habituation of the orphans.'

'Will that be straightforward?' said Isabella. 'From what I've seen, chimps are prone to fights and rivalries.'

'You've seen a group under stress because of the large number of adults in a small area. Once we divide the group, the aggression should reduce.'

'Can I help choose the chimps for the new enclosure? I've been studying Lucius's group with Hasan, and I have some ideas,' said Ten.

'Of course,' said Gupta. 'We need input from everyone on site to make this a success.'

Following their original plan, they wasted no time in separating the mother-daughter team of Sarah and Greta from the rest of Lucius's group, and moving them into the rehabilitated nursery on the right-hand side in the orphans' block. At first, they kept them separated from the orphans and only let into the adjoining cage from where they could see the orphans but only touch them through the rebar fencing.

Greta and Sarah seemed bewildered by their new surroundings and huddled together, looking around and showing their teeth. But when the orphans tumbled out of their nursery into the adjoining cage, the two females crept up to the grid separating them from the youngsters and made soft hooting and grunting noises. The orphans responded to this by flocking to the grid and trying to touch them. When they were separated for the night, the orphans showed signs of distress.

The next morning, Gupta and Isabella gave the orphans their bottles as usual, but the small chimps showed more interest in the females next door than in their food.

'They are looking around for Sarah and Greta,' said Isabella.

'They distracted even Fidget from his food,' said Gupta. 'That's unusual, to say the least.'

'What do you think?' said Hasan. 'It's been twenty-four hours now and no sign of aggression.'

'Open the door and let them mingle. They must be ready for this by now. I can't see them hurting the babies,' said Gupta.

They returned the orphans to their cage and Ten, Isabella, and Gupta stood transfixed as Hasan slid the door open between the two enclosures. Sarah put her arm through the opening and withdrew it again, uncertain, but Fidget, who had seen the door slide open, flew through the gap and latched onto Greta like grim death.

'He's getting his claim in early,' said Gupta.

A trickle turned into a flood, and soon the excited orphans surrounded the females, touching and being touched. An enormous lump appeared in Isabella's throat and she had trouble swallowing. Ten had turned away, unable to watch, with his emotions in turmoil. Gupta put her arm around him and, for once, he didn't shrug it off.

Greta and Sarah soon adjusted to their life among the orphans and their developing relationships were a source of fascination for the team at Tacugama. New bonds and jealousies flared and died as the orphans competed for the attention of their adoptive mothers.

'It's so fascinating,' said Isabella. 'I had no idea how complex chimp society could be.'

'They're like people in many ways,' said Gupta. 'Not all chimps are nice. Some of them are horrible. Look at the way poor old Miranda gets bullied in Lucius's group.'

Ten rolled his eyes.

'I don't know why you're surprised. The stronger one wins every time. Being nice doesn't get you anywhere. Humans are like chimps.'

Hasan laughed.

'I'm nice,' he said.

'And where has that got you?' said Ten, causing a tense silence at the lunch table.

'How can you say that?' said Isabella. 'Hasan and Gupta have taken you in off the streets and looked after you. They only survive because people admire them and help them with food for the sanctuary. You should apologise.'

Hasan held up his hand.

'No, Ten has a right to his opinion. He thinks powerful men get to do anything they like. That's why he admires the rebels? Am I right, Ten?'

'They offered to take me in when no one else cared about me. I could make myself a place in their group.'

'Quite right. But there is more than one type of strength. Maybe that's why you are here and not there?' said Hasan.

'What do you mean?' said Ten.

'Take Tyrone. He has grown into an alpha male, and he will soon be a threat to Lucius, but they don't fight. Why is that?'

Ten frowned.

'I don't know.'

'Because Tyrone is smart. He knows Lucius would beat him in a straight fight, so he is gathering allies around him for the battle that lies ahead,' said Hasan.

'Is that why he spends so much time grooming his friends?' said Isabella.

'He shares his food with them too,' said Gupta.

'But how can he become leader with Lucius in charge?' said Ten.

'One day, Tyrone will challenge Lucius and there will be a bloody battle. Chimps will die. I think Tyrone and his allies will win,' said Hasan.

'Is that why you want to put him in the new enclosure?' said Isabella.

'Exactly. If we move him and his allies there, Lucius will have peace again, until one of the young males is ready to challenge him.'

'So, we should move Tyrone and his buddies as soon as possible?' said Isabella.

'We can only introduce them slowly. We don't know how they will react to the orphans. If one of them shows a tendency to bully them, we need to repatriate him into Lucius's group. This is where you come in, Ten. I need you to monitor each new arrival and report on its behaviour. Isabella can help you make notes in the journal.'

'I don't need help,' said Ten.

'Isabella is a zoologist. She can use scientific terms which you don't know yet. You will make an excellent team.'

Ten looked down at his plate and pushed a grain of rice around the rim. The muscles in his jaw worked, but he did not shout or storm out as he usually would.

'Okay,' he said.

To Isabella's surprise, Ten soon adapted to their new partnership. He spent hours alternating between watching the orphans and choosing the apes to transfer from Lucius's group to Tyrone's new troop. His observation skills grew keener with practice and he had patience with detail which amazed Isabella, who missed half of the signs that Ten picked up.

He developed a code of his own for noting down unusual behaviours, an odd hieroglyphic scrawl which no one except him could understand. When he had finished his day, he would describe every interaction in painstaking detail, making Isabella desperate to get him to write his own notes. But under the eagle eye of Gupta, she held back from mentioning it, and toiled over the journal for hours every night.

She spent her own observation time watching Lucius and how he controlled group politics and arbitrated to solve disputes. Most of the time, he seemed content to get the best food at mealtimes and be groomed by the alpha females, but his presence loomed over the group. When a fight broke out, he would chase, and often bite, the perpetrator, who screamed and cried, and then begged for forgiveness by offering their rump or a hand. Lucius also played with the youngsters in the group. His different levels of tolerance amazed Isabella, who took his strength and bad temper at face value.

The youngsters in the group learned most of their survival craft from the females in the group. Hilda, the alpha female, was an inveterate tool user and constantly upgraded and developed her skills. Hasan got hold of a fresh ant hill, which he put in a massive plastic bag and sealed with masking tape. Before the chimps were let out the next morning, he put the ant hill on a piece of bare ground under the observation platform, leaving some leafy branches beside it.

When the chimps were let out of their sleeping quarters, they surrounded the ant hill. Some of the braver individuals poked at it and then leapt back as it fell on its side. Lucius approached and, noticing the ants which had been dislodged by the fall, hoovered them up with his lips. Several other chimps followed his example, being careful not to get in his way. When the supply of ants dried up, the older adults lost interest and got involved in a grooming session, but Hilda had been waiting for her chance and soon she had bitten some branches into foot long twigs and was running them through her teeth to dislodge the leaves.

'What's she doing?' said Ten.

'Be patient and watch the master at work,' said Hasan.

Hilda soon had an audience of fascinated youngsters who copied her technique for making the tools. She laid out five or six sticks in front of her and then tested them one by one for their efficacy in penetrating the holes in the underside of the ant hill. Satisfied, she selected one, which she inserted deep into the structure, withdrawing it with studied concentration. She then pulled the stick through pursed lips, sucking the infuriated ants clinging to the twig off into her mouth.

Her young audience wanted to try too, but she swatted them away until she had had her fill of ants and moved away for a nap in the shade. A free-for-all followed, with fights and tears as all the younger chimps tried to imitate her method. Finally, Lucius ambled over and stamped on the ant hill, reducing it to dust. The eager watchers scooped up the remaining ants scattered over the ground.

'Did he do that to release the ants?' said Isabella.

'He may just have been sick of the squabbling and destroyed the nest to stop the disputes,' said Hasan.

Isabella laughed

'Like any overwrought father,'

Ten, who had been transfixed by the scene, straightened up.

'When did you teach Hilda to do that?' he asked.

'Oh, I didn't teach her anything. She was two or three years old when we rescued her, so she may have had sufficient time with her mother to pick up some survival skills. Chimpanzees pass this sort of knowledge down through the generations. If you go to other countries, you will find troops of chimps that don't have any tool using abilities.'

Ten scratched his head.

'Banga says chimps are bushmeat, but they are clever, like us.'

'That's why we are trying to save them,' said Hasan. 'They are our brothers too.'

Chapter 20

Isabella picked up Fidget and sat him on her hip as she shook the formula in the bottle. Clumps of powder stuck to the bottom, refusing to dissolve. She tutted and banged the bottle on a fence post to dislodge the milk powder. It floated into the liquid and swirled around, diminishing in size as Isabella agitated the bottle. Hasan appeared from inside the Nissan hut, jingling the car keys in his hand.

'Finish that off and get ready. We're going on a road trip to pick up a baby chimp in Songo village that needs rescuing,' he said.

'But aren't we full?' said Isabella, trying to disentangle the baby chimp's hand from her hair.

'We can always fit in one more. Anyway, cook told me it's a magic chimp.'

'Magic? In what way?'

'I don't know, but it can't hurt to have a magic chimp here. Maybe it will conjure up some funds,'

'We could do with some…'

She bit her lip.

'What?'

'There's a conference about chimpanzees in London soon. The lady who wrote the textbook I brought with me is going to be presenting. I wish I could remember when it was.'

'How will that help?'

'I don't know, but there will be representatives of other publications there and rich patrons of nature conservancy. Perhaps I could raise some money for the sanctuary?'

'I don't know how we find out about it, but the money from Manu's whip-round will only last us a couple more weeks and after that, who knows?'

Isabella wiped some drool off her shirt and handed the bottle to Gupta.

'I'll see if I can find out. Let's collect the little wizard then,' she said.

As they made their way to the car park, Ten appeared, rubbing his eyes. Now that his growth spurt had sped up, he slept about twelve hours a day and ate during the other twelve.

'He grows like a bamboo,' said Hasan. 'I'll have to lengthen his bed if he stays. Come on, Ten, we're leaving now.'

Ten scampered into the Nissan Hut and returned five minutes later with his hair gleaming from some sort of pomade, and his best t-shirt on. He gulped down a banana sandwiched in a lump of bread. Hasan rolled his eyes.

'Let's go then,' he said.

Songo, like most of the villages in the capital's vicinity, had a mixture of farmers and local traders selling a selection of yams and potato leaves and local fruit on some tables, and piles of second-hand clothes on others.

'What do you think of my village?' said Ten.

Isabella, who saw only poverty and filth, searched for something positive to say.

'It's quite a place,' she managed. 'Full of life.'

Full of rats and lice and sewage. What a slum.

Hasan frowned and drummed his fingers on the steering wheel as they drove past a pickup full of men with AK47s. They wore nondescript fatigues and an eccentric selection of hats, cheap sunglasses and coloured necklaces of glass beads and cowry shells. Ten stared out at them, his nose glued to the window glass. He rattled the handle, but the window stayed closed. They didn't go unnoticed as they drove into town. Hasan's jeep had a tatty decal on its side, advertising the sanctuary, which soon made them the centre of attention. The hairs on the back of Isabella's neck prickled as the stares became hostile.

Hasan wound down his window beside a woman selling mangos. He bought her entire stock, including the rotting ones, but she didn't seem pleased. She stuffed the mangos into plastic bags like she couldn't get rid of him soon enough.

'Auntie, can you please tell me where to find the baby chimp?' said Hasan.

'There's no chimp here,' said the woman, avoiding his eyes.

'It's illegal to have a chimp as a pet,' said Hasan. 'We've come to take it away before the police do.'

The woman sighed.

'That animal is trouble,' she said, pursing her lips.

'I expect it is,' said Hasan. 'That's why we're here to collect it.'

'White Death,' said the woman, jutting out her bottom lip. 'That's what they call it.'

Tired of waiting for her to pass the mangos to him, Ten jumped down from the jeep to pick up the bulging bags. The woman's eyes lit up in recognition.

'What are you doing here, pekin? Your grandfather will be vex with you.'

'Who has the chimp, Auntie?' said Ten.

'Who do you think?' she said, sniffing.

Ten got back into the car, dragging the bags over the back seat. The smell of fresh mangos filled the car, making Isabella drool with hunger.

'You need to drive to the square down there, and turn down towards the river,' he said to Hasan. 'And stop at the house on the left.'

Hasan followed his instructions. Isabella couldn't help noticing that various people had followed behind the car.

'It's here,' said Ten, getting out.

'How do you know?' said Hasan.

'Because my grandfather lives here, and he's the witch doctor.'

Isabella stepped down from the jeep and followed Ten into the vine-covered house. A large hornet with a shiny black mask hovered in front of her as if checking her out. Having decided she couldn't be a large flower despite her pleasant odour, the hornet moved on.

'Those things have a nasty sting,' said Hasan. 'Your shampoo smells too good; you'll need to change it for something plainer.'

Isabella, who had no intention of changing her shampoo, grunted. Ten pushed his way through a front door made of latticed pieces of bamboo.

'Grandfather?' he said. 'Are you here?'

The front door swung shut, leaving them in a dark, cramped passageway. Bunches of herbs and dry twigs hung from the rafters, one of which got tangled in Isabella's curls, leading her to claw it out in panic. Small animal skulls were lined up along the supports holding the walls up. A lizard shot along another back out into the sunlight through a hole in the wall. A shaft of light broke through the thatch and illuminated the dirt floor, the only place in the house clear of curios and dried objects. A smell like a dead mouse made Isabella wrinkle her nose and took her back to the time one died under their fridge in Dublin. Graham had taken the kitchen apart to search for it.

'How can something so small, smell out the whole house?' he said, dangling it by the tail.

Graham. What would he make of their fool's errand? She hadn't thought of him for days, mostly because she obsessed about Pete. Life was so complicated.

A door at the end of the hallway opened and an extraordinary silhouette greeted them. A lion's head sat on a cloaked figure which rattled and jingled like a jewellery box in a tumble dryer.

'Ten, you are here, pekin. Come and get my blessing,' rasped a voice.

Ten disappeared into the folds of the cloak so that only the crown of his head showed. An arthritic claw on the end of a sinewy arm laid down on Ten's head and a mumbled invocation issued from the lips below the lion's head. He raised it to peer at Hasan and Isabella.

'I'm George Adams, the child's grandfather, and I am a witch doctor and a choma. Who are you?' he said to Hasan.

'Doctor,' said Hasan. 'We have come from Tacugama to collect the orphaned chimp.'

The silhouette stiffened.

'I cannot give her to you. She is not mine to give.'

'May we see her?' said Isabella.

'Who is the pomwi?' said Adams.

'She's my friend, Grandpa,' said Ten.

Startled by this declaration, Isabella stuck out her hand.

'I'm Africa Green,' she said.

Adams ignored it. Embarrassed, she gesticulated instead.

'Your house is wonderful,' she said. 'I can feel your power emanating from the walls.'

A throaty chuckle greeted this piece of hyperbole.

'Indeed? You may be right. Come with me.'

Hasan mouthed 'how did you do that' to her and she grinned. Adams led them into a backyard, which smelled even worse than the house. In a cage under a zinc overhang cowered a small chimpanzee with dirty grey fur and a face like an ancient old man. Isabella and Hasan gasped in unison.

'But she's white,' said Hasan, whose voice trembled with emotion.

'How did you do it, Grandpa? Did you use voodoo?' said Ten.

Another chuckle.

'No, boy. Mother earth has sent us a miracle. She will save the country from evil.'

Isabella crouched by the cage and made gentle grunts like she had seen the mother chimpanzees do to reassure their young. The chimp looked up in wonder and shuffled nearer to her. Hasan peered at the chimp from close up.

'She's skin and bone,' he said. 'And she's running a fever by the look of it.'

Isabella looked into the chimp's face and saw eyelids sticky with pus.

'Her eyes are pink,' she said.

'She's an albino?' said Hasan. 'That explains her colour.'

A loud harrumph from Adams indicated his displeasure at this explanation.

'She's special,' he said. 'With the strong juju she contains, she will lead the Kamajors against the government for a glorious victory. It's only a matter of—'

A loud bang at the front of the house heralded the appearance of one of the rebel soldiers at the back door. He swaggered into the yard, a large cigar clamped in his teeth, his cheap sunglasses black against his face.

'And who let these foreigners see the ape? They will suck out its power,' he said.

'Banga, these are the people from the sanctuary. They want to take her from us. She will die.'

'On the contrary,' said Hasan, drawing himself to his full height, all five foot six of him. 'This chimpanzee will die if you don't give her to us. She is emaciated and I suspect she has flu.'

Banga tapped the ash of his cigar so that it fell into the cage where the chimp poked it with her bony finger.

'Flu? Ha!'

'She caught it from someone in the village. Apes have no defence against human viruses. We can catch theirs too, you know. It can be dangerous. That's why we put them in quarantine until we are sure they are free of disease.'

'So, we can catch something from the chimp?' said Adams, backing away from the cage.

'Exactly,' said Isabella. 'She needs to be isolated and nursed back to health.'

Banga's eyes were drawn to her blonde curls, and

he put his fingers under her chin to pull her up to a standing position. A chill ran up her spine as he shoved his face with his beetle black sunglasses into hers. He pushed his glasses onto the top of his head and stared at Isabella with his bloodshot eyeballs. Fear made her stubborn, and she stared right back. *He's as high as a kite.* Before she could react, he lunged at her with a knife and cut off a strand of her hair, which he handed to Adams.

'You can have the chimp,' he said. 'But only until we need her. Adams will cast a powerful curse against you using these hairs, so you don't try to keep her.'

Isabella, whose heart hammered in her ribcage, nodded her assent. Banga handed the lock of blonde hair to Adams, who wrapped it around one of his claws, humming to himself as if he were alone in the yard. Ten let the orphan chimp out of the cage and she grabbed his leg and clung to him with all her strength. He got her up onto his hip and she gripped his t-shirt, showing her teeth and chattering.

'Poor thing. She's skeletal,' said Isabella, stroking her back.

'I don't know if we can save her,' said Hasan to Banga. 'I'm not making any promises.'

Banga balanced the point of the knife against Hasan's chest and applied pressure to it, causing a red stain to appear on his t-shirt. Hasan did not flinch.

'You'd better save it, unless you want to suffer the consequences,' said Banga, and he turned to Ten. 'I'm relying on you to keep me posted on its progress. I need to know how it's doing. Okay?'

Ten nodded, speechless. Banga turned and left the four of them standing speechless in the backyard. Ten with the chimp bound to his chest, Isabella hyperventilating, Hasan with his mouth open in an unvoiced reply, and George Adams humming to the bees in the liana flowers.

'Let's get out of here,' said Isabella.

Chapter 21

Isabella winced as Gupta dripped some alcohol over her finger.

'Bloody animal,' she said. 'We've saved her and all she can do is bite us.'

'She hasn't bitten me,' said Ten, clutching the orphan close.

'Maybe she's got good taste,' said Gupta.

'Hilarious,' said Isabella. 'What if I get rabies or something?'

'I thought you said you'd got all the vaccines.'

'Lots of them. I don't remember if one was rabies,' said Isabella.

'What are you going to call her?' said Gupta.

'Pinky,' said Ten. 'Because of her face.'

'Pinky it is then.'

'What group are we going to put her in?' said Isabella.

'We'll try Tyrone's group, but first she has to quarantine. We'll need to move Greta and Sarah with the orphans into the refurbished building so that Pinky can have a cage to herself.'

'Can she stay with me tonight?' said Ten. 'We can't put her in the refurbished building in case she contaminates it.'

Gupta raised an eyebrow.

'We don't want her getting used to being with you. She can stay in the spare room between your room and Isabella's. Why don't you put some straw in there and one of the old blankets?'

A sulky expression on Ten's face matched one so similar on Pinky's that Isabella guffawed. They were made for each other.

From the beginning, Pinky behaved like a spoiled princess, biting people at will, and demanding attention. The only person who could tolerate her constant whining was Ten. He seemed to blossom with the responsibility of looking after his querulous charge, and catered to her every whim, giving her the choicest pieces of fruit, and grooming her white fur.

The attention had the effect of increasing Pinky's self-importance and bad temper. Gupta tried to introduce her to Fidget, but when he tried to hug her, Pinky slapped the little chimp's hands away and tried to bite him. Even the long-suffering Sarah recoiled from the whining youngster and refused to engage.

'What are we going to do with her?' said Isabella. 'It's obvious that she can't go in with the orphans. There's no one who'll stand up to her nonsense.'

'What about Lucius's group?' said Gupta. 'If she misbehaves in there, she'll get taken down a peg or two.'

'But they might hurt her,' said Ten.

'She'll learn. Anyway, with that white tuft on her rump, she'll get away with murder,' said Gupta.

'Would it be wrong to introduce her to Lucius?' said Isabella. 'His size might intimidate her for long enough to get accepted by him. And Hilda will cope with her. She's brought up two rowdy boys already.'

'Now there's an idea,' said Gupta.

Hasan frowned when he noticed them approaching.

'You have the air of conspiracy about you,' he said.

'We have a plan,' said Gupta.

'A stupid plan,' said Ten, clutching Pinky tight, making her squeal with indignation.

'We thought Lucius might like to meet Pinky,' said Isabella.

Hasan rubbed his chin and pursed his lips.

'Hm, not the worst idea I've ever heard, but how do we put them in the same cage together without risking Pinky's life?'

'Ten can hold her outside first and see how Lucius reacts to her. We don't need to do it all in one day,' said Gupta.

'Of course. What was I thinking? Yes, let's give it a go. You lot should wait outside to avoid distractions,' said Hasan.

He called Lucius into the sleeping quarters and gave him a good scratch through the bars of the grid. Then he signalled to Ten to bring Pinky into the passageway. Ten dawdled trying to soothe Pinky who, as usual, mithered and fussed in his arms. He stood in front of Lucius, who had tilted his head to one side and tried to poke the white bundle with his hairy finger. Upon feeling his gentle poke, Pinky spun around, canines out, ready to bite the perpetrator. Gupta and Isabella, watching from the door, held their breath.

'Oh God,' said Hasan.

But Lucius panted, the chimpanzee equivalent of a laugh, at the sheer effrontery of the little chimp. He poked her again, and she lay on her back in Ten's arms, gazing at him with adoration.

'She's flirting with him,' said Isabella. 'The saucy baggage.'

'And he's playing along,' said Gupta. 'Well I never.'

'He likes blondes,' said Hasan. 'Look how he fawns over Africa. I think we should let them meet through the bars once a day for a while before deciding to try them together in the same space.'

'It will never work,' said Ten. 'Pinky likes me, and no one else.'

'Pinky is a chimpanzee and needs to live with her own kind. She is not a pet. When she grows up, she will be dangerous. You need to let her try,' said Hasan.

Ten sneered and did not answer.

'Put her in the cage for now and come and have lunch. Isn't it time you had a shower?' said Gupta.'

'I'll have one after lunch,' said Ten.

Isabella smiled. Ten and his priorities.

A sea of bubbles surged out of the primitive shower cabin and crept along the floor of the kitchen, tickling Isabella's toes as she sat having a cup of tea with Gupta.

'What on earth?' said Isabella, looking down at the floor. She sniffed the air and jumped up.

'My shampoo,' she said.

She walked over and hammered on the door of the shower.

'Ten? What's going on?'

A scuffling noise was followed by giggling. Isabella pulled open the door. Ten stood covered in a layer of foam which started at his head and ran down to the floor. He clamped his hand over his genitals and backed away. Isabella grabbed her now empty shampoo bottle. She stared at it in misery and then threw it on the floor.

'You used it all. How could you?'

Ten, who had not moved, bewildered at her reaction, shrugged.

'They're just bubbles,' he said. 'I've never seen so many. I only had soap before.'

'But you've used the entire bottle. Are you stupid?'

Gupta had collected a towel, and she pulled Isabella away, handing it to Ten, who snatched it from her.

'It's only shampoo. You can buy a fresh bottle,' she said.

Isabella shook her head.

'Graham gave me that for my birthday. The brand is expensive and I can't replace it here. They only have cheap stuff in the chemists, which isn't for my type of hair.'

Ten had wrapped the towel around his waist and he pushed his way past Isabella without looking her in the eye. Gupta picked up the bottle and gave it to Isabella.

'Why were you so hard on him?' she said. 'He's only a boy. He didn't realise the shampoo was important to you.'

Isabella sighed.

'I don't know. I guess I miss home and I associated the shampoo with Dublin and Graham, and now it's gone. Does that sound silly?'

Gupta patted her shoulder.

'No, but I think you should apologise, anyway. You hurt his feelings and you know how sensitive he is.'

Apologising turned out to be easier said than done. Ten sulked for days and found reasons to avoid her, spending all his time with Pinky, who matched his mood, testing even Lucius's patience. Isabella, who did not want to admit she had over-reacted, took his absence as an excuse to postpone it.

The incident might have been forgotten, but for Gupta's attempts to persuade Ten to learn to read and write. His prickly exterior protected an ocean of pent-up feelings and a rock-bottom self-esteem from being breached by kindness. He could not admit to any weakness in case someone tried to exploit it, and him. Years on the street had wrecked his confidence, and he now behaved like the invisible boy, fearing to draw attention to himself.

Soon after the shampoo drama, Gupta decided to offer Ten some reading lessons. Given his tendency to fly off the handle, she made sure they were alone together after dinner by sending Isabella and Hasan on a fake errand. Then she took an early reader, and some pens and paper out of a box under the shelf. She placed them on the table in front of him.

'Now that we're alone, I wanted to talk to you about something important,' said Gupta.

Ten eyed the book with suspicion.

'It's nothing bad,' said Gupta. 'I couldn't help noticing you are having trouble reading. I'd like to help you if you'll let me.'

Ten jumped off his chair like a scalded cat.

'I knew it. You think I'm stupid. And Africa does too. I hate you.'

'No, it's not that at all. I want the best for you. Your life will be more difficult if you can't read and write. I'm trying to help you.'

'Everyone will laugh at me.'

'No one has to be told. It will be our secret.'

Ten wavered. Just then, Hasan came in and, spotting the books on the table, he said, 'have you started already? That's great.'

'Secret?' said Ten. 'You've all been discussing me again. I'm a man, not a charity project. I'm not staying here to be insulted.'

Hasan shrugged an apology at Gupta.

'I'm sorry you feel that way. We care about you, and we want to improve your life,' said Gupta. 'Is that so hard to understand?'

Ten glared at her.

'I'm leaving for Freetown in the morning, and I'm never coming back.'

'What about Pinky? She needs you.'

Ten swallowed, and his words caught in his throat.

'She's bushmeat. Why would I care what happens to her?'

Chapter 22

The streets of Freetown were still quiet when Ten got off the bus. Pigs and dogs fought over the scraps in the gutters at the roadside and rain dripped from the roofs. The sun had not yet burned the mist off the sea and he shivered in his ripped t-shirt. In a fit of pique, he had left all his new belongings behind, an act he now regretted. He had grown so much that the rips in the t-shirt had expanded when he tried to put it on.

His stomach gnawed with hunger and he searched for something to quell the pangs. The aroma of bread being baked floated down the street, making him raise his head to breathe in a lungful. Saliva filled his mouth as he imagined the taste of sweet pastries. A flicker of regret passed through his brain as an image of Gupta's breakfasts flitted through his mind, taunting him. He shook his head to dislodge the memory and followed his nose to a small bakery on the corner with a large queue of people, many of them on tiptoe in anticipation of their breakfast. Ten fixed his most adorable smile on his face, and dropped his shoulders to appear docile. He approached the bakery with his hand out.

'I'm hungry. Can you please give me some bread?' he said to a woman coming out of the shop with a crispy baguette sticking up out of a brown paper bag.

'You don't look hungry to me,' said the woman, pushing past him. 'I've never seen such a healthy street kid. Go home and stop messing around.'

Rebuffed, Ten tried again, this time with an older man.

'Please sir, can you give me some bread?'

'A strapping boy like yourself should not be begging. Get a job.'

Ten caught sight of himself in a glass window front, and his mouth fell open. His body had filled out, and he had grown several inches. No wonder his little orphan boy act had lost its power. He wouldn't get any joy from these people.

Ten had not formed a strong attachment to anyone since his mother died. He had lived by his wits and taken chances to get by, stealing when he had to and getting beaten up by bigger boys when he didn't manage to escape. When Isabella had swept into his life, his suspicion of her motives had been reinforced by her constant interfering and criticism of him, but she had been the catalyst for the good things in his life, like Pete and Pinky. The guilt he felt for abandoning Pinky made his heart tighten. *Who would tolerate her now? Why had he run away?*

He could imagine how hurt Gupta and Hasan would be. They had taken him in with no questions, and tolerated his horrible moods, and this was how he rewarded them. It made no sense to run away from the only chance life had ever given him, but the lure of joining the rebels tugged at him too. At least they treated him like an adult. Hasan treated him like a child. And yet, they made him feel at home. Confusion ran rampant in his head, making him crazy. *How could he decide what to do?*

Pete had not been to Tacugama for weeks, but Ten had convinced himself Isabella had something to do with it. Pete understood why Ten wanted to join the rebels and be a man. He would know what to do. There must be a good reason for him staying away and leaving Ten with people who were trying to boss him around and change his destiny.

He ran after a local bus and jumped on the back, planting his feet on the bumper and hanging onto the roof rack. Another boy joined him for a few blocks, only turning to glance at him as he let go and landed on the pavement. His eyes opened wide in recognition.

'Ten, what you go do now? Where you been?'

'In de war,' said Ten.

'Dey look for you,' said the boy, running to keep up.

'I here,' said Ten. 'You find me.'

The boy shouted something else, but it coalesced with the noise of the traffic and was lost. Ten let out a deep breath, and almost got thrown from the bus as it drove through a broken drain, shuddering and rattling. His heart rate had risen as he considered the possibilities. *Could it be someone from his family? Had his grandfather sent for him?* The driver stopped at a traffic light and came to the back of the bus to remonstrate with him. Ten shrugged and leapt onto the pavement, snatching a banana off a fruit stall, and sprinting away before anyone reacted.

He made his way across the Aberdeen bridge towards Man of War Bay. As he got closer, his stride lengthened. Pete didn't know what had happened at Tacugama. Maybe they could go for breakfast at Alex's, like old times, and eat the menu, Pete's favourite joke. Ten tried to straighten the remnants of his t-shirt as he rounded the bend to the hotel. He ran a comb through his afro and stuck it back in his pocket before bounding up the hotel steps.

The reception echoed with his footsteps, but no one appeared. He approached the desk and rang the bell, which clanged in the silence. Where was Pete? Perhaps he had gone to buy some provisions for the kitchen. Ten wandered back outside and sat on the steps in the shade of a glossy Protea bush. Time went by, but Pete did not turn up.

As the heat of the morning increased, it drove Ten into the cool lobby where he sat on the floor with his back against the wall, luxuriating in its clammy embrace. Ten dozed off. He didn't wake until Demba poked him with a fat toe.

'What you doing here,' said Demba. 'You got no right to sleep in here.'

Ten scrambled to his feet.

'Waiting for Pete,' he said. 'Do you know where I can find him?'

'I do.'

'Can you tell me?'

'He's upstairs in his room.'

'Is he ill?'

Demba sighed.

'Mr Pete doesn't want to talk to anyone right now.'

'He'll talk to me,' said Ten. 'I'm his friend.'

'You need to get this into your knucklehead; Mr Pete is in no fit state to talk to anyone. Come back later.'

Ten frowned.

'What time?'

'Next week. I guess he has to stop sometime.'

'I don't understand,' said Ten.

'His mind has gone on holiday, and he is drinking the bar dry every night trying to kill the demons.'

'But I can help. I'm a soldier too.'

Demba sneered at him.

'You? I doubt it.'

'Please, just one minute.'

Demba sighed.

'Okay, but don't say I didn't warn you.'

Ten climbed the stairs and made his way to Pete's room. He knocked on the door and waited, but the only sound he distinguished was the whomp-whomp of a ceiling fan. He knocked again, louder this time, and called out, 'Pete, it's me, Ten.' When no answer came, he tried the door handle, greasy to the touch, and turned in his hand. The door swung open, revealing Pete's mattress covered in a pile of tangled sheets topped with a torn mosquito net. Ten scanned the room with nervous eyes.

In the far corner, Pete sat in an old arm chair holding the armrests as if riding a roller coaster. His puffy face made him almost unrecognisable under a thatch of unkempt hair. Stubble peppered his chin and a vomit stain had seeped into his t-shirt, making it look like it had been tie-dyed. Ten stifled a gasp. He inched forward into the room until he stood opposite Pete, whose eyes were fixed on the wall, and didn't shift focus when Ten interrupted their gaze.

'Pete, it's me,' said Ten. 'We waited for you, but you didn't come.'

Pete lifted his chin off his chest and tilted his head backwards and then forwards, as if he could not balance it on his neck.

'Ha!' he said. 'Fooled you.'

'Are you all right?' said Ten.

'Just dandy. Although, I need a little drink. There's too much blood in my alcohol stream.'

'You've had enough,' said Demba. 'Please go to bed.'

'Who asked you?' said Pete. 'Anyway, I was talking to my friend, Nine, here.'

Pete sniggered, a sound that pierced Ten's heart.

'What happened?' said Ten. 'I don't understand. I thought we were friends.'

'War happened, and explosions, and deaths, and body parts of my best buddy stuck on my uniform. You're so dumb, you think war is pure, like a religion. War is hell.'

'I'm sorry,' said Ten. 'I didn't know.'

Pete shook his head and straightened up in the chair. His grey eyes cleared, and he pointed at Ten.

'I tried to tell you. But you wouldn't listen. You need to choose between a life of misery with the rebels, or a life of hope with the chimps. There is no alternative. Now fuck off back to the sanctuary. I don't want to see you around here again.'

He slumped in the armchair and snored. Demba pulled Ten out of the room.

'He's right. It's your only hope, or do you want to be on the streets all your life?' he said.

'Hope is for losers,' said Ten. 'He's a stupid drunk, and he doesn't know anything.'

Ten ran along the passageway and down the stairs, hyperventilating with distress. He stood in the lobby, his hands on his hips, before reaching in behind the reception desk and searching around for the tip jar he knew Pete kept there. He emptied the pathetic contents into his hand and stuffed the money into his pocket.

Demba came downstairs and spotted him replacing the jar.

'You chop my tips? Now you teef too,' he said. 'You got no hope.'

Ten blushed with shame, but he did not replace the money. Instead, he burst out of the hotel and ran to the beach, where he threw himself down in the sand, hitting it with his fists. *So much for friendship. How could Pete mock his name after all they'd been through?* He felt profoundly alone. He sat up and stared out to sea, lost in thought.

The sound of familiar, raucous laughter from Alex's reached him and made him turn to search for the source. He screwed up his eyes and peered at the patio outside the bar. Sure enough, Manu and his crew were having an early evening beer at one of the tables. He couldn't bear Manu, but Pete respected him, so perhaps there was something he could do after all. He admired Pete despite the insult.

Ten shuffled through the sand, trying to appear nonchalant. He reached the patio and shook the sand from his feet. The waitress spotted him and came over to shoo him away.

'No beggars here,' she said.

'I'm not a beggar. I want to talk to Mr Faletau.'

'Don't I recognise you from somewhere?'

'I'm Mr Pete's friend,' said Ten.

'I knew it. And how is he? I haven't seen him for ages.'

'He's been ill. Malaria, I think.'

'Okay, go ahead but don't annoy the other customers or you'll have to leave.'

Ten approached the group with trepidation, but Manu gave him a wide smile and beckoned him over.

'Nine,' he said. 'We missed you.'

'I'm Ten.'

'I thought you were older,' said Manu, roaring with laughter at his own joke.

Ten flushed with anger, and turned to leave, but Manu reached out and grabbed his arm.

'The problem with you, kid, is you have no sense of humour. It's just banter. A man's got to know how to take a joke.'

Ten shrugged.

'It may be a joke to you, but it's my name,' he said.

'Give it a rest. I told you I was kidding. What are you doing here anyway?'

'It's Pete,' said Ten, a lump rising in his throat. 'He needs help,' he croaked.

'What happened?' said Chopper.

'He's drinking. A lot. Too much. I think he's trying to kill himself.'

'Why all the drama?' said Whitey. 'Pete's always drunk.'

'This is different,' said Ten. 'You've got to listen to me.'

Manu gave him a shove.

'Piss off, kid. You're blocking the view.'

'I'm telling the truth,' said Ten. 'You'll see.'

He spun around and walked back along the beach, swearing under his breath. No white person could be trusted. They were all the same. He had been foolish to trust them. He jumped on a bus going north. The bus passed back over the Aberdeen Bridge and through central Freetown to the shanty town on the outskirts where Ten descended from it. He walked to a local square and sat under a tree, waiting. He didn't have to wait for long.

Chapter 23

A stone hit the back of Ten's head, making him spin around to look for the culprit. He rubbed his head as he searched the shadows. Then he saw them lurking in the alleyway, gesticulating at him to come over. His old gang of lost boys, orphaned, and abandoned, runaways and part-timers, bound together by circumstance and the vagaries of life. He had a new gang now, but he felt a twinge of conscience at having abandoned them too, the first chance he got.

He wandered over, trying not to appear too keen, stopping to kick the ground and stare at something non-existent on the ground. Rasta, the oldest of the boys, whispered into the ear of one of the other boys. The boy took off running at full speed, not looking back at Ten. Rasta stepped out of their ranks and lifted his chin towards Ten in greeting.

'What you do here?' he said. 'We hear you got lucky. Getty saw you with a white woman. Why you didn't share the money you teef from her.'

Ten shook his head.

'I never teef money from her. She look out for me.'

Rasta sneered at him.

'You 'spect us to believe dat? We is not idiots.'

'Don't you recognise dis t-shirt? She gave me

167

shoes and a shirt, but another big boy teefed them from me. Now, I only got dis one.'

'How come you so big now?'

'I work. They feed me. I chopped all the food and licked da plates.'

The other boys giggled, and Rasta turned around to glare at them.

'We heard you give the white chimp to dem. Banga is not happy. He vex.'

'The chimp was dying. We saved it.'

'You and dat white bitch? How you do dat?'

Was she a bitch? She said stupid things, but her actions were kind. I hadn't been easy to get on with either.

'We working in Tacugama. The boss man der, he know how to save chimp.'

'Is it alive?' said Rasta.

'Yes,' said Ten. 'We save it.'

His chest swelled with pride. Rasta nodded. A chill ran down Ten's spine. Why didn't I say it had died? Africa is right; I'm stupid.

'Come stay with us now. We got food.'

Ten looked around, searching for an excuse. If I refuse, they could kill me.

'Sounds good. Where we go?'

'We got new house,' said Rasta.

New did not describe the ramshackle outbuilding in the corner of a builder's yard. It wallowed fetid in the mud, half of it open to the sky. Inside, chicken bones and rotting fruit littered the concrete floor. A pile of filthy blankets and flattened foam mattresses leaned against the far wall. As they entered, a strong smell of urine hit Ten's nose. He tried not to gag. *This is what happens when you live with rich people. You get fussy.*

168

'Hey, dis place great,' he said. 'How you stay here?'

Rasta beamed.

'De owner let us stay if we mind his yard at night.'

'You boys still clever den?' said Ten.

'We clever,' they chorused. 'We de Beach Crew.'

Dinner turned out to be a massive pile of French fries and burgers salvaged from the bins behind a burger shop. They were cold but not disgusting, and Ten's hunger got the better of him. Soon they were all tucking into the booty and Ten felt like he had never been away. They ate until nothing remained and then reminisced about their adventures on the streets, the marks they had fleeced and the frustrated police they had left in the dust.

***

Banga took a long drag on his cigar and kicked his feet up onto the railings of the porch on George Adam's house. He lifted the brim of his maroon beret and leered at the schoolgirls passing by in their pristine uniforms. Beside him, a freshly poured beer sparkled in the last rays of the sun. He tapped the cigar on the table, watching with detachment as the hot ash burned a hole in the varnish.

As evening fell, he spotted a small figure running up the road from the main street. The boy arrived at the house panting and mud splattered from charging through the puddles. He grasped two of the railings and bent over, retching with effort. Banga took his feet down and leaned over the railing. Ash from his cigar fell on the boy's back, making him jump.

'What do you want?' said Banga. 'Can't you see I'm relaxing?'

'Ten is back, sah.'

'Who?'

'Ten, sah.'

'Where is he? Does he have the chimp?'

'No, sah. He's in Freetown with de Beach Crew.'

Banga blinked twice and clenched the jaw muscles in his face.

'Come, boy,' he said, jumping up and walking to his car. 'Show me where he is.'

***

Ten had fallen asleep on a shared mattress under the roof of the shack. Around him, other members of the Beach Crew muttered and snored in their sleep. Younger members of the group whimpered and snuggled up to the older boys for comfort and safety. Outside, the buses rumbled by, taking workers to night shifts at the hotels and bars on Man of War Bay.

A strong set of headlights floodlit the yard and penetrated the shack, waking and blinding the boys with its intensity. The messenger left the car and re-joined the crew. Rasta patted him on the head and went out to the car, followed by Ten.

'You boy, come here.'

Rasta stepped forward, but the voice shouted.

'Not you. The other one.'

Ten hesitated. The voice sounded familiar, but the lights were so bright he couldn't make out a face.

'It's me, Banga. Come here, boy.'

Rasta pushed Ten forward. He stumbled around the hood to the car door, blinking as his eyes adjusted to the light. The passenger door swung open.

'Get in.'

Ten slid onto the seat, keeping his head down and

tensing his body.

'Aren't you going to greet me, boy?'

'Good evening, Major.'

'That's better. Relax. I won't bite you.'

Ten hazarded a glance sideways and caught Banga's eye.

'I thought you wanted to be a soldier.'

'I do.'

'Why are you cringing then? Face me and listen.'

Ten swung his knees around, hitting the gear stick.

'Sorry,' he said.

Banga rolled his eyes.

'I thought I gave you a job to do,' he said.

'A job? I—'

'Are you stupid? I told you to take care of the chimp. What are you doing in Freetown?'

Ten picked at the shredded edge of his t-shirt.

'I, I left Tacugama.'

'And why did you do that?'

'They were mean to me.'

Even as he said it, Ten realised how lame he sounded.

'They were mean to you? What sort of soldier are you? You're pathetic.'

Ten swallowed and cowered. Banga tutted.

'I won't hit you. I want you to listen. They trust you down there, don't they?'

'I guess so.'

'Do they, or don't they? This is important.'

'Yes, they do.'

'Okay. I want you to go back there and make sure the chimp gets well again. If she dies, it will be terrible juju. I'm planning an offensive and we need the chimp with us to succeed. People believe in its power.'

'Do you?' said Ten.

Banga coughed.

'Of course. I'll send a message when I need you to bring the chimp to me. Can I rely on you?'

'Yes, but—'

'But nothing. Go back there and stop behaving like a child. You're a soldier now. If you do this thing for us, you'll be a hero too. How does that sound?'

Ten smiled.

'Great.'

'So you'll do it? No more screw ups?'

'I promise.'

'I'll take you half way. You'll have to hitch a lift from there. Have you left anything in the hut?'

My past life.

'Nothing.'

'Let's go then.'

Chapter 24

Isabella sighed and poked at her chicken with her fork.

'You won't revive it that way,' said Gupta. 'I threw the head in the rubbish bin, if you want to give it mouth to mouth.'

Hasan snorted and choked on his mouthful of food.

'It's not funny,' said Isabella. 'Ten's run away and it's my fault. What if something happens to him?'

'It's nothing to do with you,' said Hasan. 'Rampant hormones, and the lack of a father figure, are playing havoc with his emotions.'

'What about Pete?' said Isabella.

'He's no more mature than either of you. And anyway, he's got his own problems. When he came to do the fencing, he spent the entire day swigging from a whiskey bottle.'

Isabella remembered tasting whiskey on his kiss, but being brought up in Ireland had inured her to heavy drinking as a normal activity.

'Ten needs someone stable to provide him with support. He has to believe he won't be abandoned again,' said Gupta. 'You see it all the time in the chimps. I noticed the difference in behaviour amongst the orphans, now that Sarah and Greta are in with them. No more solitary rocking or hysterical over-reactions.'

'If you're both such experts, how come you don't have children?' said Isabella, immediately regretting the question.

Gupta bit her lip and looked at Hasan, who reached out and took her hand. The glance contained a sea of pain and regret, such as Isabella had only seen before in the eyes of Liam's mother when she thought about her son. Maeve O'Connor still lived near to Isabella's parents, although all three had moved out of Kilkenny after the boys were shot. Isabella talked to Liam's sister Nuala sometimes, and was struck by how deep the hurt still ran after so many years.

'Oh God,' said Isabella. 'I'm so sorry. It's none of my business. I wanted…'

She trailed off and put her head in her hands.

'Stop charging through life without first considering what you are going to say,' said Gupta. 'Most people are dealing with pain you don't know about. We can't pretend it didn't happen just to make you feel comfortable.'

Hasan took in a deep breath.

'We had a son called Amir. He found it hard to fit in with his peers. He used to ask us if he was Muslim or Hindu, and I always told him he could choose any religion he wanted. Unfortunately, he chose drugs instead, and they killed him when he was only a little older than Ten is now.'

His eyes focussed far into the distance, remembering.

'Ten reminds us of him,' said Gupta. 'The same mercurial moods and hidden depths.'

'I'm so sorry,' said Isabella. 'I brought back terrible memories with my clumsy questions.'

'Oh, no,' said Hasan. 'All our memories of our

174

son are good ones. Allah blessed us to have him for a short time, a precious moment, and we don't regret it.'

Isabella went for a walk to clear the air and headed down the road out of the sanctuary. She relaxed a little and bent over to take photographs of plants and insects along the route. As she straightened up, she noticed a figure coming up the road to the sanctuary.

'Ten,' she said, then shouted. 'Ten!'

She ran towards him, uncertain of his reaction, and he stopped walking. *Would he run away?*

'Hello Africa,' he said.

'I'm so sorry for calling you stupid,' said Isabella. 'I'm the stupid one here. Please forgive me. I want to be your friend and I'm making a complete mess of things.'

'I came back to take care of Pinky. She needs me,' said Ten.

'But you forgive me?'

'There is nothing to forgive. I did not come back for you.'

'Pinky will be pleased. She has been pining since you left. I can't get her to eat anything.'

'She doesn't like you,' said Ten.

'It appears she's not alone,' said Isabella, but Ten did not smile.

Give him time. I deserve this.

A radiant smile appeared on Gupta's face when she spotted Ten coming towards the Nissan huts.

'Boy, am I glad to see you,' she said. 'Pinky has been sulking since you left. We need to do the one-to-one introductions with Lucius and the other chimps, and she is impossible to control without you here. Did you have a nice time in Freetown?'

'Not bad. I met Pete. He's not well. That's why he

175

didn't come here to visit me.'

Visit us, not you.

'What's wrong with him?' said Isabella.

'Oh, he has malaria,' said Ten. 'He's almost better now.'

'That's a long bout,' said Gupta. 'He must have been quite ill.'

'I suppose so,' said Ten. 'I don't know. I'm not a doctor. Where's Pinky?'

'Probably sulking in the nursery bedroom. Why don't you take her this bottle? She'll soon cheer up when she sees you.'

Ten trotted towards the nursery with a spring in his step. Behind him, Gupta sighed with relief.

'That's a turn up for the books,' she said. 'Wonders never cease.'

'One down, one to go,' said Isabella. 'Did you believe his explanation for Pete's absence?'

'Not really,' said Gupta

'Me either. There's something he didn't tell us.'

'At least Pete is okay.'

'Or not.'

'There's not much we can do from here. Let's get the lunch ready. Ten must be starving as usual.'

Gupta linked arms with Isabella, and they entered the kitchen where Hasan hacked at a goat haunch.

'Ten's back,' said Gupta.

Hasan laughed.

'There you go,' he said. 'Hormones.'

When Ten came in for a late lunch, Hasan gave him a bear hug, which he didn't resist, but neither did he return. Ten ate three servings without speaking, and then excused himself and returned to Pinky's cage. Hasan shrugged and Isabella held up a hand to stop him from speaking.

'I know what you're going to say,' she said. 'Hormones.'

'What's that about hormones,' said Manu, putting his head around the door.

'Manu! What are you doing here?' said Isabella.

'Taxi service,' he said. 'I believe you wanted to go to Tiwai? It so happens that we are due a recce in the west, and we will fly over the area. So, if you want a lift, go pack a bag, while Gupta makes me a coffee and serves me up a plate of curry.'

'That would be fantastic. But...'

'Oh, don't worry, your precious Pete will go with you and make sure you are safe. He's sobering up right now, and should be shipshape by the time we get back to town.'

'Has he been drinking?'

'Even the water from the flower vases. Don't worry, he has promised to behave.'

Isabella frowned. Another unlikely adventure. But Max would pay well for an article on Tiwai. Maybe I could stretch it to two.

She left to pack a bag, and Manu sat at the table with a glowering Hasan monitoring his demeanour with Gupta. Soon Manu had his food in front of him and tucked in with gusto, making appreciative noises.

'You should open a restaurant,' said Manu. 'It would be a roaring success.'

Gupta blushed.

'It would be nice, someday,' she said.

Ten appeared at the doorway, his face like thunder.

'What are you doing here?' he said to Manu.

'That's a friendly welcome, after all I did for your

friend,' said Manu.

'Is Pete okay?' said Ten.

'He's fine. After you came to Alex's, we checked up on him and, sure enough, he couldn't help himself, so we dried him out and stuck him in a shower. He's almost presentable now.'

'You believed me?'

'Don't look so surprised. We're human too, you know.'

'Thanks,' said Ten.

Isabella came back to the kitchen with her rucksack bulging, to find Ten, Hasan and Manu drinking coffee, an act of male bonding that surprised her. *Ten doesn't even drink coffee.*

'Ready when you are,' she said.

'Where are you going?' said Ten.

'I'm off to Tiwai with Pete to do an article for my magazine.'

'Can I come?'

'I shouldn't think you'll be welcome in their tent,' said Manu, chortling.

Isabella's face turned traffic light red.

'We're just friends,' she said. 'If you think—'

'Please stay, Ten. I need you here if Isabella's going,' said Hasan. 'I promise we'll visit another time.'

'It would devastate Pinky if you left again,' said Gupta. 'You've only been back a day.'

Ten sighed.

'Okay, but tell Pete to come and visit me.'

'I will. I'll take lots of photos too.'

'It's not the same,' sniffed Ten.

'All aboard,' said Manu. 'The Tiwai express is leaving.'

178

Chapter 25

The helicopter bounced and then settled on the dry earth of the village's football pitch, sucking a cloud of red dust into the air. Whitey unfolded the steps with a flourish for the passengers to disembark. Isabella tottered down them onto the ground and sighed with relief. She hated flying on helicopters, and couldn't escape the feeling they might plummet to the ground without warning.

'Don't do anything I wouldn't do,' said Whitey.

'That gives you lots of choice,' said Chopper, leering at Pete, who raised his middle finger.

Trevor the pilot gave them a cheery wave, and the door slid shut. Isabella waved back as the enormity of the situation hit her and a shiver of anticipation. *Alone in the jungle with a lustful soldier. No chance of escape now. I hope I'm right about this.*

'Sorry,' said Pete. 'They have a combined age of ten.'

'Younger. Anyway, you shouldn't be sorry, you're not their mother. This trip is worth any banter, and they're gone now, until tomorrow.'

Pete smiled. Did he blush?

A slight figure appeared at the edge of the clearing and a youth, wearing a pair of ragged trousers and carrying an ancient rifle, approached them smiling.

'You are welcome to Tiwai,' he said. 'Are you going to the island?'

'Yes, please,' said Isabella. 'Can you help us?'

'My father, Minah, will take you over there in his canoe. Follow me.'

Pete swung the rucksack, with the two-man tent attached to it, onto his back, grunting with effort.

'Blimey,' he said. 'What have you got in here? Gold bars?'

'I'll carry it if you're not able to,' said Isabella.

'You?' Pete laughed. 'No, you're all right. I'll do it.'

His eyes twinkled and his usual reserve had vanished. Isabella felt her heart rate quicken when she thought about the two-man tent. Since her last phone call with Graham, conflicting emotions had beset her, disturbing her sleep and peace of mind. Gupta had found her staring into space, with her charges sucking on long empty bottles.

'Hey there, earth to Isabella. The bottles are finished and the babies are swallowing air,' she said. 'A penny for your thoughts.'

Isabella removed the orphans from their slings and returned them to the nursery with Sarah.

'Just thinking about Graham,' she said.

'So, how's that going?'

'Not so good. The last time I called him, a woman friend of ours answered the phone. She said she had popped by to make sure he could cope by himself, but when Graham came on the line, his voice sounded funny, and he didn't ask me when I would come home. I...'

Isabella trailed off and shrugged, tears filling her

eyes. Gupta gave her a hug.

'Long-distance relationships are tricky. Men don't like to wait around at home. They often find an easier option.'

'But he told me he wanted to marry me only weeks ago. He kept insisting I give up my career and have babies with him. How can he have changed his mind so quickly?'

'Maybe it wasn't love? Could this be a lucky escape?'

Isabella sniffed.

'You think I should just give up?'

'I didn't say that, but you need to be sure he's the one, and from what I see, you're quite interested in Pete.'

'Pete? Don't be silly, he's not my type.'

But Isabella couldn't help thinking about Pete, his loneliness, and struggle to recover from his PTSD. He had touched a part of her she hadn't known existed. He had even made her jealous of Ten. *How ridiculous to be jealous of his friendship with a teenage boy. But I want him all to myself and now I can test the boundaries of our relationship. Can we build something from the wreckage of our emotions?*

Ahead of her, Pete moved easily under the heavy rucksack, whistling Danny Boy and chatting to the youth who had met them off the helicopter. Soon they were standing on the river's edge with a man, who, though older, looked like his son's twin brother.

'Hi, I'm Minah. Put the rucksack at the front of the canoe,' he said. 'And climb aboard.'

When they were settled, he pushed off across the chocolate-coloured river Moa, poling it through the raging current towards the sandy beach on the other side. Isabella shrank into her seat, trying not to panic. The water hit the sides of the wooden canoe and soaked them, but the heavy boat glided without mishap to the other side.

'Welcome to Big Island,' he said. 'You are lucky with the weather. The rainy season will cause the river to cut Tiwai off from the village for the next four months. The annual rains are late this year but this may be the last time I can cross the river this season.'

'Tiwai means big?' said Pete.

'It's Mende for Big Island. So, it's called Big Island island.'

'Inishmore Island in Ireland is exactly the same,' said Isabella.

'So good they named it twice,' said Pete.

'The government has just named Tiwai as a National Park. There are eleven species of monkey on the island, and some rare mammals,' said Minah. 'You'll see most of them if you search now.'

'Why are there so many here?' said Isabella

'The Paramount Chief protects them because the island is a sacred place, and Mende are forbidden to eat monkey flesh, although some hunters from other place still visit occasionally. It's tempting to come for the easy pickings.'

'And the pygmy hippos?' said Isabella.

'I'm afraid the chances of finding one are not good. They are rare, shy, nocturnal mammals, but I see from your tent that you plan to stay overnight, so you may get lucky.'

'I'd like to photograph them,' said Isabella.

'The best opportunity you will get is if you pitch your camp near the river in the middle of the island. You may see one slip into the river in the dark, but it's a long shot,' said Minah. 'If you're here for the wildlife, would you like me to give you a tour? We could use the canoe to see some of the less accessible parts of the island if you're interested?'

'I only brought a little money with me,' said Isabella. 'How much would it cost us?'

'How about thirty dollars, including fuel for the motor?' said Minah.

'That sounds great,' said Pete. His face had relaxed, and he appeared ten years younger, turning towards every fresh sight and sound like an exited schoolboy.

Loud hooting erupted from the scrub nearby.

'There are chimpanzees here?' said Isabella.

'There's a troop of about fifteen chimps. The local people think that the spirits of the dead live in the chimps so they fear and revere them. Killing them is taboo,' said Minah.

'Why do they think that?' said Pete.

'Because the chimps use stones to crack nuts, and twigs to extract them from the shells, the locals think they must contain human spirits.'

'What was the other call we heard?' said Isabella

'Those were Diana monkeys. They live high in the canopy and are called messengers because they are the first to give warning of danger approaching.'

'Can we see some?'

'They live about thirty metres up, so they are hard to spot, but we can look on the ground for fruits from the liana plants, which are their favourite.'

'Don't the monkeys compete for food?' said Pete.

'They all live at different levels in the canopy, so they don't eat the same fruits. The Colobus monkeys have powerful jaws and they are the only ones who can crack open the ugba pods from the Oil Bean trees.'

As Minah took Isabella and Pete around the island, Isabella observed this new animated version of the man she had travelled with at close quarters. As he gazed into the canopy, she glanced at his rapt face with its sandpaper stubble and long eyelashes like a gazelle. The sunlight that crept through the trees highlighted the scars on his neck and arms, ragged and faded on his brown arms. He caught her looking at him and raised his eyebrows in question, but she shook her head, unwilling to admit her fascination.

She jumped as a black ant landed on her arm, and brushed it off, shouting, 'Ow, that ant bit me.'

Minah laughed.

'You should move away from that tree. A pangolin is breaking into an ant nest and they are angry.'

'A pangolin? Where?'

'Up there,' said Minah, pointing to a scaly creature with strong claws ripping open the nest.

'I wondered what that noise was, but I couldn't see anything until you pointed at it,' said Pete. 'What's that growth on its tail?'

'It's her baby. They cling to the mother's tail for the first year of their life.'

Isabella focused her telephoto lens on the animal and took some photographs. Her heart beat fast with excitement, and she hardly noticed Pete and Minah brushing ants from her clothing.

'Wow,' she said. 'Max is going to love this.'

Her eyes shone and Minah laughed.

'You have lion's eyes,' he said. 'Do you eat men?'

'Not alive,' she said.

'Not yet,' said Pete.

'Are you sure you'll be safe on the island tonight, Pete?' said Minah, bent double with his own joke.

Isabella smirked and carried on taking photos. They can't imagine how nervous I am. At least I can take photos to distract myself.

Minah helped them to set up their camp site and light a fire.

'Don't put too much wood on it,' he said. 'It could spread if the flames are too high.'

He left, tucking his money into his shorts, and promising to come back for them the next morning.

'What if he changes his mind?' said Isabella. 'We're stranded here.'

'Hm, I should have thought of that before I gave him the money,' said Pete.

'Let's make supper. I'm starving.'

'You're always hungry. How do you keep your figure so...?'

'So what?'

'Just, um, you know. Anyway, I'll put some water on for tea.'

After a supper of tinned tuna, crackers, and some liana fruits, they took their mugs of tea to the nearby sandy bank beside the branch of the river that ran through the island. Around them, millions of insects and frogs sang and chirped in a deafening chorus. Isabella changed the films in her camera and stored the used one in her zip pocket.

'Are you physically attached to that camera?' said Pete. 'You never put it down.'

'I may never get the chance to take this sort of photograph again.'

'Are you leaving?'

Isabella didn't answer, cradling the camera on her

lap. *I can't stay here for ever.*

'Have you noticed how the jungle is only quiet at midday?' said Isabella. 'We live in a world where it goes quiet at night.'

'That's profound for you,' said Pete.

'Don't worry, it won't last.'

'Don't get in a huff. I like this version of you.'

He put down his mug and put his arm around her shoulders. The warmth of his arm seeped into her body and she leaned into him.

'I like this version of you too,' said Isabella.

They sat in their own worlds for a few minutes as the bats swooped and circled over their heads. The full moon rose over the jungle on the other side, creating ghostly shadows on the sand. Isabella's anticipation rose with it. *If Graham can do it, so can I. I know Pete likes me.*

Pete stood up, brushing the sand from his trousers.

'Okay, that's me done for the day. Are you coming?'

'I think I'll just stay here for a few minutes. I need to finish my tea and go to the bathroom.'

'See you in the tent then.'

Pete stumbled off, tripping several times on his way, and Isabella noticed he'd left his cup behind. A suspicion entered her head, and she picked it up and sniffed it. *Whiskey. I should have known.* Her desire to find out what would happen in the tent evaporated, replaced by irritation and sadness. She sat stock still in the sand, trying to breathe out her woes. *Why was life so complicated?*

She stayed there without moving for quite a while, lost in her thoughts. Just when her position became uncomfortable, a twig cracked behind her. She turned to look and a dark, wet shape reflected in the moon light. Unable to believe her luck, she grabbed her camera and focussed it on the shape which lumbered down the sand bank and stood for a second at the water's edge. Click. The perfect shot. Click. Click. Click. The pygmy hippo entered the water and disappeared.

Isabella let out her breath again, dizzy with excitement. *I've got to tell Pete.* She scampered up the sandbank and shone her torch ahead of her until she got to the tent. Bending down, she pulled up the zip and crouched down, illuminating the interior with her torch. Pete had fallen asleep, spreadeagled beside an empty bottle. His loud snoring filled the small space.

Isabella kicked him in fury and he turned on his side without waking. His snoring stopped. *Bloody man. Why did I ever imagine this was a good idea? She slid in beside him and put in a pair of earplugs. Gupta would laugh her head off.*

Chapter 26

The next morning, Isabella woke to find that Pete had already left the tent. She walked down to the river and found him standing naked in the shallows covered in lather. The dappled water twinkled around him, making him look like a muscular wood sprite. Her feeling of resentment vanished as he grinned at her without shame.

'Oops,' he said. 'You have me at a disadvantage.'

'Aren't you afraid of crocodiles?' she said.

'Minah told me his village had eaten them all. Are you coming in?'

Isabella hesitated.

'I won't bite,' said Pete, winking.

His total lack of embarrassment reminded her of her brother Michael, and his friend Sean, Liam's brother, and their river swims when she was little. They used to jump into the water shouting 'nudies' and screaming with laughter. A longing for her old life hit her. *She could pinpoint where everything changed, and she became afraid of life, but could she change back again?*

Isabella dropped her clothes on the sand and ran squealing into the river. The water felt tepid and grainy. She dropped to her haunches and splashed water over her chest and back.

'If you're going to pee, let me know and I'll move up river,' said Pete.

'Give me the soap and stop gawping.'

Pete moved towards her and held out the soap. As she reached for it, he grabbed her wrist and pulled her towards him. She did not resist as he soaped her body, starting with her arms. She played for time by turning her back on him and letting him scrub it with his rough fingers. Her blood boiled in her veins as his hands slid around her waist and pulled her against his body.

Suddenly, he stopped and moved away again, leaving her panting with frustration. He put the soap in her hand without looking her in the eye and slipped under the water, running his hands through his hair to wash out the foam. Isabella tried to recover her composure by soaping the rest of her body with her back turned to him. Waves of indignation surged through her. *What the hell was that about? Was there a male equivalent of prick tease?*

When she turned around again, he had left the river and climbed the sandbank with a towel around his waist, heading for the camp. Isabella sighed and sank into the water. She floated out into the current, and contemplated letting the river take her away, like Ophelia, but then she remembered they had only eliminated the crocodiles from this stretch of the river and struck out for shore.

She walked back to her clothes, leaving wet footprints in the soft river sand beside the hippopotamus tracks from the night before. So many conflicting emotions whirled in her head she didn't even notice them. *How could I have misread the signals? Am I so out of practice after years of living with Graham? Maybe Pete just doesn't fancy me.*

Unlike Pete, she had not brought a towel with her, so she dried herself with her t-shirt and put on the rest of her clothes. In the camp, Pete had lit a fire and put a pan of water on to boil. She ignored him and entered the tent, taking a clean t-shirt and underwear out of her rucksack, and muttering to herself. She stuffed her gear back into it, leaving her remaining camera films out on the floor and stuffing them in her pockets.

Pete had prepared a breakfast of fruit and nuts, and more tuna with crackers. Isabella picked at the food as she fought with herself, dying to talk about what had happened, or why it didn't, in the river. She threw the nut kernels away in disgust at her inability to confront Pete. He noticed the gesture and sighed.

'I can't,' he said. 'I thought, with you, it would be different, but...'

His face contorted with anguish. Isabella's heart lurched. She swallowed her first reaction, remembering Gupta's advice about not blurting out stuff.

'Is it because of your drinking?' she said.

'No, although that doesn't help. It's been this way since Afghanistan. The doctors say it's psychological, but I don't know...'

He tailed off, dropping his head. Isabella frowned.

'I'm sorry. I had no idea. I thought—'

Pete's head jerked up.

'You thought I didn't fancy you? Isabella, I'm crazy about you. I just can't...'

He looked away from her, the muscles in his cheek working. Isabella stared at him for a moment, and then she put her arms around him, looking up into his face.

190

'I'm so glad,' she said. 'Not about the, um, you know. But I'm crazy about you too.'

He raised his head off his chest and sniffed.

'You are? I couldn't figure you out.'

'Join the crowd,' said Isabella.

'What about Graham?'

'He's shacked up with a mutual friend of ours, as far as I can make out.'

'Oh, I'm sorry. Scrap that, I'm not at all sorry.'

He looked into her eyes, and she felt herself drowning in their intoxicating mix of love and sorrow. She tilted her head, and he lowered his to kiss her tenderly, and then more forcefully, pulling her so close she imagined them melding into one. Minutes passed and still they kissed, channelling all their passion into the act, neither wanting to draw apart. *Will we burst into flames like a Phoenix and be reborn?*

A loud cough intruded into their pleasure.

'I could come back later,' said Minah.

'No, it's all right,' said Pete. 'We're ready for some more exploring.'

I am too. If that's the way he kisses. Wow!

'I saw a pygmy hippo last night,' said Isabella, blushing. 'Down by the river. I think I got a couple of photos.'

'You did?' said Pete, his eyes wide. 'When was that? Oh…'

'You were sleeping like a baby by then,' said Isabella. 'Anyway, it only appeared for less than a minute and it disappeared again.'

Minah scratched his head. The poor man must be confused. I would be.

'You're privileged,' he said. 'I've seen tracks, but I've never been here late enough to see one in the flesh.

They used to trap them in pits and eat them, but the government protects them now, and the Paramount Chief thinks they will bring in tourism.'

'Can we see the otters?' said Pete.

'If we're lucky,' said Minah. 'The best place is on the other side of the island, so why don't we pack up camp and take everything with us?'

'Otters?' said Isabella.

'They came back after we had wiped the crocodiles out,' said Minah. 'They eat tilapia.'

'What are we waiting for?' said Isabella.

They left the island in the late afternoon after exploring all day and eating a lunch of tilapia, which Minah had caught using a crude line and hook, cooked over a fire on the sand bank. He handed them around, wrapped in large, waxy leaves. Their flesh tasted sweet and muddy, and they had a myriad of tiny bones. Isabella tried to pick them all out, dropping them onto the sand one by one. Pete sniggered when he saw her.

'Eat them,' he said. 'They're not dangerous. Just leave the bigger, harder ones.'

Silence reigned as they devoured the delicious fish. The midday heat quietened the animal and bird calls, and the background trilling of a million insects. Now and then the sound of a fish plopping back into the water or a fruit falling from a tree broke through their soporific nap as they lay back on the sand.

'We need to get back soon,' said Minah. 'It may rain, and I can't guarantee we will be able to cross the river anymore.'

Just leave us, we'll be fine together. I don't want to go home.

'Manu and the boys should be here soon too. Let's go,' said Pete.

Isabella got to her feet and followed Minah to the canoe. Soon they were standing in the clearing again, waiting for the helicopter to pick them up. Isabella looked at the ground hopeful Pete would make a gesture, but he seemed deep in thought and did not move towards her.

And now I feel awkward. We only kissed, for heaven's sake.

'I've been thinking,' said Pete. 'It's time I dealt with the drinking. My brother in Coventry already offered to put me up if I book into the clinic nearby. They have experience with PTSD and shell shock.'

'When will you go?'

'As soon as I can.'

'I may go there myself soon. Why don't I give you my sister Liz's number in case we have time to meet up?'

'Sure, write it down here, although I don't know if it will be possible to have visitors. Are you leaving Sierra Leone too?'

'The Fakeems are struggling to keep the sanctuary open. I thought the extra enclosures would solve their problems, but they seem to have multiplied instead.'

'What sort of things?'

'More chimps, less food, people afraid to come to work. They need a regular source of funding or the sanctuary will go broke. If I go to London, I might find an investor.'

'What would the Fakeems do with the chimps if the sanctuary has to close? The babies will die.' He scratched his chin. 'Euthanising them might be the kindest option.'

Isabella's mouth dropped open.

'How can you say that? What's wrong with you?

193

Don't you have a heart?'

'I'm being practical.'

'Should we euthanise Ten too? I thought I knew you, but I was mistaken. Go to England and get mended before you shoot us all.'

'That's not fair. I've supported you, and them, as much as I can, but I need to do something for me.'

Isabella sighed.

'How long will your treatments last?'

'I don't know. Weeks? Months?'

'Are you planning on coming back?'

Pete bit his lip.

'This country is not good for me. Too many triggers and temptations.'

'And me?'

'You shouldn't stay too long either. It's not safe.'

'And the sanctuary?'

'They managed before you arrived. I guess they'll find a way.'

'But what about Ten?'

'Ten has plans which don't include playing happy families.'

'How do you know?'

'Manu told me he got word on the grapevine. The rebels want their chimp back and they claim to have an asset at the sanctuary.'

'An asset?'

'You know. A mole, a spy.'

'And you think it's Ten? How can you say that?'

'Because I'm a realist. You need to grow up, Africa. Not everyone believes in happy endings.'

Isabella folded her arms and refused to talk any more. The chill between them discouraged banter on the helicopter, and for once Manu and his boys were silent on the trip home. Isabella had to stop herself checking her watch all the time, so desperate was she to arrive in Freetown and go home to the sanctuary. When they landed, Isabella cosied up to Manu.

'Please can I get a lift to the sanctuary?' she said.

'Sure, if that's what you want,' he said, raising an eyebrow at Pete who shrugged and sighed.

'That's what I want,' she said.

Chapter 27

Isabella spent the next few days shut into her room, writing an in-depth article about Tiwai Island. She shunned the company of Hassan and Gupta and ate by herself, unwilling to expose herself to questioning about the trip. Gupta hovered around her like a concerned mother, bringing her plates of mango and cups of tea, unable to penetrate Isabella's defences.

'You'll have to tell me eventually,' said Gupta, putting down a tray. 'You can't stay in here forever.'

'Tell you what? Nothing happened,' said Isabella. 'I'm just busy.'

'You don't fool me. I know you're upset about something.'

'Please don't ask me about the trip. I don't want to talk about it. I'm worried about the sanctuary, and thinking I should go to London to raise money for you.'

'Are you sure you should go? Who would be interested? Don't they invest in stocks and shares and precious metals? Who's going to invest in chimps?'

'I don't know, but my sister Liz works in the City, and she understands all that stuff. It's worth a shot, and no one in Sierra Leone is interested.'

'Well, we can't go on like this, that's for sure. Hasan is frantic with worry.'

Soon afterwards, the smell of fresh banana fritters seeped into her room, and Isabella left her work on the wonky table and appeared in the kitchen. Gupta hid a smile as Isabella pretended to look through the book on chimpanzees for some information. She opened the back of the book to look through the appendix, and a piece of paper fluttered to the ground.

'What's that?' said Gupta.

Isabella picked it up and turned it over.

'It's a flyer—'

She clamped her hand over her mouth to stifle a squeak.

'What?' said Gupta.

'Remember I told you about the conference before? But I couldn't think of the date? Jane Goodall is speaking in London this month, about her work with chimpanzees. If I go to the conference, I'm sure I could persuade people to sponsor the sanctuary or add it to their list of charities.'

'You sound pretty sure,' said Gupta. 'What if it didn't work?'

'We have Pinky now. People love novelty. I'm sure we can use her as the focal point of any campaigns. Liz is an expert in this sort of thing. We could print out leaflets and hand them out. She could set up some sort of bank account for donations to be funnelled to your account in Sierra Leone.'

'But isn't she busy?'

She's always hysterical because she has so much work, but this is more important.

'Not really. I'll think of something. I'll take a quick trip to Dublin to see my boss, Max Wolfe. I need to polish the articles I sent to him and deliver the photographs so he can use them. Max is dynamic. He'll have ideas.'

'I hope so. At least it's a new option for us. I don't know how we'll survive the rainy season otherwise.'

Isabella stayed in the kitchen writing notes on chimpanzee tool use to incorporate into her article on Tiwai. At lunchtime, Ten came in, excited, and tried to stick his finger in the goat and potato leaf stew Gupta stirred on the stove. She tried to bat away his fingers, and he licked them.

'You should see what Pinky did this morning,' he said. 'She's so clever.'

'What did she do now?' said Gupta.

'She stole one of Lucius's corn cobs right from under his nose.'

'I'm surprised he didn't wallop her,' said Gupta.

'He dotes on her. She's his favourite and gets away with murder.'

'I didn't realise you had introduced her into Lucius's group,' said Isabella. 'That's amazing.'

Ten beamed, and forgetting his intention to boycott her, sat opposite her at the table.

'How's Pete?' he said. 'Did he ask about me?'

Isabella looked up from her notes, chewing the end of her pen and swallowing a rebuke.

'He's better, thanks to you,' she said.

'But is he coming to see me?'

'Not right now. He needs to go back to England.'

Ten's face fell.

'To England? But when is he coming back?'

'I don't know. He needs treatment to stop him drinking so much.'

'What if he doesn't come back?'

Isabella shrugged.

'If he stays here, he may never get better. By the

way, I may go there myself in a few weeks.'

'You? Why?'

'We need finance for the sanctuary. If we can't raise some money, Hasan and Gupta will have to close it.'

'Close it? But will you come back?' said Ten.

'I don't know. I hope so.'

Ten's eyes filled with tears.

'You're leaving too?'

'I didn't say that,' said Isabella.

'But you meant it.'

Ten stood up and walked out towards the orphans' nursery where he looked into the cage, trying to control his emotions. Isabella got up to follow him.

'Don't,' said Gupta. 'Let me do it. Make sure the stew doesn't burn.'

Gupta approached Ten and put a gentle hand on his shoulder. He tried to shake it off.

'Go away,' he said. 'You can't help.'

'I know you're upset, but it may be our only hope. Africa has to go.'

'What if she doesn't come back, like Pete?'

'We don't know they won't come back.'

Ten screwed up his face and gripped onto the guard rail in front of the cages.

'I did this. I made them both go away. It's my fault.'

'Don't say that. In your own way, you have saved them both. You should be proud.'

'But they are leaving me.'

'You don't know that. And you still have me and Hasan. We're here for you if you want us, and we need you.'

Ten shook his head.

'It's all going wrong,' he said. 'Nobody wants me.'

'You're not listening,' said Gupta. 'Please come in for lunch. You can't live on air.'

'I'll come in later,' said Ten.

'Okay, I'll leave you a nice big plateful on the stove.'

When Gupta came back in, Isabella left the stove and sat down again.

'What happened with Pete?' said Gupta.

'We're too different,' said Isabella. 'I thought we could find happiness together, but we clash all the time. And he has problems...'

She avoided Gupta's inquiring glance.

'Oh, the drinking?' said Gupta.

'Yes, or the trauma of his service, I'm not sure which.'

'He loves you, though.'

'Sometimes it's not enough.'

Chapter 28

Isabella stood outside the door of the Dublin house she shared with Graham, her door key in her hand. It seemed to weigh a ton as she felt it with her fingers. Taking a deep breath, she lifted it and turned it in the lock. To her relief, the door swung open, and she stepped over the post into the hall, taking in the familiar odour of breakfast toast. She took a moment to compose herself before going upstairs.

When she had told Gupta about the plan for her trip, it seemed simple enough. She would spend a week at home in Ireland working with Max to complete her articles, and a week in London at the conference, and then return to Sierra Leone, triumphant, with funding for the sanctuary. The only spanner in the works was Ten's reaction to her leaving. He seemed inconsolable and spent all his time locked in with Pinky or the orphans. *Maybe a nice souvenir from London would cheer him up. I wonder if he knows about London buses?*

Isabella opened the door to their bedroom and took in the scene. Both sides of the bed had been slept in and a pair of woman's shoes protruded from under it. She swallowed and blew out a breath to calm herself down. Even though she had given him notice of her arrival, Graham hadn't bothered to hide the evidence that another woman had replaced her. It had been naïve of her to imagine Graham would agree to her presence without resistance, but she would not rise to the bait. Whatever else happened, she wanted to keep Max on side. She would organise for her things to go to storage until she decided about her future.

She shut the bedroom door and installed herself in the spare room where Graham had dumped most of her possessions in a corner. Her irritation at seeing them piled up like junk for a yard sale faded as she sat on the floor examining items she had missed. Her favourite dress and matching shoes still in their box made her feel like normal could return to her life. She had expected to be upset about Graham, but her heart remained indifferent. *I don't care at all. I guess it's over.*

After an hour's nap and a shower, she headed for the office where the staff greeted her like a long-lost explorer whom they had considered to be dead. Bemusement and excitement were mixed as they welcomed her back. Max loitered in the door of his office, his moustache twitching with amusement.

'Miss Green?' he said. 'Why aren't you dressed like a Victorian explorer? I'm disappointed. We need to do a handover, and I'm famished. How about lunch? On me, of course.'

Isabella grinned.

'That sounds fantastic,' she said. 'Can we go to Captain America's? I'd love a burger after all that chicken and goat meat.'

'I'm sure I can stretch to a burger,' said Max. 'Let me get my coat.'

They walked to Grafton Street through a summer

shower, pushing through the door and going up the brightly painted red stairs and hall. The restaurant itself also had red walls with a panelled bar on one side and American memorabilia scattered along the others. The waitress showed them to a table beside the window and Isabella released a sign of contentment as she sat down and examined the menu.

'How's it going out there?' said Max. 'You seem to have adapted to the different culture with no problems.'

'It hasn't been plain sailing, but I've enjoyed it so far.'

'Your articles have been fascinating. I can't wait to see the photographs.'

'I've got them here,' said Isabella, patting her satchel. 'The people who run the sanctuary are saints. I'm surprised they don't have haloes. They work twenty-four hours a day for no salary, and have spent all of their personal wealth keeping it open. It's all here in my latest article.'

'Did you manage a trip to Tiwai island?'

'Yes, I hitched a lift on a helicopter.'

'That sounds like you.'

'There are two articles about the trip on the floppy disc. You have a scoop for the magazine too, as I took a photograph of the rare, nocturnal pygmy hippo.'

'You did? I must confess, I thought they might be mythical.'

The waitress brought their food, and Isabella tried to eat hers slowly. When she noticed Max had no such intention, she cleaned her plate in double quick time. She sat back in her chair with a big grin, and Max observed her with suppressed amusement. He stroked his moustache.

'Will you come back to Dublin now?' he said.

Isabella took a swig of her coffee to buy herself some time. It went down the wrong way, and she coughed until her face turned crimson. Max laughed and thumped her on the back, almost knocking her off her chair. He waited until she had regained her composure.

'Well?' he said.

'I can't. Not yet. This is too important. It may be my only chance to do something meaningful. And...'

'And?'

'I love it. I know that sounds dumb, what with the danger and so on, but it's given me a new lease of life. Dublin sucked the juice out of me. It's so conventional. Well, maybe not Dublin, just my life there. I didn't realise how pathetic I had become until I left.'

'What will you do over there?'

'I want to go back and finish what I started. The Fakeems need me.'

Max smoothed his moustache again.

'Okay, I'll fund another trip, but I need an article on the sanctuary that will blow my readers' socks off. They loved the article on your helicopter adventure, even though there were no animals in it. Circulation has almost doubled. I'm thinking of changing the title to include more adventure and wild animals, and fewer pets.'

'It's a deal,' said Isabella. 'You won't regret it.'

'Can you work with Sheila to pull the finished articles together? I'll get the photographs developed for them.'

'Can you send the negatives back to my sister Liz's house when you finish with them?'

'What about your Dublin address? Shouldn't I

send them to your boyfriend?'

'I don't live there anymore. I'm putting all my stuff into storage.'

Max raised an eyebrow.

'What about Graham?' he said.

'He drafted in a replacement while I was away.'

'I'm sorry,' said Max. 'That's rough.'

'I'm not. This assignment has given me the space I needed to realise how much I hated being hemmed in by my suburban existence.'

'I could tell you were suppressing the real you. Why don't you give me Liz's address instead? I'll be in London in a couple of weeks and I can drop them in to her.'

Isabella wrote Liz's address on a napkin and gave it to him. Then she slapped her forehead.

'Oh, I almost forgot. Can you refund my expenses? They're itemised on the floppy disc too.'

'Sure, as soon as we get back to the office, I'll send them to accounts.'

Isabella spent the next few days rewriting the articles during office hours and packing her stuff into boxes at night. As she filled each box, she filled in a contents list, which she sellotaped to the side of the boxes. Graham did not interfere with her packing, and had been generous with his division of their music and video collections. She replaced several videos, which she would never watch on the rack in the sitting room and put clothes she would never wear again in a bin bag for the charity shop.

Once she had filled and labelled all the boxes and sent them to storage, Isabella took a bus to see her parents in Dalkey. She stayed over with them after their reminiscences lasted long into the night. Liam's mother, Maeve O'Connor, also turned up, and talk turned to Liam and Michael as it always did. For once, Isabella felt able to join in with the laughter without guilt intruding into her memories. Her mother, Bea, noticed the change in her daughter, and before they retired for the night, she beckoned her daughter aside.

'Something's changed,' she said. 'You're Isabella again. I thought the old you had gone for ever after Liam died.'

'I met some people in Sierra Leone,' said Isabella. 'Damaged people with secrets. We helped each other; I think.'

'Does that include Pete?' said her mother. 'Is he the reason Graham is history?'

Isabella blushed.

'Liz can't keep a secret to save her life. It does, but I would've left Graham anyway. I don't want to live a normal life.'

'I'm glad to hear that. You were suffocating under a heap of puppies and kittens in Dublin. Will you see Pete again?'

'I don't know. I hope so, but he's not well, and...'

'That's all right, sweetheart. Everything will work out in the end. Give my love to Liz.'

Graham refrained from having his new girlfriend in the house while Isabella stayed and even picked up a takeaway for them one evening. They hadn't had a proper conversation since Isabella had arrived, but as they sat munching on crispy pancakes, Graham cleared his throat.

'I wish you'd change your mind about all of this,' he said. 'You know I'd dump her in a second if you'd come back and get married, like a normal person.'

Isabella paused with a forkful of fried rice in the

air. She put it down and looked him in the eye.

'I am normal,' she said. 'But I don't want to get married. You should stick it out with whatshername, if she'll have you.'

'Can you put the key through the letterbox when you leave?' he said.

Chapter 29

Another journey on the underground train from Heathrow. At least the arctic chill in the air on her last visit had retreated north, leaving early summer behind. Banks of geraniums lined the stations on the overground section of the Piccadilly Line, and the hum of bees intruded as the doors opened on the platforms. After the oppressive heat in Sierra Leone, Isabella revelled in the cool summer air of the British Isles, but her heart ached as thoughts of Pete crept into her head. *Why didn't I make up with him before he left? At least he had Liz's number.*

Isabella had booked a space at the conference by fax. She had never been to a scientific conference before, but it seemed to be composed of keynote speeches and long intermissions for coffee and catch-up. She had prepared a spiel about the sanctuary with Gupta, which she had read and reread in Ireland. Pinky's presence loomed large on their leaflets and it struck Isabella how ugly the little chimp appeared in the photographs. *Would the novelty element of a white chimp, however unattractive, be enough to persuade people to open their wallets and invest in the sanctuary?*

'It doesn't count as investing,' said Liz, as they

sipped a coffee. 'If they're unlikely to get anything back. You're asking for donations.'

'They're investing in the planet's future,' said Isabella.

'If they do, they'll just be doing a box ticking exercise on their environmental obligations. They'll be wanting to use the white chimp in their brochures as proof of their newly discovered social consciences.'

'Taking an interest in the natural world is not new. Look at Prince Philip and his work with the World Wild Life Fund. And Prince Charles with his tree hugging.'

'Now, there's a better angle. There will be lots of rich donors at the conference looking for knighthoods. You should emphasise the royal credentials of the project. It's a pity Diana is AWOL. She would've been the perfect patron.'

'Did I tell you Max gave me permission to go back to Sierra Leone?'

'Max? No, you didn't. Isn't he furious with you for staying away so long?'

'He sees this as an opportunity to launch the magazine into the big time.'

'So why don't you get him to encourage his readers to sponsor a chimp like they do for snow leopards?'

'That's a great idea. Why doesn't my brain work the way yours does?'

'You don't listen to people often enough. If you stopped talking, you might hear what they wanted,' said Liz.

'That's not very nice.'

'You asked me. Don't get snotty with me. I'm trying to help.'

Isabella ran her finger through the condensation on the window. Liz was right, but it didn't mean she could accept it. The idea of approaching people for money during the conference had been fine in theory, but now the time had come, her confidence had faded. Having operated in her comfort zone all her life, her confidence in new situations had seeped away without her realising it. *Where did the brash Isabella of old go? When did I become so limited?*

'Come and sit down,' said Liz, patting the sofa. 'How did it go with Graham?'

'It didn't. He has already replaced me. When I got to the house, I found all my belongings dumped in a pile in the spare room and creases on my pillow.'

'Are you sure he didn't do it out of spite?'

'There were women's cosmetics in the bathroom.'

'Oh, so what are your plans?'

'I put all my stuff in storage for now. I'm going back to Sierra Leone before I decide about my long-term future.'

'Will you go back to live in Dublin?'

'I don't know. Sometimes I feel like a foreigner. I might try living in England for a while.'

'Why would you come here? You don't know anyone,' said Liz.

Isabella avoided her inquiring glance.

'Oh my God, you've met someone new,' said Liz. 'No wonder you want to stay out there.'

'Not exactly. I just prefer Lucius to Graham. He hypnotised me with his mournful brown eyes, and furry back. I tumbled hook, line and sinker.'

'But you can't be in love with a chimp,' said her sister Liz, flabbergasted at this revelation. Isabella hadn't ever followed the obvious path but, even for her, this appeared extreme.

'Well, not love. It's a sort of passion,' said Isabella, tossing her blonde curls in defiance. 'You wouldn't understand.'

'You're right. I don't. You can't give up your job to volunteer at a chimp sanctuary. It's not sensible, or normal.'

Isabella grinned.

'And since when have I done the normal or sensible thing?' she said.

Liz snorted.

'What if you change your mind?'

'I won't.'

Isabella avoided her sister's eyes again.

'It's not only Lucius, is it?' said Liz.

'There was someone else who interested me, but he's back in England now. I don't know if I'll ever see him again.'

'That sounds more normal. Who is he?'

'A drunken ex-soldier with PTSD.'

'For heaven's sake, Isabella, you sure know how to pick them.'

'Well, he's gone now, so you don't need to worry.'

'Hm. No one can say you don't burn the candle at both ends. I guess we have more in common than we think.'

'Talking of work, can you please help me design a leaflet for the sanctuary? I have a photo of Pinky that should slay them in the aisles.'

'Show me. I can't even imagine what a white chimp looks like.'

Isabella took a thick envelope of photographs and handed it to Liz.

'Wow, she looks nothing like I expected. She's a sort of dirty grey though, rather than white. And are those pink eyes? Yuck.'

'That's not very encouraging,' said Isabella.

Liz leafed through the photographs, putting aside the ones she liked. When she came to one of Pete in the dappled light of the Tiwai jungle, she whistled.

'Holy cow. Who the hell is that? He's drop-dead gorgeous.'

She did a mock wiping of her brow and wiggled her eyebrows at Isabella.

'Don't tell me that's your soldier?'

Isabella blushed.

'Yes, that's him.'

'Jaysus, he's a bit of a ride,' said Liz, in a broad Irish accent. 'I don't think Father Doherty would approve of those muscles out on show.'

'You should have seen him naked,' said Isabella. 'In the river, I mean.'

Liz pursed her lips.

'Graham couldn't hold a candle to this specimen,' she said. 'No wonder you took your eye off the ball.'

'I didn't. I wanted to but… Anyway, I didn't, and Graham wrote me off first.'

'What will you do?'

'I have no idea, but first I need to save the sanctuary, and the Fakeems, and Ten,' said Isabella.

'You can't save the entire world,' said Liz.

'I can try.'

'What can I do to help?'

'I need a bank account here for Tacugama donations, which automatically sends them on to the account in Sierra Leone. Do you know anyone who can organise this?'

'Sean can set up a company in a day. Just give me the name, numbers and address of the bank account in Sierra Leone and I'll get him to do it.'

'How much will it cost? I have some unspent pay checks in my bank account in Ireland, but it's not much,' said Isabella.

'Oh, don't you worry about that. I'll sort it out. They pay me a small fortune here.'

'Let's hope the investors are feeling generous too.'

Chapter 30

The conference hall vibrated with the chatter of people renewing acquaintances and having excited catch-ups with old friends. Everyone seemed to know each other, and it dawned on Isabella that raising money from people who had never met her might be a tall order. When she had explained her idea to Liz, it had seemed pretty straightforward, but now, faced with this heaving mass of specialists and experts, she felt out of her depth.

She put her hand into her satchel and touched the glossy paper of the leaflets they had made, explaining the plight of the sanctuary, and asking for donations. Liz's lawyer friend had set up a cheap trust structure, and they had opened a bank account connected to it. The next step involved handing the leaflets out to people at the conference and trying to interest them in the trust.

Isabella looked around the room for someone not involved in the large cliques of people who knew each other, speaking in tight circles that prevented easy entry. *I'm not a total fraud. I have a zoology degree.* She steeled herself for rejection and approached a mousey-looking woman standing beside a small round table, nursing a coffee, and looking nervous.

'Hello,' she said. 'Do you mind if I join you?'

The women looked at her in horror and shot off across the room, looking over her shoulder as if she were afraid Isabella might follow her. *How embarrassing. I hope nobody noticed.* She scanned the room for more welcoming territory and settled on a small group of earnest looking women who had not yet reached a quorum for making a defensive wall. She approached them with a sunny smile.

'Hello, I'm Isabella Green.'

A woman wearing a pince-nez turned to glare at her over the top of it. The other women in the group looked her up and down as if examining a new species. Perhaps her outfit had been a bad choice. When she had decided on the white dress with yellow flowers, it had been to make her stick out in a crowd, like a bloom attracting the bees. However, most of the attendees were wearing grey, navy or olive dowdy suits and tweed skirts. Grey hair predominated. She felt as if she had worn a tracksuit to a black-tie ball.

'Yes?' said the woman. 'Are you the entertainment?'

They all sniggered.

'Honestly, Davina,' said one of them. 'Do you have to be so snobby? What do you want, dear?'

Was this how rabbits stuck in an Irish boreen with an oncoming tractor and no escape felt? She fumbled inside her satchel and handed the top leaflet, now creased and crumpled, to the woman.

'I'm raising funds, for a chimp sanctuary. I wanted—'

The woman reached into her handbag and pulled out her purse.

'Why didn't you say so? We all like a good cause.'

She handed Isabella a fifty pence piece and put the

leaflet in her bag without a second glance. Isabella stood holding the coin, her mouth open, unable to speak.

'Off you go now. We're busy here,' said the woman addressed as Davina, giving her a shove.

Isabella backed away, humiliated, still holding the money. She could see people pointing at her and whispering. *What a disaster.* She headed to the beverage table at the back of the hall and poured herself a cup of strong tea with milk to settle her nerves.

The tea had been stewing for hours, but fresh milk made it more than drinkable. All the UHT milk she drank in Sierra Leone had represented an ordeal for someone brought up on a farm. Mrs O'Reilly used to let her have a glass of fresh milk straight from the cow whenever she asked, despite Isabella's father complaining about it being unpasteurised.

'Filthy stuff,' said a voice at her shoulder.

'I quite like it,' said Isabella. 'It's been a while since I had fresh milk.'

'I meant the seething masses,' said the man. 'Worse nepotism than the Popes of the Renaissance era.'

Isabella examined the speaker who sported a massive set of sideburns under a bald head whose dome shone under the bright lights in the hall.

'I'm Isabella Green,' she said, extending her hand.

'Henry Farthingale, Earl of Heathcott at your service.'

He took her hand and lifted it up to his mouth to kiss it. His appalling breath almost knocked her out, but she faked pleasure at meeting him.

'I've never met an Earl before. How do I address

you?' she said, looking at him from under her eyelashes.

'Oh, don't bother with all that guff. It's Henry. And are you a doctor or a professor? I must admit, you don't resemble either. Most of the women around here are dreadful; ferocious bluestockings all.'

Isabella bit back a retort. Don't scare off the investors.

'Oh, my stockings are quite blue, I assure you. I'm just different to them on the outside.'

He raised a monocle to his eye. Liz would laugh herself silly when she told her. A monocle? In this day and age?

'What finds you here then, Miss Bluestocking? I presume you have a passing interest in the great ape.'

'I came here to raise funds for a project that saves baby chimpanzees from a life as beach photographers' props.'

Henry's eyebrows danced on his forehead, which was as shiny as his bald crown. They looked like caterpillars on an ice rink, and Isabella had to bite her lip to stifle a giggle.

'I don't mean to be rude,' he said. 'But you won't raise any money here dressed like that.' He ran his hand over his head. 'However, if you would let me take you to lunch, I am not as stuffy as that lot, and I have stacks of money for the right cause.'

'And what cause is that?'

'Pretty young women who need wining and dining,' he said, leaning in with a leer and almost gassing her. Isabella pulled her satchel around to her front and removed a leaflet, which she held out to him.

'I haven't got time for lunch,' she said.

After a day of embarrassing failures, and more

offers of small change, Isabella slunk home, defeated. The conference only ran for two days, and she had raised five pounds and fifty pence on the first day, which she had used to buy a smoked salmon sandwich and a packet of cheese and onion crisps for lunch. Some people had taken a leaflet from her, but no one wanted to talk about the sanctuary.

'They didn't take me seriously,' she said to Liz.

'Don't tell me you wore that dress?' said Liz.

'What if I did? It's a smart one.'

'For a garden party. You need to dress the part if you want people to listen to you What were the other people wearing?'

'Dowdy, tweedy, sludge-coloured suits and skirts with ghastly high-necked frilly shirts and polo necks,' said Isabella.

'Ah, that explains it. You need to fit in, not stand out. I have just the suit which will make you appear like you live in a library. Have you got a pair of reading glasses?'

'Reading glasses? I'm in my thirties.'

'Of course, you are. I forgot. Never mind. I've got a fake pair I wore to a fancy dress once. They should do the trick. And I think we'll put your blonde curls in a turban too.'

The next morning, Isabella strode into the conference hall in her tweedy suit and turban, with the fake glasses perched on the end of her nose. She wore a pair of Victorian lace-up boots, like those worn by Mary Anning. *Quite apt considering I am entering the company of fossils.* The reception she received this time made her see the error of her ways. Liz was right. As usual. She blurred into the crowd and soon found people willing not only to take a leaflet but to read it and ask questions.

Extracting money from them turned out to be another matter. Despite several people asking for more information about the sanctuary and the possibilities of using the white chimp in promotions, doubts assailed her. *What if this turned out to be a complete waste of time?* She kept a smile on her face, but anyone examining her closely would have seen the strain.

She approached a group of men who looked as out of place as she was. They looked up in interest as she handed out her leaflets.

'This is just the sort of thing I was talking about,' said one.

'A white chimp? It looks grey to me,' said another.

'It's an albino,' said Isabella. 'They are incredibly rare.'

I hope he doesn't ask me how rare because I don't have a clue.

'Are they now? Tell me more about the sanctuary,' said the first man.

'It's full of orphaned chimps. The guerrillas ate their mothers.'

'I didn't know gorillas ate chimps. I thought they were vegetarian,' said the second man.

'Rebels, not gorillas,' said Isabella.

'Make up your mind love. He has a short attention span,' said another of the men, rolling his eyes in a droll manner.

'The rebels in Sierra Leone eat chimps and sell their babies as pets. The sanctuary saves the babies and brings them up with a group of chimps on site.'

'So, what do you want us to do about it?' The first man again.

'They need funding,' said Isabella. 'The sanctuary is about to go bankrupt.'

'Ah, so we send money to Sierra Leone, and some corrupt politician buys a flat in Mayfair,' said the second man.

'Mayfair? Steady on. More like Shepherds Bush, unless you are emptying your trust fund,' chimed in a third.

They all laughed, reminding Isabella of a stable full of neighing horses.

'The people who run the sanctuary are honest and hardworking. They have spent all their money on keeping the chimps alive,' she said, fighting for self-control.

'Oh, so they will be the ones buying the flat?' said the second man.

Isabella put the leaflets back in her satchel and turned to go.

'Wait,' said the first man. 'My name's Tristan Horton. My editor might be interested in doing a documentary. Here is my card. Why don't you send me some details and I'll see what I can do?'

'Your bleeding heart will get you into trouble,' said the second man.

Isabella smiled and took off her glasses to read the card.

'That's the first time I've seen someone take off their glasses to read,' said the first man.

'Congenital clear sightedness,' said Isabella. 'The glasses are to prevent me seeing through people.'

'You'd better not look at Harry then.'

Another roar of laughter and Isabella left to search for more victims.

Chapter 31

Ten had been subdued after Isabella left for England, and loud sighs had punctuated his resentful silences. Pinky did not take kindly to his lack of attention to her antics and sulked in her cage, only becoming animated on her continued introductions to Lucius's group. Hasan let Ten take on more responsibility for the meetings and watched as he grew into his role.

'What do you think about letting Pinky into the sleeping area with Hilda?' said Hasan. 'It has to be done eventually.'

Ten scratched Pinky's head and gave her a piece of banana.

'She's ready,' he said. 'I can take her in to meet Hilda. I just need you to be ready with the water hose in case it goes wrong.'

Hasan ran his hands through his hair.

'Okay, let me get set up. I'll see if Joe can be here too.'

Ten smoothed down Pinky's fur and fed her some more fruit.

'I need you to behave,' he said to her. 'Hilda is not tolerant of naughty children.'

Pinky stretched her hand up and stuck one of her

fingers in his ear, trying to excavate the wax. He shook himself free, giggling.

'Stop that, you silly girl. Ear wax is disgusting.'

Hasan came back with Joe and he rigged up the hose, while Hasan enticed Hilda indoors and shut her in the sleeping quarters. She sat on the floor, selecting the choicest morsels from a plate of fresh fruits, and popping them in her mouth with appreciative slurping noises.

'Come on in,' said Hasan, sliding the door open.

Ten walked in without looking at Hilda and sat on a tyre with Pinky who wriggled in his arms, desperate to investigate this stranger.

'Let her go,' said Hasan.

Ten placed Pinky on the ground. She sniffed the air and spotted the plate of fruit and headed for Hilda without preamble.

'No, Pinky,' said Ten.

Pinky did not take any notice of him. She sidled up to Hilda, who looked up and used her hand to shield her plate of goodies from the intruder. Pinky tried to lift Hilda's hand so she could steal a piece of mango, but Hilda batted her across the floor. Pinky screeched in indignation and fear, showing her teeth and wrapping her arms around herself for comfort. Ten started to get up, but Hasan signalled at him to stay put.

When no one came to her aid, Pinky tried again. She shuffled across the floor and sat out of reach of Hilda in her line of vision, raising her eyebrows and trying to look cute. Hilda pulled the plate across the ground and turned her back on the baby chimp. Pinky moved back into her line of vision and make pleading squeaks. Hilda pretended not to hear her, but Pinky persisted. Finally, an irritated Hilda threw her a scrap end of mango, which Pinky sucked loudly, before returning to Ten's lap to complain.

Hasan laughed.

'That'll teach her to have some manners,' he said. 'Okay, I think Hilda needs to go back to the group. Baby steps will be best for this relationship.'

Joe opened the door and Hilda scooted back outside where the troop examined her for damage. Hasan let Ten back out of the cage with Pinky.

'Well done,' he said. 'Hilda trusts you as much as Pinky does. You have a way with chimps.'

Ten shrugged.

'It's easy,' he said, but his eyes glowed with pride. 'Unlike writing, which is impossible.'

'You're making great strides,' said Hasan. 'Imagine how amazed Isabella will be to see your progress.'

Ten frowned.

'But will she come back?'

'Off course, she loves us. She wouldn't just disappear.'

'That's what you think.'

The next afternoon, Hasan mixed the sugar into his coffee, his spoon clinking against his cup and the aroma rising into his nostrils as Ten traced the letters into his notebook. Ten shifted and grimaced as his pencil slipped. He grabbed the eraser and scrubbed at the page, his tongue protruding from between his lips.

Gupta put her finger to her lips and winked at Hasan who moved into the corner and sat on a stool, watching Ten graft. Outside, the din of insects whirring and chirping reached a crescendo, and a butterfly balanced on the window sill, its wings quivering. The minutes slipped by as both of them waited for Ten to finish his task.

He pushed the notebook across the table to Gupta, who checked his work, beaming.

'That's much better. You're such a quick learner.'

'Can I go now?' he said. 'Pinky needs her bottle.'

'I was hoping we could practise some reading this afternoon.'

Ten had already stood up, and Gupta, knowing his moods could turn from sunny to thunderous in a sentence, nodded. He took the bottle from the sideboard and trotted down the path to Lucius's quarters. Gupta smiled at Hasan who sipped his coffee and rolled his eyes.

'It's never going to be easy,' he said.

'What do you expect? He's a teenager. Remember Amir? Just the same.'

Hasan rubbed his chin and tilted his head to one side.

'Have you thought about the future?' he said.

'I'm getting through one day at a time right now. Who knows if we have a future? I wish Isabella would come back with some good news,' said Gupta.

'She may never return.'

'Don't say that. She won't let us down. I know her.'

'Like you know Ten?'

Gupta sighed and sat at the table, taking Hasan's hand and examining the callouses.

'I've been thinking,' she said.

'That sounds ominous,' said Hasan.

'This is no time for joking.'

'Sorry, habibi. What about?'

'About Ten,' said Gupta. 'And us…'

She tailed off and gave him a pleading look. He

squeezed her hand.

'Ah,' he said. 'I thought this moment might come.'

He drank the last mouthful of coffee and wiped his mouth on the sleeve of his t-shirt. Gupta noted the gesture and tensed herself for an answer. He looked up and smiled.

'If that's what you want,' he said.

Gupta blinked.

'You don't mind?'

'Mind? It's the first time I've seen you happy for years.'

'But what about you?'

'I've got a free helper. I'm not complaining.'

Gupta clipped him around the ear.

'Honestly, can't you be serious for one minute? This is important.'

Hasan took her face in his hands.

'You're not the only one who is happy,' he said. 'Ten is not perfect, but Allah sent him to us for a reason. Who am I to question the will of Allah?'

Gupta kissed him, eyes shining.

'Why don't we do a ceremony tonight? I can light some candles and wear my special sari. Oh—'

Hasan laughed.

'You silly woman. Do you imagine I don't know about it? Put it on and cook a nice curry. I'll kill a chicken for you.'

Gupta embraced him and showered him with more tender kisses, which he returned. After a short time, Hasan pulled away, patting her face.

'Stop that now, woman, or I'll be stuck in here all afternoon. I have chickens to kill, and places to go.'

Pink in the face with passion and excitement,

Gupta made paper flowers from a stained and faded roll of pink tissue paper, which she had kept in the box with her sari. She removed some treasured old sticks of incense from a bag in the same box and planted them in cracks in the wood around the kitchen. Soon the room vibrated with colour and aroma as she hummed along to an old Indian song on a tape containing theme songs from some of her favourite Bollywood movies.

When Ten came to the hut for dinner, he remained rooted in the doorway with his mouth open, taking in the candles and the paper flowers, before spotting Gupta in her beautiful sari. Even Hasan had oiled his hair and beard, and wore his best t-shirt. The smell of spices and incense hung in the air, intoxicating Ten. He inhaled a lungful, savouring their rich mixture of aromas.

'Is it someone's birthday?' he said. 'I don't have a present.'

Gupta shook her head and Hasan pulled out a chair, bidding Ten to sit down.

'No birthday,' said Hasan. 'But this is a special occasion.'

He took Gupta's hand, and they stood opposite a bemused Ten. Gupta glanced at Hasan and he nodded his assent.

'We'd like you to join our family,' she said, her voice quavering. 'As our son, if you want.'

Ten rose to his feet, knocking his chair to the floor. His mouth worked, but nothing came out. He stared at them in disbelief.

'Why are you lying to me?' he said. 'This isn't funny.'

Hasan put his hand on Ten's shoulder.

'Calm down. No one is lying.'

Ten backed away

'You. Want. Me?' he said. 'Why?'

'Because we love you. So, if you'll have us, we want to adopt you.' said Hasan. 'We can't offer you any luxuries, but we have lots of love to give.'

Ten shook, and a croak escaped from his throat. Gupta reached out and touched Ten's face, wiping away a stray eyelash. He winced as if scalded, but the couple reached out and took his hands, forming a chain.

'Stay with us,' said Gupta. 'Look how you complete our circle.'

Ten looked down at their hands in wonder and swallowed. Then he nodded his head.

'Yes,' he said.

Ten floated to bed that night, full of curry and rice and love. What had just happened to him? He had nothing to compare it with. All the years of misery had hollowed him out and the black hole beneath his sternum, which sucked all the joy from his life, had disappeared, replaced with a warm glow. He did not recognise the feeling, but he wanted to hold on to it.

Someone knocked on the door of his room, and Hasan came in.

'I hope I'm not disturbing you,' he said.

'I wasn't asleep,' said Ten. 'It's difficult for me to sleep well.'

'Gupta told me you had nightmares.'

'How does she know?'

'We hear you shouting sometimes.'

Ten bit his lip.

'Sorry, I can't help it.'

'Ah, but maybe I can,' said Hasan. 'Hold out your hand.'

Mystified, Ten did as he was told. Hasan dropped a small medallion into Ten's hand.

'What's this?'

'It's a sleep charm, belonging to our son, Amir. He swore it helped to keep the demons away. Just put it under your pillow and you'll see.'

Ten wrapped his fingers around the charm and put his fist under his pillow.

'Thank you,' he said, overcome.

'You're welcome.'

Ten lay in bed afterwards and gazed out of his window at the blanket of stars. Isabella like to stare at the heavens. He'd never understood why before. *Would she come back? And what about Pete? What would they say about his new family?* Finally, sleep took him and he lay motionless, worn out by all the new emotions whirling around his brain.

Chapter 32

The next morning Isabella leapt out of bed and made a pile of the documents to photocopy and copied the addresses of interested parties on A4 sized envelopes. She included photos of the miserable orphans behind the bars of the old nursery.

'Tug at their heart strings to open their wallets,' said Liz, appearing dressed for work.

'Will you be back in time for me to say goodbye?' said Isabella.

'I doubt it, it's bonus day today. We all get to go to a strip club and have a great time.'

'That doesn't sound great to me.'

'Me either. It's not like they have any male strippers. But I have to go if I want to be one of the boys. That's how it is in the City. Participation is not up for discussion. Wimp out and I'd soon find myself without a job.'

'I don't know how you stand it.'

'Says the girl working in a country beset by civil war.'

'No one's shooting at the sanctuary.'

'It's only a matter of time,' said Liz. 'Promise me you'll leave if it gets too dangerous.'

'How will I know?'

'I've created a monster. I should have let you marry Graham. At least you'd be safe.'

'I'd be miserable too.'

'Give me a hug then. I've got to go to work. Call me from Freetown so I know you landed safely.'

'Okay, sis.'

Isabella left the flat to find a shop with a photocopier and a post office, and soon found both, side by side on the high street. The photocopier churned out the copies and she stuffed them into their envelopes, sealing them with masking tape. She queued up in the post office to send the fat envelopes, handing them over with fingers crossed. *Would any of the people donate or would the increasing violence in Sierra Leone would put them off? Should I be going back there at all?*

Chores finished, she had fun replenishing her supplies of tea and shampoo, feeling guilty for her earlier tantrum, when she bought herself another bottle of the same brand Ten had wasted. He hadn't deserved it, poor lad. She needed to get her priorities straight. A barrow of tourist souvenirs caught her eye, and she wandered over to look at the t-shirts. *Would Ten recognise a London double-decker bus, or Tower Bridge?*

Deciding it didn't matter, she bought him two t-shirts and a baseball cap with a Union Jack on it. As she paid, she spotted a pair of rip-off Ray Bans, so she bought those too. While her buying urge reigned, she also bought a beautiful silk scarf for Gupta and a bar of Cadbury's Fruit and Nut for Hasan. Happy with her purchases, she headed back to the house and packed her suitcase, anticipation rising. *But what would it be like without Pete?*

Since he had left, she had missed him like a part of her had been chopped off. Their relationship had never got off the ground floor, but she had hoped that they could resurrect it under the right circumstances. A deep longing to hear his voice rose in her chest, making her choke with emotion. She lifted the telephone and rang directory inquiries.

'Hello, how may I help you?'

'I'd like the phone number for the Renewal Clinic in Tandsforth, please.'

'How are you spelling that?'

'R e n e w a l.'

'Right, yes, I have the number here. Have you got a pen?'

Isabella tapped her fingers on the counter. Is this foolish? I need to hear his voice before I go back. I have to tell him how I feel about him. Finally, she dialled the number and waited.

'Renewal Clinic, Tracy speaking.'

'Hello Tracy, I want to speak to Pete Hawkins, please.'

'Is he a member of staff?'

'Oh, no, he's in there for treatment.'

'I'm afraid it's not possible to talk to patients.'

'But I need to speak to him. It's important.'

'Are you family?'

'No, but—'

'I'm sorry. There are no exceptions.'

'Can you at least tell me how he's doing?'

'I can see from my screen that Mr Hawkins is suffering from trauma, but he's making good progress. That's all I can tell you.'

'Can you tell him that Isabella called?'

'No, I'm sorry. He needs to be one hundred per

231

cent focussed if he's going to get better.'

Isabella rang off. She sat on the sofa, fighting her emotions until they calmed. *Maybe he will call Liz when he recovers.* As she drank her last cup of tea, the telephone rang. *Could it be Pete after all?* Unsure if she should pick it up, she let it ring a few times before answering.

'Oh, you're still there. Thank goodness, I thought I'd missed you,' said Liz.

'I'm about to drag my bag down to the underground station.'

'Don't bother. I'll send you a taxi on my account.'

'You can't do that. It will cost a fortune,' said Isabella.

'I don't care. I rang to tell you about my bonus. It's enormous, humongous, epic. I never imagined I'd ever see this much money.'

'That's fantastic. I'm so proud of you.'

'Anyway, I checked with Sean and if I donate to a trust, it will be tax free, so I'm putting a lump sum in to the Tacugama account to keep them afloat a little longer.'

'But—.'

'No buts. The vast majority would have gone to tax otherwise, so I'm only giving a small amount of actual cash. Anyway, I'm glad to do it. I've never seen you care about anything before. Sean doesn't know what I earn. He won't miss the money.'

'I don't know what to say.'

'Just come home safe. I've got to go now; the strip club awaits.'

The phone went dead before Isabella could reply. She replaced the receiver and sat watching her tea go cold. *The money won't last that long but at least I can hold my head up when I get back, and it gives us a welcome breather.* The doorbell rang just as she washed her cup in the sink.

'Taxi for Miss Green?'

***

Max Wolfe turned up at Liz's flat a couple of days later, bringing back Isabella's negatives and copies of the Tiwai photographs. By coincidence, Liz was at home because of a power cut in her office building. She recognised him from Isabella's colourful description.

Soon they were sipping a glass of Beaujolais Nouveau at the kitchen counter, admiring the photographs of Tiwai and the rare hippopotamus.

'Was she always like this?' said Max.

'Like what? Infuriating? Opinionated. Yes, always,' said Liz. 'Why ever did you choose her for this trip. You were asking for trouble.'

'Have you met the other writers who work for the magazine? Some of them haven't moved for so long they have moss growing on them. Your sister, on the other hand, stalked me for days when I first started there. I could feel her eyes on me all the time, willing me to put her out of her misery.'

'But you left her until last. How cruel.'

'I wanted to be sure she'd be desperate enough to accept the assignment. I knew it would be a tough one.'

Liz examined him in a new light.

'You played her?' she said. 'No one plays Isabella. How did you know which buttons to press?'

He guffawed.

'Officer training. I've always got the most out of my men, sorry, people.'

'But how are we going to help the sanctuary? We

can't let it sink without trace.'

'We? How did I get embroiled in this Green family endeavour?'

'Come on, Max. Don't be a bore. Anyway, I've had an idea that could work.'

Max looked at her and stroked his moustache.

'Oh my God,' he said. 'Another one. Are all the Greens like this?'

Liz ignored him.

'I noticed an advertisement in a travel magazine for a subscription to the World Wildlife Fund. You pay them every month and they send you a newsletter and a cuddly toy and use your money to save rare animals. I think Greenpeace does something similar.'

Max pretended to shudder.

'Greenpeace? Those women, with hairy legs and infestations of head-lice, who camp at Greenham common?'

'I'm serious. Why don't you run Isabella's column above an advertisement for a subscription to the Tacugama sanctuary? I have set up a trust fund here in London and can organise an automatic transfer of any deposits to the sanctuary's account in Sierra Leone.'

'And how does this help me?'

'You told me yourself, subscriptions to the magazine have jumped after Isabella's first few columns.'

'So, I continue to run the column in the magazine?'

'Of course. Your readers get the option to donate to the trust. We could design an ad with a cute picture of Pinky and her pals. It would be irresistible to animal lovers.'

Max rubbed his chin.

'Hm, that's not the worse idea I've ever heard. Okay, I'll give it a go.'

'You won't regret it.'

'That's what Isabella says.'

Chapter 33

Ten did not believe in miracles. His life had been a series of disasters and tragedies, some self-inflicted, but most of them random. He struggled to accept the good luck that had befallen him, waiting for the punchline of cruel fate. As the days passed, he allowed himself to relax a little. Bathed in the subtle, but fierce, love of the Fakeems, he dared to hope, a luxury he hadn't allowed himself since his mother died.

He had little time to question his luck. They had introduced Pinky to several of Lucius's group and another female chimp, who had lost an infant, showed signs of wanting to breastfeed her. Plans were afoot to put Pinky in with the group for good, and Hasan had abandoned his usual jokey persona and had become business-like and serious.

Ten reacted to this change by applying himself to his lessons with more than the usual application, garnering praise from the Fakeems. He tried reading words in the Jane Goodall book but gave up in disgust.

'Why does that stupid book have such long words?' he said, shutting it with some violence. 'I'll never be able to read it.'

Gupta wiped her hands on her apron and put a tin of homemade biscuits in front of him.

'I don't understand half of those words myself,' she said. 'So, I'm not sure being able to read them will help that much. But there's no hurry. The book will still be here when you are ready for it. Maybe Isabella can help you with some words when she gets back.'

'How do you know she's coming?'

'I just know. She told me she'd be away for two weeks. It's two weeks today, so she could arrive any minute.'

Ten shrugged. He hadn't wanted to miss Isabella, but he couldn't help remembering some things she said, and the bluster she employed to keep people away. A bit like him. *Had she said something to Pete to make him leave?* Gupta told him Pete had left to get treatment for alcoholism, but Ten didn't understand what that meant. His grandfather would have performed strong voodoo spells to chase out the evil spirits, but Isabella had told him that there were no witch doctors in England. *How could people heal with no voodoo?*

Hasan told him science had the answer to everything, but if that was true, why did it not stop wars? The local newspaper, brought in to the sanctuary most mornings by Joe, had stories of renewed hostilities between the rebels and government troops. Ten made Hasan read them out loud at lunchtimes so he could keep up with the news. He had not forgotten his promise to Major Banga. It made him sick to the stomach to remember it. *Maybe the newspapers would bring good news about government victories. Perhaps Banga would die in battle.*

After another tough day foraging enough food for the growing group of chimps needing solid food, Ten fell into bed. He slipped his hand under his pillow and felt for the medallion given to him by Hasan 'to keep nightmares away'. His fingers closed on it and he felt all the day's tension melt away as his breathing became shallow and his eyes heavy. Soon he fell sound asleep, impervious to the sounds of the night.

He woke with a start several hours later when someone sat at the end of his bed. He could not make out a silhouette in the pitch-black night and terror seized him. His heart in his mouth, he reached for his torch and switched it on. The weak beam picked out the teeth of Rasta from the Beach Crew, who shielded his eyes and smiled at Ten's groggy state.

'You sure sleep good now, in a proper bed and everything,' he said. 'I could have stuck my knife in your heart.'

Ten pushed himself up into a sitting position, laying the torch on the mattress with the beam pointed at the wall in between them.

'What you want?' he said, although he knew.

Rasta snorted.

'You know why I is here,' he said. 'De Major, he want de chimp.'

'But she's not strong enough yet.'

'He don't care. He say it's time for the juju. Your Grandpa is ready now.'

'My Grandpa?'

'Yes, Major Banga is living in his house. He say if you don't bring chimp, he kill de old man.'

A chill rose up Ten's spine.

'He can't do that. He will bring the evil spirits down on the rebels.'

'Major Banga don't care. He want de chimp, now, and he want you to bring it to him.'

'Why do I have to go? Why don't you take her to

him?'

'Would she come wid me? I could slit her throat so she can't bite me.'

Rasta spat on the blade of his Bowie knife, which caught the torchlight, and he rubbed it between his thumb and forefinger. Ten could not see Rasta's expression, but he did not need to. Rasta had long since lost any empathy or sympathy for anyone except himself. He swung his legs off the bed.

'You tink I want to stay here wid dees people? I'm a soldier. I take the chimp to Banga myself.'

As they headed for Pinky's sleeping quarters, Ten glanced back at the Fakeems' hut, but only the idea of a silhouette loomed behind them. A wave of regret hit him as he understood the finality of this act. But if he called for help, Rasta would murder them without a second thought. So much for happy families. He lived in the real world and it had come to claim him.

Leaving Rasta outside, Ten entered the passageway behind the cages as quietly as possible. Pinky woke as he entered with his torch, blinking in the dark and whining. When he called her, she shot across the cage and wrapped her arms around his chest. He scratched her head and left the cage, finding Rasta in the passageway.

'What you doing here?' said Ten. 'Don't you trust me?'

'I don't trust anyone.'

'Be useful and get dat bottle and de tin of formula.'

'What for?'

'She got to eat.'

'I don't think she gonna be eating much.'

'I don't care what you think. Major Banga asked

me to bring her to him alive, and that's what I'm going to do.'

Rasta grumbled, but he took the items, and they walked out of the sanctuary gates to find Major Banga's driver waiting for them in the parking area. Ten climbed into the back with Pinky and Rasta sat up front with the driver. When Rasta tried to stroke Pinky, she showed her teeth, and he whipped his hand away.

'Why she not bite you?' he said.

'Cos she know class,' drawled Ten.

'And Beach crew is class,' said Rasta, laughing. 'Man, we miss you. Why you don't stay wid us?'

'No choice. Banga need me to do war tings.'

'After da war, we gonna rock da town.'

'You right.'

Ten's head soon nodded with sleep, and Pinky snored on his shoulder as they drew into Songo. The car halted with a judder and the boys woke with a start. They descended from the jeep and entered the house. Ten walked through to the back and put a sleeping Pinky in her old cage. She would go ballistic when she woke up, but he had no choice. Then he opened the door of his grandfather's bedroom.

'Grandpa, it's me, Ten.'

The old man stirred, but he lifted his wizen arm for Ten to lie under and they both fell back asleep.

Loud screeching woke them after dawn, as Pinky awoke to find herself imprisoned in the tiny cage. She had grown since her time living there and it had become a tight fit. She screamed blue murder and rattled the cage so much it fell on its side. Ten slipped out of bed and made a bottle. He let himself out into the yard and fought to get the cage back on its base, not helped by the antics of Pinky who threw herself around inside it.

After a while, he managed to calm her down, and he opened the cage so she could come out and drink her bottle. She snuggled up to him and emitted baby squeaks, something she hadn't done before. Maybe finding herself back in the horrible cage had frightened the sass out of her. Ten scratched her under the chin and encouraged her to chase him around the yard. Soon they were absorbed in their game, laughing and tumbling in the dirt. Rasta watched them, his eyes hooded and dark.

'Why you play wid de bushmeat?' he said. 'We make fetishes soon.'

Ten stopped in the middle of the yard, ignoring the entreaties of Pinky to follow her around it. He panted with exertion.

'What you say?'

'Dat bushmeat be made fetishes soon.'

Pinky scampered into Ten's arms and poked at his face, trying to stick her fingers up his nostrils. He brushed her hand away, staring at Rasta, waiting for the laugh that never came.

'Dey make fetish wid her?'

'Sure nuff.'

Ten patted Pinky on the head, his mouth open in shock. Had he brought her to her death? He couldn't believe it. Rasta laughed at his consternation.

'You gone soft now?' he said.

Ten did not answer. He sat on the ground and groomed Pinky's fur while his mind whirred. It had never occurred to him they might kill her, but maybe he had been naïve. On the other hand, Rasta loved to bait him. He knew who would tell him the truth.

George Adams fingered his cowrie shell necklace

and shook his head at Ten.

'Banga wants to defeat the government, but they have chased his troops out of the capital. He has convinced the men they will be invisible and invulnerable to bullets if they wear fetishes made from White Death and they will win a glorious victory. He wants me to conduct the ceremony to kill the chimp, and anoint its body parts with black magic to protect them.'

'But you must protect her. She's only a baby. I won't let you kill her,' said Ten.

'If I don't use her in the service of voodoo, Banga will kill me, and you,' his grandfather replied.

'How do you know he won't kill us anyway?'

Adams frowned.

'Do you want to die for this chimp? She is just bushmeat not a human. Your Western friends have polluted your mind.'

'You won't save her?'

'No. I am trying to save you instead. Be patient, there is a chance his troops will not want to fight. We have a few days. Just enjoy your time with her, but, understand, I must act when I am told to.'

Ten nodded his head, but his mind revolted. He would not let them kill Pinky. As soon as he got the chance, he would flee back to the sanctuary and hide there. The Fakeems would call Manu to protect them. Even the best rebel fighters were afraid of him and his men. They would not dare to attack the sanctuary.

Chapter 34

Pete sank into the armchair and sipped his can of fizzy apple juice, wrinkling his nose as the bubbles tickled its lining. Outside, his brother Jim's children chased the dog around the garden, screaming with glee as he ran round and round the big oak in the centre of the vast lawn. A robin yelled out his claim to the territory as a rival had the temerity to sing nearby. Pete breathed in the normality with relief after his sojourn in the clinic.

He found it hard to believe he got classified with those broken men, each one of them more lost than the last. His alcohol cravings had calmed almost as soon as he had entered the main atrium of cool marble and seen the unmistakable signs of military service; the cropped haircuts, the wary looks at strangers, the shrapnel scars. He had rubbed his neck in sympathy, running his finger over the ridge below his right ear. A young doctor, who had noticed the gesture, put a hand on his shoulder.

'You'll be safe here,' he said.

This marked the first time Pete cried, but not the last. The kindness of strangers broke through the wall he had constructed to keep out the pain, and his emotions flooded out like a dam being breached, sweeping away everything before them. The first time he slept through the night, he blamed the pills, but when it happened again with none of the morning grogginess he associated with sleeping tablets, he knew something had changed.

He threw himself into the therapy sessions, willing them to hollow him out and replace the old workings with new ones. Even the group therapy offered him the relief of knowing he helped not only himself but also the other men who had foundered on the shores of the clinic. But with the relief came the pain of knowing how badly he had failed his friends, old and new. He had abandoned Ten without a thought, even though he knew Ten had no one to rely on.

And as for Africa, Miss Isabella Green, he cringed when he remembered Tiwai and her incomprehension as he pushed her as far from him as he could, making sure to kill their budding relationship. And that moment in the river as she melted under his fingers. *How could I have missed the chance to make her mine?* The incomprehension and regret he felt about her and Ten represented the last stumbling block in his therapy. He couldn't square the circle as far as they were concerned.

'Time heals all ills,' said his therapist.

'What if they die because I left them?' said Pete.

'They are in charge of their own fate. You need to let go.'

'And if they die? How will I ever get better if I leave them in danger?'

'You can't save everyone. Let's just concentrate on saving yourself for the time being.'

And he had. But the fate of Isabella and Ten still nagged at him, despite his successful treatment. *How can I pretend they don't need me when I know they do?*

'Everything okay?' said his brother, coming in. 'I see you've made yourself at home.'

'Thanks for having me here. I really appreciate it.'

'Where will you go next? Not that I want to get rid of you, of course.'

'I'm not sure. It's all been a bit of an ordeal to tell you the truth. I don't know who I am any more.'

'It'll keep. Come and have some supper. June's made lasagne as a treat.'

A treat. June disapproved of Pete and she made it pretty clear, always hovering on the brink of a tut when he came near. No doubt the lasagne was low fat, low carb, low flavour mush. June couldn't stand for anyone to enjoy themselves. Her puritan upbringing pervaded everything she thought and did, poisoning the simplest of pleasures and making everyone feel guilty all the time. Pete tried not to bait her, but it often proved impossible. He steeled himself for battle and followed his brother into the kitchen.

'That smells fantastic,' he said.

June almost smiled, but her need to make him feel unwelcome won over her pride in her cooking. Pete smirked and sat down between his two pink-cheeked nephews, sweaty faced after their game in the garden. June served everyone a portion of watery lasagne and some tinned peas and removed her flowery apron. She sat down and held her arms out to the sides.

'Grace,' she said.

Pete stretched out his hands and took his nephews' small, sweaty ones. He bowed his head and let June complete the ritual. Visions of Ten weeping into his chest on the beach swamped him and he had to swallow hard to prevent a sob escaping. *Can I escape my old life if I don't fix this?* He felt the small hands slide out of his grasp and looked up to find June staring at him.

'What?' he said.

'I asked you if you wanted to add anything to the prayer?' said June. 'Have you gone deaf as well?'

As well as what? A drunk, broken burden sponging off my brother? Pete looked deep into her eyes for compassion or comprehension, but saw only disdain and judgement. He shrugged.

'Amen,' he said. 'This is delicious by the way. Thank you.'

She nodded and picked up her cutlery. Jim caught his eye and winked. *How could he stand living with this awful woman? Attraction of opposites? Masochism?* Jim might understand Pete's longing for Isabella, his polar opposite, so far out of his league as to be almost mythical. Pete chewed his way through the unappetising meal without a thought. He had eaten much worse on his travels, and he had to build up his strength again. For what, he wasn't sure.

After dinner, June went upstairs to put the children to bed.

'Let's watch the news,' said Jim, pulling the remote control out from under the dog.

They watched the last five minutes of a documentary about whales and then the headlines came on. Pete stiffened as the newsreader mentioned Sierra Leone.

'Now there's a coincidence,' said his brother. 'You were lucky to get out of there.'

Pete didn't reply. He sat transfixed as they broadcast the section on Sierra Leone.

'Renewed fighting between the Kamajors and

government troops has caused people to flee from their towns in the surrounding area and take refuge in the capital. Our correspondent, Kevin Tolly, travelled to Songo where he interviewed Major Banga in the house of George Adams, a local witch doctor.'

George Adams? Wasn't that Ten's Grandfather?

'Major Banga, it's Kevin Tolly from the BBC, thank you for agreeing to speak with us.'

Banga looked over the top of his sun glasses at the reporter and then shoved them against his nose.

'What do you want to know?' he said.

'My sources have informed me that you are gathering your forces for an attack on Freetown. Have you any comments?'

Banga sneered. 'My comment would be that informants should have their hands cut off.'

'But is it true? Are you planning on breaking the cease fire?'

'Cease fire? I didn't sign any cease fire. Only cowards and losers sign cease fires.'

'So, it's true then? You are planning to attack the capital? What about the Royal Irish Rangers? They are heavily armed and protecting the roads into the capital.'

'Their guns cannot harm us. We have juju on our side and are invisible to bullets.'

'Invisible? But how does that work?'

'I don't expect you to understand. We have White Death on our side and we will be invincible.'

'White Death?'

'Yes, they cannot kill us if we have her on our side.'

'Can I see her?'

Major Banga snapped his fingers and a small boy

ran inside the house. Seconds later, another boy came out carrying a white chimp. Pete leaned forward and then he gasped.

'Record this please,' he said to his brother, who pressed the button on the remote.

'Show the weapon to the cameras,' said Banga, and Ten moved forward, his eyes wide with fear. Pinky showed her teeth and tried to flee, but Ten held her tight. They both stood transfixed as the flashes went off.

'So this is White Death, your secret weapon,' said the reporter, suppressing a snigger. 'It doesn't look dangerous to me.'

Banga grimaced.

'That's because you are a stupid man who doesn't understand the power of voodoo. When the time comes, my warriors will carry pieces of White Death with them and bullets will pass them by, causing no harm. You will see.'

Ten's lower lip appeared to quiver. Banga dismissed him with a wave of his hand.

'It's time for you to go, BBC, unless you want to feed the pigs,' said Banga.

'Thank you,' said Kevin Tolly, backing away and turning to the camera again.

'This is Kevin Tolly in Songo, Sierra Leone. Over to you at the desk.'

Jim pressed stop recording and turned to his brother.

'What's up, Pete?' said Jim. 'You look as if you've seen a ghost.'

'It's Ten. That boy with the chimp. I didn't recognise him for a second. He looks so much older.'

'Ten, isn't that the boy you befriended out there?'

248

'Yes. I can't believe it. How did he end up with Major Banga? I thought he'd returned to the sanctuary to live with Hasan and Gupta. They'll be worried sick.'

'Didn't the therapist tell you to forget Sierra Leone and move on?'

Pete sighed.

'How can I? Did you see the state of him? That poor boy is terrified, and I'd like to bet he hadn't realised that they planned to cut Pinky up for fetishes until he heard it just now. He dotes on that creature.'

'There's not much you can do from here. Is there any way of finding out what's going on?'

Yes, but do I want to go there again?

'I have a phone number for Isabella's sister.'

'You kept that quiet,' said Jim.

'I never intended to use it.'

'And yet you didn't throw it away either.'

Chapter 35

Isabella jumped out of the taxi and paid the driver. She breathed in the humid air, and looked around her at the secondary undergrowth around the sanctuary, noting the depletion since her last trip. *Funds must be short again. Thank goodness Liz gave me the money.* She heaved her suitcase up the path to the Nissan huts and into her bedroom. She called for Ten but he didn't appear. Still sulking then. She smiled to herself and rolled her eyes.

She took Gupta's scarf, and Hasan's chocolate, out of her suitcase and went next door to put the chocolate in the fridge before it turned to liquid. To her surprise, Gupta sat at the table weeping into a dishcloth, her shoulders shaking as volcanic sobs racked her chest.

'Gupta, whatever's wrong,' said Isabella.

Gupta raised her head. Her eyes had swollen and her face had become puffy with crying. She gasped and launched herself at Isabella, weeping onto her shoulder and soaking it in tears. Isabella waited until the torrent had abated, and then she pushed Gupta away from her.

'What's happened?' she said, pulling her eyebrows together.

'Our son has gone,' said Gupta, hiccupping.

'Your son? I don't understand,' said Isabella.
Hasn't he been dead for years?

'Ten, he left.'

Isabella's face relaxed.

'He's run away again? Why are you crying like this? He always comes back.'

Gupta croaked.

'The rebels took Ten and Pinky away in a jeep. Joe saw them going towards Songo.'

Isabella slumped into a chair, her head in her hands.

'Oh no,' she said.

'I don't believe he would have gone willingly,' said Gupta. 'He had agreed to stay with us and be our son. His delight shone from his eyes. You should have seen him.'

'Can we rescue him?'

'Ten won't leave Pinky alone with the rebels. They don't know how to look after her. Anyway, they have re-armed for an attack on the capital, and she is their talisman.'

'Hm. They may hold his grandfather to ransom too. We need Manu's help,' said Isabella.

'We tried to contact him, but he has disappeared on some secret mission to Liberia.'

'He's been there at least once before, when he dropped me and Pete at Tiwai. I doubt he'll be gone long, but we'll have to wait until he gets back.'

Isabella put Hasan's chocolate in the fridge and returned to her room to unpack. She took out the presents she had bought for Ten, and she laid them out on his bed. She moved the pillow, and the medallion Hasan had given Ten fell onto the floor. Isabella picked it up and brought it into Gupta.

'I found this under Ten's pillow,' she said.

Gupta's eyes opened wide.

'It was Amir's. Hasan gave it to him. Ten would never leave without it, not by choice.'

A wave of fear hit Isabella. *I wish Pete were here. He would know what to do.*

After a quick nap, she visited the orphans with Hasan and helped give them some bananas. Two of the bullied males from Lucius's group were being introduced into the nursery group, and Hasan wanted to let them loose outside with the group. Isabella watched with bated breath as they emerged from the sleeping quarters into the outside enclosure. Curious orphans, being supervised by Sarah and Greta, soon surrounded them. Both of the adult males appeared confused by all the attention and unsure of what to do. Luckily, Fidget started a game of tag, and soon most of the chimps, including the two males, were scampering around the enclosure together, mouths open in enjoyment.

'It's going even better than I hoped. I wish Ten could be here to see this after all his effort to make it happen.'

'He'll be back,' said Isabella.

Hasan sighed.

'I wish I could believe that. I don't even know if the sanctuary will survive the renewal of hostilities in the civil war. How did your trip go? Is there any chance of funding?'

'Let's go in for lunch and I'll tell you both how I got on,' said Isabella. 'Gupta cried so much I didn't manage to tell her.'

The mood improved after Isabella recounted the tale of her trip to London. She employed hyperbole and bravado to make the Fakeems laugh, and skipped the bit about having to pack her belongings and move out of Graham's house.

'Well, that all sounds positive,' said Hasan, wiping his mouth with a napkin. 'How soon will you know about the investors?'

'I'm not sure. I'll give them a week to receive the information packs and then I'll call them to check the water.'

'I don't mean to seem ungrateful, but we still have to survive until then, and we don't have any funds,' said Gupta. 'We can't pay the bills this month.'

Isabella smiled.

'That's the bit I hadn't told you yet. My sister Liz received a generous bonus last week, and she has deposited five thousand pounds in the bank account we set up for Tacugama in London. It should be transferred automatically to the account in Freetown.'

Hasan's eyes opened wide.

'That's incredibly generous of her, but we can't accept it. We'll never be able to pay her back.'

'She doesn't want it,' said Isabella. 'Liz works in finance in the City of London. They're swimming in money in her company. She pays so much tax that the donation was almost free, as it's a deductible. I don't understand.'

'I do,' said Gupta. 'She must love you very much.'

Isabella blushed.

'Oh, and another thing, Max, my boss, is going to set up a subscription service to Tacugama, which also funnels into the account in London. He just needs photographs of the chimps once a month and reports on their progress. I can tidy up the articles when they come through.'

Gupta looked at Hasan.

'That's wonderful, but I guess that you're leaving too?' he said.

'Not yet. But soon,' said Isabella. 'I have to go back to my life. But first I want to be sure I set you up for a more regular income.'

'Why are you doing this?' said Hasan.

'I'm doing this for me,' said Isabella. 'I need to do something selfless to convince myself I'm a good person.'

'I've never had any doubt,' said Gupta.

As they waited for news of the investors, the tension at the sanctuary increased. Ten did not reappear and Gupta's mood collapsed, making Hasan miserable too. Isabella tried to avoid talking about anything not chimp related. She spent lots of time with Lucius's group, making notes on suitable candidates for transfer to Tyrone's group. Tyrone himself remained unaware that his promotion approached.

A loud knocking woke Isabella from a restless sleep, and Gupta burst into her bedroom, hair free from her usual immaculate bun.

'Come quickly, there's something wrong with Hasan.'

Isabella, groggy from lack of sleep, jumped out of bed and pulled on her shorts and slipped her feet into her sandals. She followed Gupta back into the other hut and found Hasan sitting at the kitchen table, his hand on his chest, and a grimace of pain on his face.

'What happened?' said Isabella, anguished to see him double over.

'He woke up shouting in pain,' said Gupta. 'I'm afraid it might be a heart attack.'

'You should take him to hospital.'

'But what about the sanctuary?'

'I can cope for a couple of days. Joe will be here.'

'I can't ask you to do that.'

'Who asked me? Get dressed and go into Freetown. I'll hold the fort.'

After the Fakeems had left, Isabella sat at the table drinking a cup of coffee and feeling deflated and scared. She shivered in the cold light of dawn as she struggled to make up the orphans' bottles. The female chimps gave them constant company and physical comfort, and the orphans were thriving in their new environment, but they still needed feeding. Now that the orphans lived in a mixed group, it was no longer safe to enter the sleeping quarters to fetch them for their bottle feed. They had become accustomed to reaching out through the grid and holding the bottles for drinking through it.

The shock of Hasan's potential heart attack reverberated with her. She felt lost without Gupta's good sense and motherly company to get her through the day. And she had the sense of a sad ending to her African adventure. She had alienated Pete, and failed to get funding for the sanctuary, and now Ten had joined the rebels taking Pinky with him. On top of that, Hasan had shown signs of giving up the struggle to keep the sanctuary open. Could things have gone any worse?

She heaved the basket off the table and took it down to the lean-to on the new enclosure where Tyrone's group were still groggy with sleep and hardly noticed her enter, or leave the basket on the bench covering it in a piece of tarpaulin. A box of foxed papayas and a stalk of bananas were all that remained in the storage shed. After that, the chimpanzees would have to survive on leaves and bark and any insects they could find. Hasan had shown her the vegetation they included in their diet, so she could hack down enough at ground level to keep them going until he got back. *If he comes back.*

Chapter 36

As the sun rose higher in the sky, Isabella sat in the kitchen eating a quick breakfast, and making notes in the sanctuary journal. She felt a tear leak from her eye and it splashed on the page, blurring the surrounding writing. A sob rose in her chest and she dropped her head into her hands as a fit of weeping overtook her. She cried out all the sorrow and frustration until her eyes were dry and her throat raw. A stray tea towel acted as a substitute handkerchief, and she blew her nose into its comforting smell of curry and spices.

When she looked up, there was a silhouette in the door, standing against the strong morning sunlight. She gasped and looked around for a weapon, but then the figure spoke.

'Africa, it's me, Ten. I've brought Pinky back.'

'Ten? Oh my God. I thought we'd lost you.'

Isabella rushed over to Ten, intending to hug him, but Pinky coughed and screeched at her. *I hate that bloody animal.* Instead, she shut the door, pushing Ten into the kitchen.

'But how did you get here?' she said. 'I thought you were in Songo. And what—'

Ten slumped onto a chair. He had cuts and grazes all over his face and body. Pinky headed for the fruit bowl and grabbed a banana, crouching in the corner with it.

'Have you got something to eat?' he said. 'I haven't eaten for two days.'

Isabella fried four eggs and reheated a large bowl of rice, which she put in front of him. Ten launched himself at the food, gulping it down until nothing remained. Then he sat back in his seat, sorrow etched on his face.

'What happened?' said Isabella. 'Why have you brought Pinky back?'

'They killed him,' said Ten. 'My grandfather. I thought they cared about us, but they were going to murder Pinky in a ceremony and cut her up for making fetishes. My grandfather tried to stop them, but they shot him. They would have shot me too, but they didn't know how to look after Pinky, and they were waiting for another witch doctor to perform the ceremony.'

'Do they know you came here?' said Isabella.

Ten sniffed.

'I don't know. Where else would I go?'

A chill ran down Isabella's spine. They were on their own at Tacugama. *The sanctuary does not have a telephone, and who would I call anyway?* Pete had not contacted her before he left for England, and they had sent Manu to the south to quell a rebel group. Most local staff had fled the region when the rebels reignited the conflict. Only Joe remained to help them, and he had not arrived yet. If Banga and his crew came for Pinky, they would kill Ten if they found him.

'We need to get out of here,' she said.

'What about the chimpanzees? They'll starve to death,' said Ten.

'What if we left the cages open?'

'If we leave them here, the rebels will eat them.

And the orphans will die. I'm not leaving,' said Ten. 'Anyway, there's only one road into Tacugama. If the rebels are on their way and see us walking, we won't stand a chance.'

Isabella sighed. *Caught between a rock and a hard place. How the hell did I get myself in this position? I know nothing about weapons or self-defence. Think Isabella, there must be something we can do.*

'Okay, first have a shower. You smell terrible. There are some clean clothes on your bed. And don't use all the shampoo.'

The twinkle in her eye gave Ten a second to consider his reply.

'You're so bossy,' he said. 'No wonder Pete hates you.'

But he smiled.

Isabella felt a wave of emotion course through her and she turned away so he wouldn't see it. She sat back at the table and sipped her tea, struggling to regain her composure. The journal lay in front of her and she opened it and started to write again. The Fakeems needed to know about Ten coming back, even if they didn't make it out alive.

She had just finished writing when Ten appeared in the doorway wearing his London t-shirt and his fake sunglasses. He posed for a second and then came in, his shoulders shaking with laughter at the look on her face. His expression changed, and he rushed to her and hugged her tight, knocking the wind out of her. They stood together, holding on tight to each other.

Finally, Ten pulled back from her, his face a picture of puzzlement.

'I don't understand,' he said.

'What?'

'How did you know I would come back?'

'This is your home now. Where else would you go?'

'And why did you buy presents for me when I treated you horribly?'

Isabella cocked her head to one side.

'You seriously don't know?' she said. 'That's what friends do.'

'I never had a proper friend before,' said Ten.

'But you have now. You've got me and Pete, and Gupta and Hasan, and Joe. You've got lots of friends.'

Ten's face crumbled.

'But we're going to die,' he said. 'And it's all my fault.'

'No, we aren't. It's not our time.'

'What can we do?'

'Let's put Pinky in the sleeping quarters with Hilda. She won't make a fuss if she has Hilda to hold her. We can shut Lucius and the rest of the group in the adjoining room so the rebels can't see them from the road. Come on, we may not have much time.'

Ten persuaded Pinky to enter the sleeping quarters with a bribe of bananas, and while Isabella distracted Lucius with a box of mango juice, he led Hilda by the hand into the same room as Pinky, and shut the doors. Isabella persuaded the other chimps to stay inside without fussing, using as bribes the half rotten papayas. They could not resist the sweet treats even though their keepers rarely kept them indoors during the day. Ten turned to Isabella.

'Now what?' he said.

'We do the same with Tyrone's group. I'll bribe the orphans with milk bottles, and we can keep them in one room with the adults in the other. Then I want you to get in with the orphans and give them their bottles to keep them quiet. If you hear anyone coming, lie down on the floor and cover yourself with straw.'

'And what are you going to do?' said Ten.

'I'll think of something. Come and get the basket of bottles from the kitchen.'

Before giving Ten the basket, Isabella wrapped a sandwich in a sheet of greaseproof paper and put it beside the bottles with a mango. She filled a bottle with clean water and put it in too.

'That should keep you going,' she said. 'I know what you're like if you don't get fed. I don't want you stealing the orphans' bottles.'

Ten managed a wan smile, but his face was grey with worry. When he had gone, Isabella did the washing up, scrubbing the frying pan long after she had cleaned the egg off. Her head swam with lurid imaginings of their plight. Hope seemed like a luxury in these circumstances.

Why did I lie to him? We're both going to die. Did Michael know the IRA men were going to shoot him? I've never talked to him about that dark day. He had never wanted to revisit the horror of losing Liam, and I've never pressed him. Had he told Liz? Maybe. But she never talked about it either. Even our parents never referred to it. It was as if it never happened, but now it would happen to me. Should I write a will? Apologise to Pete. Or Graham. Leave an article for Max. I don't know. A bit of Dutch courage might help calm my nerves.

Isabella went next door, into the Nissan hut she shared with Ten, and dug a bottle of gin out of her suitcase. She had bought it in Duty Free Shopping on her journey back from the Jane Goodall conference in London, and had been saving it for a special occasion. She had left it in her bag when she remembered Hasan was a Muslim and didn't drink, intending to drink it with Pete if they ever talked again.

This occasion seemed to be special enough, so she made herself a cocktail with some lime cordial of Gupta's and a splash of Seven-Up and raised her glass to herself - On the occasion of my death – and took a gulp. She screwed up her face at the taste but drank another mouthful anyway. She banged her fist on the table as it burned its way down her throat.

Banga had been watching her from the doorway, a sardonic smile on his face. He swung the AK47 off his shoulder and hung it on the back of a chair, sitting down opposite her.

'So, little miss perfect is downing gin at eleven o'clock in the morning. That's not the sort of behaviour I would expect from you,' he said.

'The sun must be over the yard arm somewhere,' said Isabella. 'I was just about to have another.'

'Make me one too,' said Banga.

Isabella shrugged. At least if he were drunk, he might forget to shoot her. She made them two more, being sure to make Banga's drink extra strong. She slammed the glasses down on the table, daring him to complain. His eyes narrowed, but the expression in them was of excitement rather than annoyance. He grabbed his drink and downed it in one. She smirked and did the same.

'Another,' he said. 'And bring the bottles over here.'

Chapter 37

The airliner skidded to a halt on the runway at Lungi airport, and the passengers made their way to the terminal and the immigration queue. Pete pushed his way to the front of the queue, a scowl on his face. Any mild recriminations ceased as he spun around, his muscles rippling in his t-shirt, ensuring no one had the guts to complain. He wiped the sweat coating his brow in the oppressive humidity, dark circles appearing under his arms. The immigration officer took one look at him and stamped his passport without questions.

Pete avoided the baggage scrum, slinging his kitbag over his shoulder and heading for the hoverport. He sat near the staircase on the ferry and drummed his fingers as it filled up with passengers for its trip across Tagrin Bay to Freetown. A plump woman wheezed onto the ship and headed for the seat beside him, but he growled, 'it's taken,' at her, worried she would slow him down.

Finally, the hovercraft lifted up on its cushion of air and sped across the water to Man of War Bay. Pete tried to still his heart rate, which threatened to make him sick with the accompanying adrenaline rush. *What the hell am I doing? I should have left them to fend for themselves.* But visions of Ten's frightened face kept invading his mind and the dread of what the rebel soldiers would do to Isabella if they found her unprotected. *Why did I go home at all? What was I running away from?*

The hovercraft sped over the waves in the estuary, bouncing rhythmically. Through the clouded Perspex windows, the coloured wooden boats of the fishermen headed back from night fishing at sea. The water calmed as they entered the Man of War Bay, and the hovercraft glided up to the foreshore and shuddered to a stop.

As soon as they opened the door, Pete bounded up the ramp and looked around, breathing hard, panic rising in his chest.

'All right, mate?' said a voice. 'Back so soon?'

Whitey stood apart from the crowd of welcoming relatives, grinning broadly. Pete calmed down in an instant.

'Am I glad to see you,' said Pete.

'Couldn't stay away, uh?' said Whitey. 'I thought Isabella might fancy me with you gone.'

Pete grinned.

'She's class, mate. And miles out of your league. But it's not her I'm worried about right now.'

'Talk in the car,' said Whitey, and headed towards the jeep where Manu and Chopper waited, strain on their faces.

'You've got some cheek,' said Manu. 'Calling a code red for that snotty faced kid.'

'He saved my life,' said Pete. 'I owe him. Aren't you always telling us to leave no man behind?'

'I like Ten,' said Chopper. 'He's got some guts approaching us to help you. And Isabella loves him…' He hesitated. 'And we love her, so it's not that complicated.'

Pete almost choked up at his macho friend's confession.

'What the hell is all this mushy stuff?' said Manu. 'We're going to war. I need everyone to be sharp. Get in the car.'

They drove through town to the barracks, cursing the traffic, which seemed designed to frustrate them. The streets were full of people shopping in bulk. Manu sounded the horn as they staggered across the streets in front of the jeep, carrying their supplies home.

'They're hoarding again,' said Whitey.

'It must be bad in the countryside,' said Manu. 'They always do this when they think the rebels are getting close. Nobody trusts the government troops to keep them out.'

'Will the rebels go to Tacugama?' said Pete.

'Unlikely. There's nothing of interest for them there, unless they need bushmeat, and then it will be like a free supermarket. Major Banga wants the capital. Everything starts and finishes with Freetown,' said Manu.

'Where is the boy?' said Manu.

'He's with Major Banga.'

'How on earth did you find out?' said Chopper

'I saw him on television,' said Pete

'Are you sure it was him? These street kids are pretty similar looking,' said Whitey.

'I know Ten, and he looked terrified. He's not there of his own accord. I guess they made him take the chimp from Tacugama for them.'

'Major Banga has set up his headquarters at Songo, but his troops are scattered in villages nearby, stealing people's food and raping their daughters and wives,' said Chopper.

'We were planning on paying him a little visit,' said Manu. 'Our sponsor is quite keen to eliminate the problem before it gets out of hand.'

'Maybe we should kill the white chimp. If they are relying on it for juju, it will burst their bubble and they'll slink off home,' said Whitey.

'You'll have to find Ten first. He's the only person the chimp likes, and she's a vicious little brat,' said Pete.

'Most women are,' said Manu.

The traffic unclogged, and they made their way into the outskirts of town, where they turned into Manu's compound, coming to a halt beside the weapons' storage shed. Manu opened the massive padlock and shoved open the reinforced door. Sunlight flooded the gloomy room, which smelt of cordite, an odour which made the hairs on Pete's arms stand to attention. Oily Armalites lined one wall, and belts of ammunition sat in boxes underneath the guns.

'Okay,' said Manu. 'Take what you need.'

'I thought you'd never ask,' said Chopper.

Whitey seized a box of grenades, and Chopper slung some M2 bullet belts over his shoulders, grunting with effort. Pete stood open mouthed at the arsenal.

'What are you staring at?' said Manu. 'Get us a few Armalites and I'll sort out some bullets.'

By the time they came outside again, Chopper had mounted an M2 heavy machine gun on an armoured car and was feeding a belt into it.

'Those bastards won't know what's hit them,' said Manu.

Pete's heart rate had risen again, and he got into the front of the armoured car with a couple of

Armalites with clips full of bullets, ready to fire at will. He had taken a Fairbairn Sykes double-bladed knife from Manu's extensive collection of close quarter weapons, and he attached the scabbard to his belt. Manu had raised an eyebrow at his choice.

'Oh, we're serious now, are we?' he said. 'Good to have you back, soldier.'

Pete grinned and saluted. The weapons had centred him. He felt like a warrior again.

Almost no traffic ventured along the road to Songo. The presence of the rebel force had caused an exodus of the local population who camped in the fields and the burned-out houses along the route. Small children played football in huge numbers, all running after the ball at the same time. Only the goalies stood between the stones at the ends of the pitches.

'They could do with a coach,' said Pete.

The countryside showed signs of attack. Blackened vehicles sat in the ditches beside the road and bullet holes scarred the whitewashed walls of local houses. As they drew close to Songo, a roadblock manned by rebels barred the entrance to the village. One rebel started shooting at the armoured car, but Chopper mowed him down and the others ran away. Whitey drove straight through the tree trunks and oil cans, scattering it into the ditches.

No further rebel troops impeded their progress. They had melted away, leaving the streets of the town eerily quiet in their wake. The streets were littered with beer cans and chicken bones being chewed by stray dogs wagging their tails in delight.

'They don't have any stomach for a fight without their fetishes,' said Whitey.

'Where are they keeping the chimp?' said Manu.

'I don't know,' said Pete. 'I think Ten's grandfather is the town's witch doctor, so it shouldn't be that hard to find him.'

They drove around for a while, keeping an eye out for someone who could give them directions. The streets seemed deserted, but Whitey spotted a woman cowering in a doorway and asked her for directions. Quaking with fear, she pointed downhill at a house covered in flowers and vine plants.

'White Death awaits you if you disturb the holy man,' she said.

'What the fuck is White Death?' said Manu. 'I thought that was us.'

Pete laughed.

'That's Pinky.'

'Pinky? And is Perky there too?'

'No, Pinky, she's an albino chimp. They're going to cut her up to make fetishes to keep them safe from bullets,' said Pete.

'And I thought I was primitive,' said Manu.

They pulled up in front of the house. The front door hung wide open and a trail of blood led through to the back yard. The men entered with caution; Chopper trained the machine gun on the house, looking for the slightest sign of trouble. A crumpled heap of clothing lay in the back yard. Manu poked it with his toe and it moaned. Pete turned over the body of George Adams. His eyelids flickered, and he tried to speak.

'Get him some water,' said Pete.

They sat Adams against the wall of the house and held a cup up to his lips. He sipped some water, swallowing with difficulty. A bullet hole through his left side seeped blood onto the gravel. His wiry arms waved about in the air as he tried to communicate.

'What happened here?' said Pete. 'Where is Ten?'

'Ten?' said the old man. 'I tried to stop him.'

'Where did he go?'

'He wouldn't listen. He love dat bushmeat too much.'

Adams pulled at his clothing, trying to straighten his kaftan. His fingers found the blood leaking from his side and he lifted them to his face, examining them with peculiar interest.

'It ends,' he said, and his head flopped onto his chest.

Pete lifted his head again and looked straight into his eyes.

'You must tell us. Ten's in danger.'

Adams breathed in with difficulty and coughed up some blood. His eyes focussed for a second and he reached out with his hands, trying to stand up. He fell back against the wall, sighing.

'Ten took White Death. Major Banga will kill them both,' he said.

'Where did they go?' said Pete, shaking his shoulders.

'Tacugama,' said Adams.

Chapter 38

Banga's gaze ran over her body, lingering on her breasts. Isabella kept her eyes on his face, taking in the pock-marks and the scar slashing through his chin. He drummed his fingers on the table, making her feel nauseous. Her t-shirt stuck to her back where the cold sweat had run down to her trousers. She shifted in her seat, fighting the effects of the alcohol, wishing she had never started this game. Banga seemed unaffected by it, and his eyes had regained their blank shark-like quality. He narrowed his eyes.

'Where is the boy?' he said. 'Tell me and I'll let you live.'

A lie.

'He's not here,' she said. 'He dumped Pinky and ran away.'

'Pinky? You mean the white chimp?'

'Yes, she's here.'

'Take me to it and give me the bottle.'

She handed him the gin. He let the gun slip down to a horizontal position at his hip, pointing it at her abdomen.

'This way,' she said, trying to keep the tremble out of her voice.

He swung the gun, indicating that Isabella should

walk ahead of him. She walked down the pathway, avoiding looking at Tyrone's block, and led him to the passageway under the viewing platform. The chimpanzees, who were normally voluble in their recognition of visitors went strangely quiet. *Was it Banga's gun that had silenced them? The Fakeems had originally rescued most of them from the beach photographers, or from villages where they were being kept as pets, but poachers had shot their mothers. Perhaps they recognised the gun as a dangerous object?*

Isabella stood in front of the cage containing Hilda and Pinky.

'She's in here,' she said.

'So, go in and get her for me,' said Banga, pointing the gun at her.

'Pinky doesn't like me. Hilda may attack me if I try to take Pinky from her.'

'I don't care. Go in there and get her, or I'll shoot you.'

'Pinky knows you. Why don't you come in with me? I'll try to distract Hilda and you can get Pinky.'

Banga examined her face for signs of subterfuge, but Isabella had not bothered to lie. Drink had made her brave. She would not die for a bad-tempered ape.

'Okay, open the door.'

Isabella pulled the sliding door open and entered the cage with Banga. He held out his arms, but Pinky showed no signed of wanting to go to him. She whimpered and held on tight to Hilda who bared her teeth in fear. Lucius had approached the barrier between the sleeping quarters and he seemed to inflate as his chest and arm hairs stood up in fury. He tried to shake the bars, but they were solid and would not move. Banga laughed.

'I don't know why I'm wasting my time,' he said, and he lifted his gun.

A quick retort of several shots rang out and Hilda fell backwards, releasing Pinky who also rolled to the floor.

'You shot her?' said Isabella, faint with shock. 'I thought you needed her.'

'Oh, I need her,' he said, smiling. 'But only to make fetishes. The witch doctor told me she doesn't have to be alive.'

He bent over and picked up Pinky's limp body, slinging it over his shoulder. His lip curled, and he pointed his gun at Isabella.

'Take your clothes off,' he said.

Isabella's eyes opened wide. He'll kill me anyway.

'No.'

Banga moved towards her and shoved the gun's barrel into her stomach.

'Now.'

Isabella shook her head and squeezed her eyes shut, waiting for the shot. Suddenly, the gateway between the cages opened with a crash. Banga swung around in fright. In one bound Lucius had entered the cage and grabbed Banga's gun, wrenching it from his grasp and throwing it on the floor. He pounded the floor of the cage with his feet, and slapped his chest with his hands, roaring in fury. When Banga tried to pick the gun up again, Lucius threw him against the wall. Isabella had shrunk into a ball on the floor, covering her head with her hands as Lucius ran around the room, bouncing off the walls and pounding Banga's prone body as he ran by.

'Africa, are you all right?' said Ten. 'You need to come out of the cage, now, before the others enter. Is Pinky dead?'

'I'm not sure. I'll try to find out.'

'Be careful of Lucius. He's crazy right now.'

Isabella moved to where Lucius, who had calmed down a little, prodded the body of Hilda. He lifted Hilda's arm and let it fall again. In the adjoining cage, the chimps hooted and moved towards the door. Isabella crouched down and put her hand on Pinky's body, feeling her small chest rise and fall with shallow breaths. She slipped her arm under Pinky and cradled her. Lucius loomed over her and she cringed, waiting for the blow, but he put a gentle hand on Pinky, hooting at her. When she didn't respond, he let Isabella stand up and back towards the door leading out of the cage.

Her heart thundered in her chest and she almost fell out of the cage as she tripped on the step. Ten slammed the door shut just as several of the larger males in the troop came through the doorway from the adjoining cage and supported Lucius in his display of force. One of them jumped up and down on Banga's body. Ten took Pinky from Isabella and stroked her. She panted but did not open her eyes.

'Should we try to rescue Banga?' said Isabella.

'I think it's too late. Anyway, we should get out of here. The troop is agitated. If we tried to calm them, it might make it worse,' said Ten.

'But what will happen to him?'

Ten scratched his head.

'They might eat him. If not, we can take the body out later.'

'Pinky's badly injured. I think she's dying.'

'But you are alive.'

'Thanks to you. How did you know we were in here?'

'When the chimps went silent, I knew something had happened. I couldn't leave you to face Banga alone. It's my fault he came here.'

'But how did he get here?' said Isabella.

'He must have driven,' said Ten.

'Maybe he's not alone.'

'I hadn't thought of that.'

'Can you reach Banga's gun?'

'Lucius might tear my arm off. I'll look outside and see if we can get to the house. Hasan has a pistol there somewhere that he uses to shoot injured animals.'

Ten slipped out of the door. Isabella tried to examine Pinky's wound but Pinky bared her teeth.

'I don't know why I bothered to save you,' said Isabella. 'You're still horrible.'

'Come out or I'll kill him,' shouted someone outside the building.

Isabella froze in terror. The nightmare isn't over. We are dead if I don't think of something.

Isabella clutched Pinky and forced herself to step out into the blinding sunlight.

'I'm here. Don't hurt him,' she said.

As her eyes became accustomed to the light, she made out the silhouette of a rebel fighter pointing a machine gun at Ten, who stood with his arms up. She walked in front of Ten, whispering 'stay behind me' and held out the chimp.

'I have White Death,' she said. 'You can't shoot us. The bullets will fly backwards and hit you.'

'Not if she is dead,' said the rebel.

'She is alive,' said Isabella.

Isabella poked Pinky who screeched in protest.

The rebel frowned and looked around for support, unwilling to call her bluff.

'Where is Banga?'

'He is in there,' said Isabella, gesturing with her head. 'He is cutting up the bushmeat.'

'Why doesn't he come out?'

'Why don't you ask him?'

'Major, sah, I have the prisoners,' shouted the rebel.

When no one answered, he rubbed his chin and shuffled from foot to foot, pointing the gun at them.

'You lie,' he said. 'You die.'

He lifted the gun and focussed it on them. Isabella put her arm around Ten who had emerged from behind her. Suddenly, she spotted movement behind the rebel, and Pete and Manu appeared, running at him. She gasped in surprise, and the rebel spun around, spraying bullets in an arc in his fright. Manu fell to the ground and Pete shot back, hitting the rebel in the arm. He fell to his knees, trying to fire at Pete, but his weapon jammed. He took a knife from his belt. Pete reached him with his knife out too. They rolled over and over, grunting with exertion. Pete yelled out as the rebel knifed him in the ribs. He lay on the ground without moving.

The rebel picked up his gun and pointed it at Pete's head. A shot rang out. The rebel spun around and collapsed. Manu limped over to Pete and lifted him into a sitting position. Blood trickled from Pete's mouth. Isabella and Ten ran to Pete and knelt in the dust. Manu examined the wound. He shook his head at Isabella who tried not to sob. Ten buried his head in Pete's shoulder.

'You came for me,' he said. 'I didn't believe in

you. I'm so sorry.'

'Don't be sorry. I ran away to England and left you at the mercy of Banga. I only came back because I missed you hanging around,' said Pete.

Ten sobbed and flung himself at Manu who patted him on the head in embarrassment. Isabella moved closer and took Pete's hand, stroking his face.

'Fancy seeing you here,' she said. 'There's no point trying to impress me, you know. You screwed up big time.'

'I thought you liked a bit of macho action,' said Pete, coughing. 'Can we start again, please? I'm ready now.'

Isabella wiped the blood from his chin.

'Me too,' she said, and kissed him tenderly.

When she raised her head, his eyes were blank.

'He's gone,' said Manu.

Chapter 39

The rest of Manu's crew arrived up at the sanctuary not long after Pete's death, having been scouring the area for more rebel troops. Manu had strapped up his calf with a length of bandage he found in the kitchen and he limped down to meet them at the gate. Whitey and Chopper carried automatic weapons and looked around in expectation.

'What happened?' said Whitey. 'We heard shooting.'

'Where's Pete?' said Chopper. 'Trust him not to wait for us. Glory hunter.'

Manu shook his head.

'Pete bought it,' he said. 'He saved Ten and Isabella like the hero he was.'

Chopper's shoulders slumped and Whitey bit his lip.

'Where is he?' Whitey said. 'We need to take him home.'

Whitey and Chopper replaced their weapons in the vehicle and took a wooden pallet out of the back. They found Ten and Isabella sitting on the ground with Pete, holding his hands. Whitey hugged Isabella and put his arm around Ten's shoulders. Chopper saluted Pete's body. Then they picked him up and placed him on a wooden pallet. They draped a blanket over Pete and lifted the pallet onto their shoulders. Isabella and Ten followed them to the truck.

Ten went over and put his hand on Pete's body before they loaded it into the back of the truck. Isabella stood rigid with misery, twisting her fingers and biting her lip. Manu saluted the truck as it rumbled out of Tacugama in a cloud of dust. Then he came over to Isabella, limping from the flesh wound in his calf.

'Do you want to come back to town with us?' he said.

'No. I promised Hasan and Gupta I would keep the sanctuary going for them, and I keep my promises,' said Isabella.

'Where are they?'

'They're in the hospital. Hasan had a heart attack.'

'It never rains,' said Manu, shaking his head. 'What about you, Ten? We could do with a brave young man like you in our barracks, if you want to throw in your lot with us.'

Ten managed a smile.

'Thanks,' he said. 'But Pinky needs me.'

Isabella punched him in the arm, and he gave her a wry grin, rubbing it. Manu looked from one to the other.

'The rebels don't stand a chance with you two here,' he said. 'We'll clean out their officers' mess, so you won't have any more trouble with them. The Medusa will die as soon as it loses its heads.'

When Manu had left, Isabella and Ten examined Pinky, who lay in a box of blankets.

'The injury must be bad. She hasn't tried to bite me once,' said Isabella.

'She bites you because you make her nervous.'

'It's her who makes me nervous.'

Ten rolled his eyes. He scratched Pinky behind her ears and crooned to her.

'I'll take her into my room tonight,' he said.

'Call me if you need anything,' she said.

Isabella lay in bed that night thinking about Pete and fate. Pete had loved her in his infuriating way, with a ferocity she hadn't experienced before. Her romance with Graham now seemed so beige and drab. *What on earth did I see in him?* Love is blind. Pete had not been perfect, but he had opened her eyes to real passion, and she wouldn't compromise again. A shooting star crossed the sky outside her window and she hoped it was Pete, on his way to heaven.

Ten came into her room in the early hours of the morning, his head bowed, and she knew, before he said anything, that Pinky had died. Lifting her blanket, she let him lie beside her. She put an arm around him, and he cried for Pinky or for Pete. She couldn't tell. A lump rose in her throat as she listened to his heart breaking. *I know just how you feel.*

The next morning, Hasan and Gupta arrived from Freetown, ignorant of all the drama. They found two broken people sitting in the kitchen filling the orphans' bottles. Gupta's eyes opened wide when she spotted Ten.

'You came back,' she said, and hugged Ten to within an inch of his life before releasing him.

Only then did she realise how unresponsive he was.

'What happened?' she said. 'What's wrong?'

Ten looked at Isabella.

'Tell them,' he said.

'Pete and Pinky are dead,' she said. 'The rebels

came looking for Pinky, and Pete came to rescue us with Manu. And Banga…'

She trailed off, choking on her words. Hasan and Gupta looked from one to the other in horror.

'Pete dead?' said Hasan. 'But what was he doing here? He returned to England.'

'I don't know how he knew we were in trouble, but he turned up with Manu, just when we were going to be shot,' said Ten. 'He's a hero.'

Gupta put a hand on Isabella's shoulder.

'I'm so sorry,' she said. 'He came back for you after all.'

'He came back for all of us,' said Isabella. 'Mostly for himself.'

'Paradise regained, thank Allah,' said Hasan.

'How did Pinky die?' said Gupta.

'The rebels shot her. They only wanted her to make fetishes. I'm such an idiot. Why did I take her to them? Can you ever forgive me for running away?' said Ten. 'I wanted to come home the minute I left.'

Gupta hugged him again.

'You silly boy. Did you imagine we'd give up on you? You may be a pain, but you're our pain now.'

'Literally,' said Hasan.

'What about you?' said Isabella. 'Didn't you have a heart attack?'

'False alarm,' said Hasan. 'Angina.'

'The doctor told us that the stress of running this place brought it on.'

'No surprise there,' said Isabella.

Pinky's funeral threatened to be a solemn occasion, but in the end, it offered everyone the chance to tell stories about what a prima donna she turned out to be. Isabella showed everyone the scar on her finger, and Ten told a long and rambling story about how clever Pinky was. After the burial, behind the Nissan huts, Isabella visited Lucius who had reverted to his gentle self. She groomed his massive hands and fed him strips of mango.

'Maybe this is the actual love story,' said Hasan, watching them. 'Will you be leaving soon?'

'Not before I've made you safe. It's even more important now that Ten is staying.'

But doubts assailed her. What will the investors say when they learn Pinky is no more? Will they still want to invest? And as for the documentary...

Chapter 40

To Isabella's surprise, the rhythm of the sanctuary re-established itself almost immediately after Pinky's burial despite the hopelessness of their situation. Hasan whistled, and Gupta cooked and gave Ten lessons like nothing had happened.

'Aren't you worried about the sanctuary?' said Isabella.

'Allah will deal with it. Inshallah,' said Hasan.

'And the condemned man ate a hearty breakfast,' said Isabella.

She tried to carry on as usual, helping Ten by reading excerpts of the Jane Goodall book to him, and cosying up to Lucius in her spare time. With the threat of civil war receding, the staff reappeared and food supplies improved. Liz's money proved to be a lifesaver for a while.

'It won't last forever,' said Hasan. 'When are you going to hear about the investments?'

'I'll go into town and make some calls,' said Isabella. 'They should have received their information packs a few days ago. Hopefully, I can persuade them to donate to the fund in London.'

Hopefully.

Ten would not come into town with Isabella, as he

feared bumping into Rasta. Isabella had to negotiate the call centre by herself, a process she found tedious in the extreme. She faxed an update to Max, telling him of her fears for the sanctuary and the disaster of Pinky's demise. She did not hold back on her expectations that the funds would run out and the horrible possibility of euthanising the orphans. *Have I been over dramatic? Nothing I wrote was untrue.*

She booked a call through to Tristan Horton, the media guy who had laughed at her with his friends. He had mentioned a documentary, and it occurred to her that might be the best way to get people interested in the sanctuary. He took the call and came on the line, his voice excited.

'Miss Green. I've been waiting for your call? Are you in Sierra Leone?'

'Yes, I'm calling you from Freetown.'

'Great. Listen. My editor loves the concept of making a documentary about the white chimp. He thinks we can sell it to the big networks in America, not just the BBC. It's such a rare thing I—'

'Sorry to interrupt you, Mr Horton—'

'Tristan, please.'

'Okay, Tristan. The rebels attacked the sanctuary and the white chimp got shot.'

'Even better, we can follow its progress as it recovers. We could make a series.'

'I don't think you understand,' said Isabella. 'The chimp died.'

A long silence ensued. Then muffled noises, as if someone had their hand over the receiver, were audible.

'Hello. Is anybody there?' said Isabella.

'Um, yes,' said Tristan. 'Listen, I'm sorry, but my

283

editor says it's a no go. With the white chimp dead, it's just another hard-luck story from a war zone.'

'But, the sanctuary will go bankrupt.'

'Not my problem, I'm afraid. You've got my card. Let me know if you ever get another story like this one.'

Click. *The bastard has hung up on me. But the other investors are interested in saving wildlife, not just the white chimp. Someone will stump up.*

But their reaction to the news of the death of Pinky was identical. As much as Isabella tried to argue for the orphans, the interest of the investors died with her.

A dispirited Isabella left the call centre and went to have a coffee and a torta de nata in the Portuguese café. As she flicked the flaky pastry off her lap, the defeat overwhelmed her. She had lost her boyfriend and home, her new boyfriend had died, she had failed to save the sanctuary and she had nowhere to go next. The temptation to get on the next flight out and abandon ship nagged at her. *But how can I desert Gupta and Hasan? And Ten?* Instead, she bought a bag of pastries and got on the bus back to the sanctuary.

Hasan and Gupta received the news with resignation.

'Allah has willed it,' said Hasan.

'We knew this might happen one day,' said Gupta. 'It's not a complete surprise.'

'When the money runs out, we will have to close the sanctuary and release the chimps into the wild to take their chances.'

'What about the orphans?'

Hasan avoided looking at her.

'We'll have to shoot them. They'll starve to death in the jungle, or get eaten by locals.'

'Pete told me this would happen, but I got angry with him. He was right,' said Isabella.

As the days went by, the effort of maintaining a sunny exterior became too much, even for Hasan. The death sentence hanging over the sanctuary and most of its inhabitants took all the joy out of life. When Isabella found Hasan counting his bullets, she knew the end could not be far away, but she could not leave either. *How can I desert them now?*

Hasan looked up from his morning coffee, huge black bags under his eyes.

'We're not going to make it,' he said.

'But what about Liz's money?' said Isabella. 'I thought that would keep you going for weeks.'

'We owed almost all of it. And now we don't have any left for the monthly bills.'

'Won't people wait for their payments?'

'No one wants to give us credit in case the civil war starts up again, and most of our donors have left the country for safety. This is the end of the road,' said Gupta.

She put her hand on Hasan's shoulder.

'Is there nothing we can do? My family might help if I begged,' she said.

'I don't want to go on my knees to them again. They'd just laugh at us,' said Hasan.

Gupta sighed and sat down beside him.

'What will you do?' said Isabella.

'I'll have to shoot the orphans, and release the adults into the forest to fend for themselves,' said Hasan

'But do they know how?'

'They'll have to learn fast.'

'But they won't be afraid of the locals. The locals

will catch them and eat them, won't they?'

Hasan looked away, and Isabella knew the answer.

'There is no other solution,' said Hasan. 'Listen, I need you to help me.'

'Anything.'

'Ten mustn't be here to see this. It would break his heart. I want you to take him away for a day.'

'But what will I tell him?' said Isabella.

'Why don't you take him to visit Manu and have dinner at Alex's. You can work your magic to persuade Manu to lend us his biggest truck to transport the chimps to the jungle in batches.'

'That might work. But don't you need me here?'

'We have brought these orphans up by ourselves for ten years. We have shared their triumphs and their pains. Allah willing, we will share their deaths and they will not be afraid.'

'It will be difficult, but you mustn't let on our plan, or Ten will not stay away,' said Gupta.

Isabella took a deep breath.

'Okay, I'll do it.'

The prospect of a trip to town excited Ten, who put on his London bus t-shirt and his sunglasses and paraded in front of Gupta and Hasan.

'What do you think?' he said.

'Hoards of girls will follow you down the street, screaming, like the Beatles fans,' said Hasan.

'Why do they scream at insects?' said Ten.

'The Beatles were a pop group,' said Isabella.

'Oh. Let's go then,' he said. 'I'm hungry.'

'You're always hungry.'

The Fakeems waved Ten and Isabella off from the gate of the sanctuary. Once they had disappeared down the road, Gupta and Hasan gathered the workers together for a solemn announcement. Consternation and tears greeted the news of the closure and the massacre of the orphans. Hasan took Joe to one side while Gupta make a vat of coffee and calmed people down. They chose a site in front of a small copse beside the car park to dig a pit for the orphans.

Joe took the tools from the shed and chose the strongest staff members for digging the pit. They dug in shocked silence, the only sound being the scrape of the spades against the stones in the ground. The orphans sat in the new enclosure watching this strange activity and imitating the movements of the men. Hasan and Gupta observed them together, their hearts breaking.

When the workers had gone home for the evening, and the chimps were in their sleeping quarters, the Fakeems sat down for supper together. Gupta raised her beaker of pineapple juice.

'To you, my husband. You are the light of my life. I don't know what I did to be so lucky.'

'It is me who is lucky, habibi. But I'm dreading tomorrow. I don't know if I can do it.'

'Think of what would happen to them if we left them to fend for themselves. You will do them a kindness.'

'I'm being cruel to be kind? I hope I find the strength.'

Chapter 41

As the bus rattled and bumped its way towards Freetown, Isabella sneaked a look at Ten. His boyish face had animated with the excitement of the trip, and betrayed no knowledge of the dreadful fate planned for his charges. Guilt surged into her chest where it competed with misery for dominance. Losing Pete had broken her heart, and she found it hard to hide her feelings. This trip felt like a betrayal to both of them.

'We're here,' said Ten, heading for the door of the bus.

Isabella dragged herself out of her seat. She took a deep breath and plastered a smile on her face, forcing her gloom into the recesses of her brain. Manu came to meet them at the gate of the compound.

'I heard there might be trouble at the gate,' he said. 'Now I know there is. Did you change your mind, Ten?'

'No, I'm just visiting. We're going to Alex's tonight.'

'Is that so?' said Manu, catching Isabella's eye. 'Why don't you go to the armoury and see if you can get into trouble with Whitey?'

Ten walked off, trying not to run, and disappeared through the door.

'I presume you have an ulterior motive for being here?' said Manu. 'We're about to go out on a raid. Let's have a quick coffee, but then you must leave.'

Isabella followed Manu into his office and sat down on an upturned tea-chest. She avoided Manu's enquiring glance.

'Spit it out,' said Manu. 'We're busy.'

'The sanctuary is bankrupt.'

'Oh, I thought that might happen.'

'The worst thing is that Hasan and Gupta will have to shoot the orphans. It would traumatise Ten. So, they asked me to take him away.'

'Does he know?'

'I haven't told him. The Fakeems wanted me to take him away for the day so they could dig a grave and prepare the ground. I'm supposed to entertain Ten until tomorrow.'

'Poor kid. He loses everything he ever loves. How will he get over this, so soon after Pete?'

'I know how he feels,' said Isabella.

'Hey, I'm sorry, but Ten's a kid. You should be used to disappointment, at your age.'

'My age? You really know how to flatter a lady,' said Isabella, only half joking.

'Did you love him?' said Manu.

'Pete, yes, more than I knew. I'd like to kill those bastards. I almost lost my brother to the men who killed our friend Liam, and we never got justice.'

Manu chewed on the nail of his index finger, watching her with his beady eyes as she squirmed under his gaze.

'Would you like some revenge?' he said. 'It might not feel as good as you think it will.'

'Revenge? Like what?' she said.

289

'We're going to clear out Banga's headquarters near Songo for the government. It will be over quickly, but it will be an adrenaline rush.'

'Can Ten come too?'

'Only if you both stay in the armoured car until it's over.'

Isabella knew that any reasonable person would refuse the offer, but her blood rose to her head as the idea of avenging Pete took over her better nature. The memory of the adrenaline rush of the helicopter raid was still fresh in her mind. *What an article this would make. Like a war correspondent instead of a reporter on kittens and puppies.*

'You've got a deal,' she said, colour in her cheeks.

Manu smirked at her.

'You've got a strong blood lust for a woman. Are you sure you wouldn't like to join us? I need someone who likes violence.'

'Who said I liked violence? I like revenge. It's not the same thing at all,' said Isabella.

'So you say,' said Manu, winking. 'Do you want to break the news to Boy Wonder?'

A smell like rotting carrion permeated the inside of the armoured car. The oppressive heat made it worse. Isabella fell her stomach rise in her throat as she got the urge to vomit. She wasn't the only one. Ten had turned a peculiar shade of green. She distracted herself by doing the twelve times table in her head. *I must be out of my mind, but at least I've stopped dwelling on the fate of the orphans.*

'Brace yourselves,' said Manu.

The armoured car drove straight through the barriers protecting the rebel compound. Chopper manned the machine gun and mowed down the rebels as they tried to run for shelter. Bullets pinged off the armoured car but did not penetrate. White threw a grenade into one building, which collapsed when it exploded.

Ten held on to Isabella, forgetting his macho front and cowering for protection. Despite the danger, Isabella revelled in the sound of the machine gun over their heads. The rebels fell to the ground one by one, like in a movie, until Chopper called the all clear.

'Stay inside while we recce the area,' said Manu.

Isabella nodded unable to speak. Ten pulled himself upright, pretending he had fallen into her arms instead of taking refuge there. They sat inside the carrier, gazing out of the windows at the surrounding destruction. Chopper, Whitey and Manu collected the rebels' weapons and rolled over the bodies, checking for hidden weapons. Finally, Manu came back to the car and opened the door.

'Would you like a quick look around?' he said.

'Yes, please,' said Ten, jumping out.

Isabella rolled her eyes at him, but she also got out and wandered over to the main building and put her head around the door. Inside, the floor was littered with rubbish and discarded flip-flops. An old map on the wall attracted her attention, and she wandered over to have a look. Meanwhile, Ten opened the drawers on a large desk, which looked out of place among the more rustic furniture and homemade beds.

Suddenly, a bullet flew through the glassless window and buried itself above Ten's head. Isabella launched herself at Ten and dragged him down to floor level. She pulled him under one of the single beds with her.

'Don't move. Don't even breathe,' she said.

Outside, she could hear Manu shouting orders while Ten's shallow breathing whistled in her ear. The door of the house burst open and a pair of bare feet stood on the threshold. Blood ran down the right leg onto the floor. A burst of machine gun fire echoed around the room and bullets sprayed into the walls and floor just beside them. Ten whimpered and Isabella pulled him closer. The feet came towards the bed and stopped as the sound of someone trying to un-jam his gun reached them. Isabella hugged Ten to her and shut her eyes.

A single shot rang out, and the man fell to the floor, his face with its surprised expression landing on the floor inches from their faces. Manu burst through the door.

'Are you all right?' he said. 'The bastard played dead.'

'I think so,' said Isabella, and pushed Ten out from under the bed.

As she tried to extricate herself, her hand closed around a small wooden box. The bed rose into the air as Manu lifted one end up.

'Get out before I drop it on you,' he said. 'This is heavy.'

Isabella stood up and moved out of the way. Manu dropped the bed back down, narrowly missing the body of the rebel who lay with his eyes wide open. He patted Ten on the head.

'You can't stay out of trouble, can you?' he said.

'I found this under the bed,' said Isabella, handing Manu the box.

Manu opened it and his eyes almost fell out of their sockets.

'Holy shit, Africa. You've hit the jackpot.'

He held out the open box and Isabella picked up a large crystal.

'Honestly, voodoo, chimp fetishes, quartz crystals, what sort of army is this?' said Isabella, brushing the dirt off her trousers.

'Let me see that,' said Whitey, who had entered the room and turned it over in his fingers. 'I need to try something,' he said.

He strode over to the back window of the jeep followed by the others, and pulled the crystal over it, leaving a long cut.

'Blimey,' he said. 'It's a massive diamond.'

'Don't be ridiculous,' said Manu.

'Give it here,' said Chopper. 'Let the expert have a look.'

He twisted it around and held it up to the light. He whistled.

'It's got a couple of minor flaws in it, but Whitey's right. It's a whopper.'

Isabella took it back and looked at it again.

'It doesn't look like a diamond. What's it worth?' she said.

'Millions,' said Whitey. 'Probably.'

'It's not the only one,' said Chopper. 'There are about a dozen small ones in here with it.'

'We'll keep the small ones for expenses, but the big one is Pete's now,' said Manu. 'What would he want us to do with it?'

'As if you didn't know,' said Whitey.

Isabella stood mute with her mouth open and her arm around Ten.

'What's wrong, Africa?' said Manu, and then he slapped his forehead. 'We gotta go, boys. Like the wind.'

'Where to, boss?' said Whitey.

'Tacugama. As fast as you can.'

Chapter 42

It had been a long day at Tacugama. Hasan had given mango and pineapple treats to the orphans and cuddled them one last time. Joe had locked Lucius's troop into the sleeping area early, and there were hoots of dissent coming from their building. They separated Sarah and Greta into a cage with the bullied males, and then Hasan walked back into the hut where Gupta made up the last bottles. He picked up his pistol and shovelled the bullets into his pockets.

'I don't know if I can do this,' he said.

'Focus on the good in this,' said Gupta. 'Would you prefer to let them out into the jungle where they will starve to death?'

'I don't know how you can be so calm.'

'I believe in Karma. We have defied our fate so often; we have annoyed the Gods. It is time to accept it now.'

'Who shall we shoot first?'

'Fidget and the more excitable babies are the best option, in case they get wind of what is happening and cause distress to the others.'

'Okay, will you come out and distract them for me?'

'Of course. You didn't think I'd let you do this

alone, did you?'

They took the handle of the basket containing the bottles and carried them down to the cages where loud hooting and jubilation greeted their arrival. Hasan wept in misery, and Gupta put her arms around him while he emptied his sorrows on her shoulder.

'We're not finished yet,' she said. 'We can start again with Ten.'

'If he ever forgives us.'

Gupta sighed.

'Get Fidget,' she said.

Hasan did not have any trouble extracting Fidget who ran into his arms when called. Shutting the door behind him, Hasan walked out towards Gupta, his face blank of expression.

'How will we do this?' she said.

'Let's carry him down to the car park. Joe can put him in the pit so that the other chimps don't see what happens.'

They gave Fidget his bottle and Hasan carried him down to the car park and put him on the ground. As usual, the little ape gave one hundred per cent of his attention to sucking the milk out of his bottle and didn't notice as Hasan walked behind him and took out the pistol. Hasan whispered a prayer to Allah and took aim at Fidget's head.

A loud horn blast broke the silence. Hasan lowered his gun.

'What on earth—?' he said.

The armoured car roared up the road, klaxon sounding, with Manu shouting out of the window, 'don't shoot!'

Hasan turned to Gupta whose bewildered expression matched his. Manu flung open the door and jumped out. He took in their tear-stained faces.

'Don't tell me. Someone else died,' he said. 'You two never have any luck.'

Hasan put his head in his hands.

'How could you, Africa?' he said.

'Have you shot anyone?' said Isabella, looking at Fidget, who had the empty bottle in his hands and feet and still tried to suck milk out of it.

'No yet,' said Gupta. 'You need to leave, now.'

'No, we don't. Pete has saved us.'

'What are you talking about?' said Gupta. 'He's dead, sweetheart, he can't save anyone.'

'That's where you're wrong,' said Isabella, and held out the massive diamond.

The incredulous looks on the Fakeems' faces were something Isabella would never forget. Gupta pretended to be furious with Isabella for taking Ten into a war zone, but she couldn't pull it off. Instead, she made one of her famous curries and Manu produced a bottle of whisky, which they used to toast the sanctuary.

'The money from this diamond will keep us going for years,' said Hasan. 'I never thought we'd get out of debt, never mind having money in the bank,'

'Pete would be so pleased,' said Manu.

'You should name the new enclosure for him,' said Ten. 'The Pete Hawkins Enclosure.'

'Tyrone won't like that,' said Joe.

'Tyrone likes bananas and grooming,' said Hasan. 'He can't read.'

Crawling out of bed the next morning, Isabella screwed her eyes up and put on her sunglasses. She stumbled into the kitchen to find Manu and the crew tucking into a big breakfast.

'You should open a restaurant,' said Chopper, gorging himself.

'I already told her that,' said Manu.

Isabella drank a cup of tea and took several pain killers for her headache.

'You're a lightweight Africa.'

'I can't drink anything. My sister Liz is the one with hollow legs.'

'You should go home to her then. Someone has shot me twice since I met you. You're bad luck.'

Chapter 43

Isabella shut her suitcase and heaved it outside. It felt a lot lighter than when she had arrived. Joe insisted on carrying it down to the taxi. The Fakeems took her arms and walked to the car park with her. She looked around, but she couldn't see Ten.

'You know what he's like,' said Gupta.

'It doesn't mean he doesn't love you,' said Hasan.

They both hugged her twice, and she had such a large lump in her throat she could hardly speak.

'Don't forget the monthly progress reports. You have fans now,' said Isabella.

'We won't. Come and visit us some day,' said Gupta.

'Don't be a stranger,' said Hasan.

Isabella got into the taxi and the driver reversed it and pointed it down the road. She waved out of the window until they were out of sight, trying not to cry. The taxi shuddered to a halt.

'What dat boy do in da road?' said the driver, leaning on his horn.

Ten had jumped out of the ditch in front of the car, waving his arms.

'I know him,' said Isabella. 'Give me a minute.'

She got out of the car and put his arms around Ten,

sniffing his dusty hair and feeling his ribs under his t-shirt.

'You need to eat more,' she said. 'You're too skinny.'

'Gupta is starving me,' said Ten. 'Maybe you should take me to England with you and feed me there.'

'I can't cook,' said Isabella. 'I think you should stay, don't you?'

'I'll miss you too much,' said Ten.

'Me too,' said Isabella. 'But I'll be happy knowing you are happy. And Pete will watch over you, now he's got his own enclosure, you'll see.'

Ten stepped back to let her get into the car.

'Goodbye, Africa.'

'Goodbye, Ten,'

The flight from Sierra Leone landed in the mist at Heathrow. Isabella dragged her suitcase onto the tube and fell into a seat. She slept most of the way to Green Park where she took a taxi to Liz's flat. By the time she arrived there, she had nothing more to give. She let herself in with the spare key and went straight to bed. When Liz came home, she soon noticed the state Isabella was in and let her sleep for days without commenting.

Grateful for her sister's care, Isabella did her bit by washing up the dishes and tidying the flat when Liz worked at the office. While using the vacuum cleaner in the hall, Isabella noticed a thick envelope on the sideboard with her name on it. The postmark read Dublin, and the writing was Graham's. Isabella switched off the vacuum and put it back in the hall cupboard. She made herself a cup of tea and opened the envelope.

It contained items of mail from the last couple of months; bank statements, credit cards, postcards, and one envelope with a London post mark. She put the London letter to one side and opened the other letters one by one. They contained nothing startling. Her bank balance looked healthy, which didn't surprise her, considering her absence from the country for months. She picked up the London letter and turned it over. The hairs on her arms stood up as she recognised the crest, and she dropped it on the table.

It took her five minutes of pacing the apartment to get her courage up to open it. She slid a knife under the flap and prised it open. Inside a letter on thick paper with another raised crest on it. She pulled the letter out and unfolded it with exaggerated care. 'Dear Miss Green, We are delighted to inform you.' Isabella let out a shriek of excitement and bounced around the flat. She read, and reread, the letter before Liz arrived home from work.

By the time Liz arrived, Isabella had worked herself up into such a state of anticipation that she couldn't speak. She just handed her the letter and waited with bated breath while her sister read it.

'Oh my goodness. I can't believe it. It's your dream job.'

'It's only an interview.'

'When is it?'

'I'm not sure. I was too excited to take in the date.'

'Hang on. I didn't read past the bit where they were delighted.'

Liz picked up the letter again and wiped her brow.

'This is too close for comfort. The interview is tomorrow morning,' she said.

'Why didn't you give me the envelope before?'

said Isabella.

'I saw it was from Graham. I didn't want to upset you.'

'Can you imagine if I only found it after the interview?'

'Don't even say that. Have you got a suit?'

'What about the frumpy one you lent me for the conference?'

'I think we can do better than that. What will you do if they give you the job?'

'Slow down, I need to interview first.'

'You could live here until you find somewhere to move to.'

'Let me get the job first.'

The man doing her interview looked over the top of his glasses at her.

'You worked at a chimpanzee sanctuary in Sierra Leone and went on commando raids on the rebels? Don't you think the BBC nature documentaries might be a little tame for you?'

'I'm well trained, that's for sure,' said Isabella, laughing.

The man wrote something down and she wondered if she had said something wrong, but the next letter from the BBC contained a job offer.

Isabella and Liz celebrated with a glass of Chardonnay and a Chinese takeaway. Liz took a fax out of her handbag and handed it to Isabella.

'This came for you today,' she said.

Isabella unfolded it and screwed her eyes up to look at some fuzzy black and white photos, which Hasan had faxed from Tacugama. She realised she was looking at a picture of Ten smiling and pointing upwards at a sign over the new chimp corral. It read

'The Pete Hawkins Enclosure'. Isabella swallowed hard and tears gathered in her eyes. She passed it to Liz who smiled.

'Pete won't be forgotten at the sanctuary,' she said.

'Or here,' said Isabella, patting her heart.

'I'm sorry you lost him,' said Liz. 'Are you sure you won't go back to Graham? He's so desperate, he's even been calling me asking me to intercede.'

'I'm sure. I've been looking at houses near the BBC in Shepherd's Bush. They're cheap.'

'There's a good reason for that,' said Liz.

'I've lived through a civil war,' said Isabella. 'Anyway, it will gentrify. One day my house will be worth millions.'

'Dream on,' said Liz.

~~~~~~~~~~~~~~~~~~~~~~~~~~~~~~~~~~~~~

Thank you for reading my book.

Please leave me a review if you can. Reviews are vital to help authors sell books, and useful to help readers work out if they would enjoy the book too. Short and sweet is fine.

If you enjoyed this book, I highly recommend my Sam Harris Adventure Series about a pioneering female geologist who had a talent for getting into trouble.

The first book in the series, **Fool's Gold, is free to download** so what have you got to lose?

Tacugama Chimpanzee Sanctuary is a real place in Sierra Leone and it is still open. Please visit the site and adopt a chimp if you would like to help their important work.

The Complete Sam Harris Adventure Series is available at all online retailers. Please go to my website, www.pjskinnner.com for links to your favourite site.

All my books are available in regular paperback and large print paperback

Other Books by the author

The Sam Harris Series

Set in the late 1980's and through the 1990's, the thrilling Sam Harris Adventure series navigates through the career of a female geologist. Themes such as women working in formerly male domains, and what constitutes a normal existence, are developed in the context of Sam's constant ability to find herself in the middle of an adventure or mystery.

Sam's home life provides a contrast to her adventures and feeds her need to escape. Her attachment to an unfaithful boyfriend is the thread running through her romantic life, and her attempts to break free of it provide another side to her character.

The first book in the Sam Harris Series sets the scene for the career of an unwilling heroine, whose bravery and resourcefulness are needed to navigate a series of adventures set in remote sites in Africa and South America. Based loosely on the real-life adventures of the author, the settings and characters are given an authenticity that will connect with readers who enjoy adventure fiction and mysteries set in remote settings with realistic scenarios.

Fool's Gold - Book 1

Newly qualified geologist Sam Harris is a woman in a man's world - overlooked, underpaid but resilient and passionate. Desperate for her first job, and nursing a broken heart, she accepts an offer from notorious entrepreneur Mike Morton, to search for gold deposits in the remote rainforests of Sierramar.

With the help of nutty local heiress, Gloria Sanchez, she soon settles into life in Calderon, the capital. But when she accidentally uncovers a long-lost clue to a treasure buried deep within the jungle, her journey really begins.

Teaming up with geologist Wilson Ortega, historian Alfredo Vargas and the mysterious Don Moises, they venture through the jungle, where she lurches between excitement and insecurity. Yet there is a far graver threat looming; Mike and Gloria discover that one of the members of the expedition is plotting to seize the fortune for himself and is willing to do anything to get it. Can Sam survive and find the treasure or will her first adventure be her last?

Hitler's Finger - Book 2
The second book in the Sam Harris Series sees the return of our heroine Sam Harris to Sierramar to help her friend Gloria track down her boyfriend, the historian, Alfredo Vargas.

Geologist Sam Harris loves getting her hands dirty. So, when she learns that her friend Alfredo has gone missing in Sierramar, she gives her personal life some much needed space and hops on the next plane. But she never expected to be following the trail of a devious Nazi plot nearly 50 years after World War II.

Deep in a remote mountain settlement, Sam must uncover the village's dark history. If she fails to reach her friend in time, the Nazi survivors will ensure Alfredo's permanent silence. Can Sam blow the lid on the conspiracy before the Third Reich makes a devastating return?

The background to the book is the presence of Nazi war criminals in South America which was often ignored by locals who had fascist sympathies during World War II. Themes such as tacit acceptance of fascism, and local collaboration with fugitives from justice are examined and developed in the context of Sam's constant ability to find herself in the middle of an adventure or mystery.

The Star of Simbako - Book 3

A fabled diamond, a jealous voodoo priestess, disturbing cultural practices. What could possibly go wrong? The third book in the Sam Harris Series sees Sam Harris on her first contract to West Africa to Simbako, a land of tribal kingdoms and voodoo.

Nursing a broken heart, Sam Harris goes to Simbako to work in the diamond fields of Fona. She is soon involved with a cast of characters who are starring in their own soap opera, a dangerous mix of superstition, cultural practices, and ignorance (mostly her own). Add a love triangle and a jealous woman who wants her dead and Sam is in trouble again. Where is the Star of Simbako? Is Sam going to survive the chaos?

This book is based on visits made to the Paramount Chiefdoms of West Africa. Despite being nominally Christian communities, Voodoo practices are still part of daily life out there. This often leads to conflicts of interest. Combine this with the horrific ritual of FGM and it makes for a potent cocktail of conflicting loyalties. Sam is pulled into this life by her friend, Adanna, and soon finds herself involved in goings on that she doesn't understand.

The Pink Elephants - Book 4

Sam gets a call in the middle of the night that takes her to the Masaibu project in Lumbono, Africa. The project is collapsing under the weight of corruption and chicanery engendered by management, both in country and back on the main company board. Sam has to navigate murky waters to get it back on course, not helped by interference from people who want her to fail. When poachers invade the elephant sanctuary next door, her problems multiply. Can Sam protect the elephants and save the project or will she have to choose?

The fourth book in the Sam Harris Series presents Sam with her sternest test yet as she goes to Africa to fix a failing project. The day-to-day problems encountered by Sam in her work are typical of any project manager in the Congo which has been rent apart by warring factions, leaving the local population frightened and rootless. Elephants with pink tusks do exist, but not in the area where the project is based. They are being slaughtered by poachers in Gabon for the Chinese market and will soon be extinct, so I have put the guns in the hands of those responsible for the massacre of these defenceless animals

The Bonita Protocol - Book 5

An erratic boss. Suspicious results. Stock market shenanigans. Can Sam Harris expose the scam before they silence her? It's 1996. Geologist Sam Harris has been around the block, but she's prone to nostalgia, so she snatches the chance to work in Sierramar, her old stomping ground. But she never expected to be working for a company that is breaking all the rules.

When the analysis results from drill samples are

suspiciously high, Sam makes a decision that puts her life in peril. Can she blow the lid on the conspiracy before they shut her up for good?

The Bonita Protocol sees Sam return to Sierramar and take a job with a junior exploration company in the heady days before the Bre-X crash. I had fun writing my first megalomaniac female boss for this one. I have worked in a few junior companies with dodgy bosses in the past, and my only comment on the sector is buyer beware…

Digging Deeper - Book 6

A feisty geologist working in the diamond fields of West Africa is kidnapped by rebels. Can she survive the ordeal or will this adventure be her last? It's 1998. Geologist Sam Harris is desperate for money so she takes a job in a tinpot mining company working in war-torn Tamazia. But she never expected to be kidnapped by blood thirsty rebels.

Working in Gemsite was never going to be easy with its culture of misogyny and corruption. Her boss, the notorious Adrian Black is engaged in a game of cat and mouse with the government over taxation. Just when Sam makes a breakthrough, the camp is overrun by rebels and Sam is taken captive. Will anyone bother to rescue her, and will she still be alive if they do?

I worked in Tamazia (pseudonym for a real place) for almost a year in different capacities. The first six months I spent in the field are the basis for this book. I don't recommend working in the field in a country at civil war but, as for many of these crazy jobs, I needed the money.

Concrete Jungle - Book 7 (series end)

Armed with an MBA, Sam Harris is storming the City
- But has she swapped one jungle for another?

Forging a new career was never going to be easy,
and Sam discovers she has not escaped from the
culture of misogyny and corruption that blighted her
field career.

When her past is revealed, she finally achieves the
acceptance she has always craved, but being one of the
boys is not the panacea she expected. The death of a
new friend presents her with the stark choice of
compromising her principals to keep her new position,
or exposing the truth behind the façade. Will she
finally get what she wants or was it all a mirage?

I did an MBA to improve my career prospects, and
much like Sam, found it didn't help much. In the end,
it's only your inner belief that counts. What other
people say, or think, is their problem. I hope you enjoy
this series. It was written to rid myself of demons, and
it worked.

You can order these books in paperback at your
favourite retailer. Please go to the PJSKINNER.com
website for links.

Connect with the Author

If you would like updates on the latest books by PJ Skinner or to contact the author with your questions please click on the following links:
Website: www.pjskinner.com
Facebook: www.facebook.com/PJSkinnerAuthor
Twitter: https://twitter.com/PJSkinnerAuthor
Amazon Author page;
www.amazon.com/PJ-Skinner/e/B01ABVE7J2

About the Author

PJ Skinner is the author of the Sam Harris Series of adventure-thriller novels. A geologist who has spent thirty years roaming the planet and collecting tall tales and real-life experiences, she now writes fact-based novels from the relative safety of London. She still travels worldwide collecting material for the series and having her own adventures.

The Sam Harris Adventure Series is for lovers of adventure thrillers happening just before the time of mobile phones and internet. It has a unique viewpoint provided by Sam, a female interloper in a male world, as she struggles with alien cultures and failed relationships.

The author is considering writing a third book in the Green Family Saga, or a series of Cozy Mysteries, or a book about… You'll have to wait and see. Join my newsletter on my website to get updates and offers at pjskinner.com

Printed in Great Britain
by Amazon